A MORE PERFECT UNION
By RW Richard

Published by WEB Press a subsidiary of WEB Pacific Commercial

This is a work of fiction. Names, characters, places and incidents are products of the author's imagination or are used fictitiously and are not to be construed as real. Any resemblance to actual events, locales, organizations, or persons either living or dead is entirely coincidental except for some media types and politicians who have always been fair game.
They deserve a certain special tweaking. To accomplish this, the author employs irony, satire and general humor. You may notice a dose of lampooning. Yet, there is a very serious point to this story.

The author dedicates this novel to an ex-CIA agent friend who has passed on. He made numerous suggestions for the story and came up with the unlikely title*. For your brilliance, Orin, the author will be eternally grateful.

The author also wants to thank the Writers Bloc critique group and the local RWA chapter (San Diego) for their professionalism and comradery.

* Author's note: The title, A MORE PERFECT UNION, comes from the preamble to the U.S. constitution. Of course, you literally can't have something more perfect. Were the founding fathers taking the politically expedient path of glorifying the articles of confederation and then replacing them with the constitution or had they intended more? Religious men they were. They understood there was more to life than could be measured as perfect. Create a 'perfect' system of government, as they envisioned it, and make it 'more perfect' by acknowledging and practicing certain inalienable truths. In this way, the whole becomes greater than its parts. They called on all of us to practice the greatest truth. Love thy neighbor even if they're stupid enough to belong to the other Party.

Other novels and novellas by RW Richard
The Carlos series will be offered in both paperback and e-book formats. The series below have some continuing characters and story lines. I list them in alphabetical order because the chronology is not important to enjoying the story. Each novel stands alone.
AUTUMN BREEZE will be out late 2014
A MORE PERFECT UNION out now
BLINDFOLD CHESS will be out in early 2015
Expect more in the Carlos series.

Stand alones:
THE WOLVES OF SHERWOOD FOREST a novella in e-book format only
DOUBLE HAPPINESS a novel in paperback and e-book out late 2014
NEANDERTHALS AND THE GARDEN OF EDEN, a novel in e-book and paperback

Chapter links in blue for the e-book format.

If you like music in the background while reading, the author recommends the songs that inspired the theme and tone for each chapter.

Song References and the author's pick for artist:

Chapter One: "Big Girls Don't Cry" by the Four Seasons

Chapter Two: "True Colors" by Cyndi Lauper

Chapter Three: "Matchmaker, Matchmaker" a song from "Fiddler on the Roof" lyrics by Sheldon Harnick

Chapter Four: "You Only Live Twice" by Nancy Sinatra

Chapter Five: "Hot Hot Hot" by Buster Poindexter

Chapter Six: "Diamonds are a Girl's Best Friend" by Marilyn Monroe

Chapter Seven: "You're Getting to be a Habit with Me" by Bebe Daniels

Chapter Eight: "Que Sera, Sera" by Doris Day (with all my love – author's comment)

Chapter Nine: "Fallin'" by Alicia Keys

Chapter Ten: "Who Let the Dogs Out?" by Baha Men

Chapter Eleven: "The Days of Wine and Roses" by Andy Williams

Chapter Twelve: "All of Me" by John Legend

Chapter Thirteen: "Poker Face" by Lady Gaga

Chapter Fourteen: "Girl on Fire" by Alicia Keys

Chapter Fifteen: "Getting to Know You" by Marni Nixon

Chapter Sixteen: "Put 'em in a Box, Tie 'em with a Ribbon, and Throw 'em in the Deep Blue Sea" by Doris Day

Chapter Seventeen: "Hit the Road, Jack" by Ray Charles

Chapter Eighteen: "New York, New York" by Frank Sinatra

Chapter Nineteen: "I Feel Pretty" from "West Side Story" by Marni Nixon for Natalie Wood

Chapter Twenty: "Promises, Promises" by Dionne Warwick

Chapter Twenty One: "You Give Love a Bad Name" by Bon Jovi

Chapter Twenty Two: "Peace Train" by Cat Stevens
Chapter Twenty Three: "Honeymoon Hotel" from Footlight Parade music by Harry Warren, Lyrics by Al Dubin, sung by the cast (Dick Powell, Ruby Keeler, and gang)
Chapter Twenty Four: "From This Moment on" by Bryan White and Shania Twain
Chapter Twenty Five: "Can't Take My Eyes Off You" by The Four Seasons
Chapter Twenty Six: "The Times They are a Changin'" by Bob Dylan
Chapter Twenty Seven: "Like a Star" by Corinne Bailey Rae

A More Perfect Union
RW Richard

Chapter One
Big Girls Don't Cry

Senator Starblanket's head swam with confusion and her vision focused like a bad camera. She knew from the antiseptic stink and the tubes irritating her arm that she lay in a hospital bed. A reassuring doctorly voice whispered she'd be okay.

A very short and blurry version of Governor Arturo Arnez, her unworthy presidential opponent, held her hand for reasons beyond her muddled mind. All she could remember was shaking this hand at their comedy roast and then being bashed against the back wall. Must have been a bomb or his handshake was something to avoid.

She blinked her eyes for a clearer image to positively identify the bastard. "I fell down a-ah rabbit hole." She couldn't believe she just said that.

"Thank God you're alive, Ayita."

He seemed sincere and off his rocker. She remembered him much taller and then a wheelchair came into focus. She hoped he was okay.

"What…happened?"

"They tried to kill us."

Obviously.

She fell down the rabbit hole, endlessly tumbling. A little dizzy, she formed so many questions with not enough focus and power to push words out. She squinted again and focused on Arturo's blotchy red eyes. She tried to reach up to touch his cheek.

"Don't move yet, Ayita," the doctor ordered.

"I can't move my arms."

"Let the drugs wear off."

"Somebody fill me in. Is Jason here?" She hoped her Secret Service team leader lurked somewhere in this huge room.

"Yes, ma'am," Jason's breaking-falsetto voice rose from behind a curtain. "I'm sorry to inform you that we lost both vice-presidential nominees."

"That's too much just yet, Jason," the doctor said.

Interrupted, Jason promised to go into detail when the impatient doctor allowed him more time. The doctor assured her that both she and Arturo would fully recover. *Although, Arturo could use a brain transplant.*

"Oh no. How could this happen?" Devastated, she struggled to get her feelings under control. Her popular far-left running mate, Arturo's charismatic far-right running mate, and possibly others gone. Impossible. Tragic. Ugly. She cared for all these people. Yep, even the way-out righties and lefties. Her parents and grandparents had raised, Mary Ayita Starblanket in both Cherokee and Christian cultures and traditions. She didn't have to like or agree with both VPs' political bent, but she'd loved them as human beings. Agape, the nuns had called it. Balancing and celebrating diverse political thought ensured the health of the country.

The Secret Service needed to answer for this breach in security. The nation would mourn while they tracked down the culprits. Again, she tried to will her recovery and stop speculating. She had no facts. Thinking about endless scenarios slipped beyond useless, especially when her mind tumbled down rabbit holes.

They, whoever they were, wouldn't get away with this, if she had to pull the trigger herself. Better yet, she'd have the infamous Colonel Carlos Petrovich and his sidekick, Moon, eliminate the threats. Carlos, her campaign security chief, had long ago gained a reputation as the most feared assassin of assassins and Nazis, but nowadays his younger sidekick was better.

"Work with Carlos. Okay, Jason?"

"Yes, ma'am."

"We need to give her some peace and quiet for a while. Evac the room, everybody," the now mostly-in-focus doctor snapped. She read his badge, Navy Captain George something. His stethoscope swung back and forth from his starched sweet-smelling white uniform while he leaned over to examine her eyes. *My nose's working, Doc.*

The strapping physician could cure with his looks. At least her eyes functioned well enough to notice the differences between men and women. She hadn't hunted men since she lost her husband. Too busy, too powerful for most men. God, what drug had he put into her? And, her tummy felt like it would explode.

She'd likely live through the doctor peering into her eyes, if he didn't knock her out with his pendulous stethoscope.

Adrenalin kicked in. No matter his rank or hunkyness, she would wrest command. She summoned her strength and barked, "Belay that order." As a former NSA chief engineer and then CIA director, she knew how to command counter-threat activities, shut up Navy doctors and get men, in general, to jump. Of course, she hoped the doctor wouldn't balk. In a hospital, he commanded. All her bluster wouldn't stop him.

"But, Senator, I must insist."

"Where the hell are we?" She'd attack the doctor's resistance, sideways.

"Deep underground at a SAC base, ma'am."

"How long have I been out?"

"A week, Senator."

A week. "I'll take fifteen minutes, that's all, Captain," she said, taking command of her voice. She gathered strength, breathed in and out and took her time. "I need a quick—" she swallowed to let her words flow, "—debrief from the Secret Service, and get me a line to the president. My dear Arturo, I know you're distraught, but *could you*—" she clenched her teeth, "—please let go of my hand." He would have to explain his taking liberties with her very lovely hand later.

"Ten minutes, ma'am," the doctor said. "That's it." Great, her bluff worked. She'd take fifteen.

She scanned the drab, windowless gray-walled hospital room, an obvious bunker. No one had smirked, giggled or run away over her rebuking Governor Arturo Arnez. To her, fun equaled pushing him around. He'd have to get used to it. She intended more of the same in the upcoming debates.

But he looked so sad, forlorn, so somewhere else. Something ate at him besides the horror of the deaths. If her remarks angered or flustered him, he didn't show it. He had gripped her hand like a boyfriend or family member, and he let go with the same gentleness.

Her tummy, other aches and fuzzy head were secondary right now. She could help, having been the best sleuth the CIA had ever employed. Also, she'd never allow a little thing like being blown up get in the way of justice or an election.

"All we have now is each other," Arturo said.

She scoffed inwardly, but then the idea that they only had each other made weird sense. You couldn't have a Mohammed Ali without Joe Frazier. You couldn't run a real presidential campaign against fill in the blank. America needed two parties, if only to aggravate each other. Arturo had so far done an excellent job of doing just that, aggravating her.

"Have you seen a doctor?" She wanted to say, *perhaps a psychiatrist.* She held her well-known wicked tongue.

"Why aren't you crying? You're a woman. You can."

He dropkicked her right back to being pissed off at him. "A glass ceiling should fall on your head."

She softened. Arturo, merely a man with too much testosterone, belonged to a party in which some of its members had not yet realized embracing women's equality meant more victories, besides it being right in the eyes of the Lord. She mused, women were superior, anyway. So men would just have to get used to it. She smiled at a joke almost true.

"I suppose, I deserved that." He seemed to grasp how sexist his remark had sounded. If she could get him to repeat that on the campaign trail, she'd win in a landslide.

"You look like you cried enough for the both of us." She handed him an imaginary peace pipe. But since neither of them smoked...

Arturo said nothing. He offered no explanation for why his normally rugged, handsome face resembled a Jackson Pollock painting. He still had his thick black curls, square-cut jaw, star-athlete's body—one season, major league baseball, was it?—and Latin charm. It got the women voters swooning if not voting for him.

"Big girls, they don't cry-y-y. I wonder why."

Arturo had a winning quick wit. She almost laughed, but her tummy felt like she'd swallowed a balloon. *Gassy or internal injuries? Surgery?*

No wonder he had beaten out everybody in his party during the primaries. Incisive, brilliant, caring, a resilient mind able to change people's moods instantly. However, now he'd have to court the middle class to win. *We'll see.* At least for the country's sake, he embraced the center. A Rockefeller Republican. Ayita wouldn't have to move back onto the reservation if she lost.

"Big girls on drugs do get bi-i-itchy," she tried to sing, but her voice came off flatter than a beaver's tail. Actually, she could not claim the soft curves of a big girl's body, although she understood the song. Having worn her birthday suit before the closet mirror, she appeared tall and a tad too skinny these days.

"Five minutes left," the doctor said as if they had wasted time.

They had *time* for a quick Secret Service report.

Jason listed the dead—the two running mates, two comedians, and one Secret Service agent. The deceased Secret Service agent had thrown his body in front of the bomb to try to save the presidential nominees.

No matter their valor, she wouldn't go easy on the service. These patriots who protected her and Arturo need only explain how this could have happened for now and then work with the nominees. Nothing in this world was perfect, except for souls.

Shit.

The inhumanity of it all, crushed her. She could no longer hold off tears, even if pegged as a weak *woman* in Arturo's eyes. *Forget him. Grown up girls do cry.*

Jason added, "Another reason you were saved, ma'am— is that we had just reinforced the podium."

"You can thank Arturo for saving your life, as well," the doctor said.

"I grabbed you and offered my body as your shield, but really I wanted to steal a hug," Arturo said.

She'd ignore that complicated comment until her brain could engage his wit. Then she'd kick his ass or somewhere where it would actually hurt.

Arturo spoke up again. "Can you believe this? We're scheduled to debate in D.C. next Tuesday."

"We need to carry on," she said weakly. Is this all she had to offer? She longed for full strength. Would she be able to bob and weave arguments on behalf of the citizens of the United States at a debate? With him?

"We can't let the assassins win," Arturo said.

"Where are your sons, Arturo? And where's my baby?" She worried about her daughter. The last time she'd texted Daya, the day of the explosion, she was listening to a poetry slam in Catholic University's student center.

Arturo had lost his wife, Sheryl, to cancer two or three years before. Now all he had left of his immediate family was two college-aged sons.

"They'll be joining us tomorrow in Washington."

"We don't know for sure who's behind this yet," Jason said.

11

"Once I talk to President Carthage, he'll agree to let me at least help the counter-threat team."

"I want in." Arturo said.

"But you're…" She was about to say busy winning the election.

"You want to know why I cried…I cry for the American people, Ayita. I want justice for the dead, and you know I can help."

True, Arturo, a former U.S. Attorney General under the often denigrated—by Democrats—previous administration, had received high praise from both parties. During his tenures as Miami City and then District Attorney, he'd severely weakened the Cuban mob. If the president would grant both of them clearances again, she'd have no problem working with Mister Law and Order. He'd be a grounding asset to her black ops background. A hell of a team. Besides, they could keep an eye on each other.

In addition, his visage eased her recovering eyes.

Don't think about men.

First, she liked the way the doctor looked. Now, she was ogling her opponent. When she got off these drugs she'd reassess her inner horny, in the meantime, she gave herself, normally Ms. All Business, a pass. The embarrassment of being off focus, less woman of steel, made her stomach turn, which then made her release a long, squeaky fart. A small sound—maybe nobody heard. Had to be the drugs or maybe an operation. She had never ripped one in public. Her face felt red.

No one reacted, not even mister comedian, although the glimmer in his eyes gave his merriment away. Or it was simply one more tear for fallen friends? "I was about to say, you're busy winning this election." She decided to test his mettle and change the subject.

"Not after the latest polls. We're in a statistical tie." *Honesty, a willingness to share, to ignore my pains and embarrassing noises, hmm.* She'd investigate the nuances embedded in election statistics as soon as she grabbed ahold of her campaign manager. Still, Arturo's caring ways portended a new era of cooperation.

"Polls, Arturo, we need justice. By living, both of us will have won."

* * *

He knew what she meant. In her own muddled drugged reasoning, polls were just a footnote and she was right. If they sought justice and conducted their campaigns in a just manner they would never have to second guess the election results.

Yet, Ayita had no idea what drove him to pursue the presidency. Not yet. If she'd concede that he loved this country the same way she did, they'd have something to build on. A radical, not fully formed idea intrigued him. "Let's do a joint press conference when they let us out of here, where instead of blasting each other, we speak to this feeble attempt to influence an American election."

"I don't think either of us should debate without rest and prep."

He planned a surprise that would change American politics *forever*, if only his pretty opponent would agree. Nope, he wouldn't dare spring it on her in her Alice in Wonderland state of mind. He'd have to check with his legal team and the party. He pretty much knew the answer. It had been done before, when the nation was just starting.

Change the country forever. Well, at least shine a light on a new path.

"I agree. No debate." He tried twisting her words to mean no debates at all.

"Why did you hold my hand, Arturo?"

Her gorgeous Cherokee eyes, her wavy torso-length locks, this proud face to behold intrigued him. "Not because you had won that beauty contest." Long ago, she had won Miss Cherokee Nation. Today, in spite of a scrape or two, she was more beautiful.

"I'm getting older."

"No, Ayita, it has nothing to do with your stunning beauty." They both looked at the bemused doctor.

Stunning beauty. Did she remember the day she had kissed him some twenty years ago.

...The Miami bar smelled of stale cigar, the dust of too slow ceiling fans. He was wingman and key holder for his bachelor buddies. In walked a beauty beyond beauties.

"Who is that?"

"Oh, I know her. Forget her. She's married." He couldn't understand why he wouldn't give his friend a chance at the widowed Miss Cherokee Nation.

No. He'd rather flirt with adultery. At least he did nothing but sneak peeks. He watched as the sweat formed on the top of her breasts as she danced the rhumba with her girlfriends, the sway of her body, the shape of her legs, her proud face, her long glistening raven hair. She kept stealing glances, until so wobbly drunk she made her way to him holding chairs. She planted a luscious kiss. He gave back, his heart thumping, his guilt rising. He took her by the shoulders and gently pushed her away, holding up his wedding ring, besides he was a nobody city attorney, a washed up major leaguer and married for Christ's sake...

The kiss she'd planted on him had eaten away at his soul for twenty years. He'd allowed that wet kiss to become his only indiscretion. He'd permitted his fantasies to soar at times of stress over the years. He'd take her, ravish her, time after time, in the closet or out in the parking lot against his Lincoln. Then he'd kiss his wife's neck, feeling guilty. That one moment where he had come remotely close to cheating seared him.

Ayita's driven eyes suggested she didn't remember him. With her reputation, she had no room for a past, for being a woman.

"Somewhere along the way I have lost my looks," she insisted again. *Not like her.* He speculated she really wanted someone to tell her she was still that girl in the white beaded dress with the crown, banner and bouquet. She needed to feel good about herself after the attack.

"No," he said, almost saying no, honey, but that would be entirely inappropriate. "You're still easy on the eyes, but that's not the reason I held your hand." He'd have to think quickly now. He had loved his wife, deeply, completely. Yet he'd always believed in soul mates—and here with the splendor of Cleopatra, laid his. Or at least he'd thought after one stupid, liquor-ridden kissin' another world ago. A world that would never be. He'd been dumb, naive.

He apologized to his deceased wife. *I'm sorry, Sheryl. The boy in me had wanted an impossible world. I played the fool to harbor such a fantasy. I couldn't have loved you more, my darling.*

"I held your hand, Ayita, reminding myself that we are both patriots. We both love our country. Frankly, Ayita, I'm tired of the partisan bickering. We have so much more in common than we have in differences."

"That's a fine display of buffalo chip tossing by the b.s. master himself."

"Okay, I held your hand because you are so damn cute...when you're unconscious." He swatted a ball over the centerfield bleachers.

Now was not the time to tell her he pictured the two of them holding their hands aloft at a press conference, announcing to the world they would not let the assassins win.

They would run on each other's tickets.

He'd be her vice-president if she won.

She'd be his vice-president if he won.

Chapter Two
True Colors

Four weeks before the election

The Secret Service had won the argument. The nominees cancelled the first debate at Washington University in Saint Louis over security concerns. The Air Force jet flew both nominees to Washington, D.C. Ayita had managed to avoid Arturo, feigning the need for sleep and recovery, for the entire trip. In reality, he drew her off focus. She needed to win and he was just an all too attractive obstacle.

A nurse wheeled Ayita through the doors of the White House in her temporary wheelchair. They left the plush-carpeted anteroom to enter the wood-planked White House pressroom. She grinned at Arturo when he asked his nurse to step on it so he could beat Ayita to the podium. *He's such a boy.* They had agreed to stand together, but not on who'd get there first. The last time they'd stood on stage together behind a podium, it had saved their lives. She wanted the symbolism of standing together to strike home with the American electorate.

The press corps went wild with cheers and clapping. Obviously, getting blown up had made them almost as popular as if they'd been assassinated. Ayita preferred almost. All the networks and online news outlets had been running their life stories back-to-back ever since the assassination attempt. It was good to be alive, and it was great to have free publicity.

First, a rabbi offered a prayer and a moment of silence for the dead.

Second up, their Navy doctor bored the crowd with a Q&A session in which he answered repeatedly that they were both going to recover completely and their injuries were private.

Then the president took the podium.

After inspiring words about the heroes lost, the president, a notorious, passionate and lengthy speaker surprisingly relinquished control.

"And so, without further ado, I present to you what I know will be a difficult choice for the American people, the two finest nominees for president this country is blessed with. The senior senator of the great state of Virginia, Mary Ayita Starblanket, and the esteemed governor of the great state of Florida, Arturo Arnez."

Wheeled up, Arturo stood first. Ayita wobbled trying to stand. Arturo leaned over and grabbed her arm at the same time the nurse righted her by taking her other arm. She stood, clasped his shoulder to inch up and whisper into Arturo's ear, "Please stop touching me." *Our little joke.* First he had held her hand, then he told her how beautiful she was. What could possibly be next?

He smiled as if agreeing to something pithy. The press corps ate up their interplay. Some tears were yanked here and there and the applause continued. *Maybe he should head for Hollywood and leave her to a very hard job.*

"Ladies first," he said while raising her hand in a sign of unity. She had enough leg strength to stomp on his foot. The guy exhibited an obsessive, insufferable hand fetish. She didn't stomp, though. She might lose the stop-the-violence-against-republican-governors-from-Florida vote.

"Arturo and I..." She waited for the applause to die down. "Please, please, we've got voters to see. Arturo and I have been forged like steel by this unfortunate event. The steel of our great American democracy. We must vanquish our assassins for the sake of the dead. We have reached a finer appreciation of our love for this country. I have no doubt that whoever wins will serve you well in these trying times. Me, a little better." She put her hand on Arturo's broad shoulder.

Arturo said much the same and offered the mic back to Ayita. "I'll start with Joan." Ayita pointed.

The NBC Capitol Hill correspondent rose. "How do you feel?"

"I feel like I visited a Nazi dentist for a never-ending root canal. Aside from that, I'm fine." The crowd laughed. "Please continue, Joan."

"With your background and resources, can you tell us anything about the bombing investigation?" Of course, Joan referred to Ayita being the former CIA head and before that, the NSA's chief engineer. Now off the doctor's narcotics, she wondered what she'd been thinking when she had wanted to lead the bombing investigation. She had to beat this guy standing next to her, nothing more. Of course, she'd influence the investigation if the president would deal her in, deal them in.

"Arturo and I agree that we would best serve this country by campaigning and staying focused on the needs of the American people. The investigation is in more than competent hands." She peered into the journalist's eyes for a tell. Joan had always been easy to read. Ayita noticed Joan's furtive eye movement. Joan would come back to the subject at some point.

Then both nominees were asked questions about aspects of the campaign. Richard from CNN asked Arturo, "Governor. Will you agree to include Edgar Rice in the remaining debates? And the same question to you, Madam Senator."

"If I read Edgar's pamphlets properly, he stands for *no government*," Arturo said, "On this issue, I couldn't agree with him more. Since the closest thing we have to no government, is less government, I'm all for keeping the debaters down to two. No Edgar is also less Edgar." The guy would get one to two percent max, most of the votes sapping the Republican side. Allowing him to debate would open the door to all the other tiny party candidates.

Ayita smiled broadly. "I agree with my opponent, but for a different reason. I need to keep Arturo around, otherwise I'd have nobody to bash." Laughter filled the room. The crowd loved having their favorite politicians back.

Arturo chimed in, "Actually, I see no need to debate at all. Ayita and I are both centrists at heart. There's really not much difference in our positions. Mine are slightly better. I'd prefer—" he put his hand on her shoulder and she pretended to like it, "— press conferences."

Ayita realized they'd likely be with each other quite a lot more than planned before the terrorists attack so she jumped on board to take the initiative. "I believe we can travel the country together and have open forums, town-hall meetings. If the governor will join me, I propose we eliminate all our commercials and give any excess campaign contributions to help our veterans." There. That topped him.

As is his way, Arturo furrowed his bushy brows and paused, for dramatic effect. "I don't know, Ayita, if it's that easy to turn off our supporters and PAC money. This is a free country and I really enjoy all those ads showing you as a citizen of a foreign country." This stunk of debate. The crazies hounded her for being part of the Cherokee nation. Telling her to go back to where she came from. *Oh, really.* Like most crazies, they'd never read or understood the constitution and the laws that had followed to increase the fundamental rights of Native Americans, all of whom were citizens of the United States of America, all of whom were here before anybody else.

Ayita grabbed the mic. "I really enjoy those ads showing you sipping champagne while southern Florida disappears underwater." She knew Arturo had no problem acknowledging global warming and that solving the problem was good for business.

"Governor Arnez. Governor Arnez." The Fox correspondent jumped out of her seat. The way she dressed, she should have shown up naked.

He touched Ayita's hand and stole the mic back. "Yes, Elaine."

19

Have you chosen a vice presidential candidate, and if not, who are you considering, and how will the voters pick your choice?" Elaine referred to the ballot, many absentees already printed and mailed and the use of write-ins.

Arturo looked down at Ayita as if to ask permission. *For what?*

"Before I answer, I'd like Ayita's thoughts."

She realized she was being set up for one of his notorious zingers. In slight pain and in no mood to be bested, she tossed the ball back into his court. "Whatever Arturo conjures up to help with this ̄dilemma, we'll discuss at length in any case. We'll recommend write-ins soon, no doubt." She looked up at him.

Arturo winked and she knew she had done nothing to brunt a nasty surprise.

"The assassins, in a feeble attempt to influence an American election, wanted to get rid of Ayita and me. We aren't going anywhere. Voters can write in whomever they want for vice president, but I'd like to recommend for their consideration as my running mate someone who is almost as qualified as me, almost as popular, shares ninety-nine percent of my views, believes as I do that once in office, the president is not of one party or the other, but for all the people. I'd like to recommend as my running mate the great senator of Virginia, Mary Ayita Starblanket."

Ayita's jaw dropped, maybe to the floor. The crowd of otherwise organized journalists went wild. If there had been a line of phone booths in the back they could all stampede into, it would have toppled over. The Secret Service had confiscated their cell phones, so the reporters would have to wait to file their stories.

Arturo and she would have a fight with party leaders, their campaign staff, most bloggers, Rush Huffington, etc., but not with the American people. They'd love his idea and he'd become president for being so philosophically perfect. *Bleep him.*

Now that Arturo had let this little gem out of the bottle, there would be no stuffing it back in. The press would push this 24/7 as the top story for the remaining four plus weeks of the campaign.

There would already be voters out there right now writing in her name as vice president on their mail-in ballots. She was *so* screwed and he was *so* rude not to have confided in her. Yet he'd asked more than once to talk to her on the plane. So it was her fault? She'd have her physician pull out the dagger from her back. She peeked up at the handsome Cuban American. *Later, baby.* But for now, unless she could perform a miracle, she was going to lose the election.

She needed a diversion, to balance the damage Arturo had inflicted on her campaign. She'd need to top his attempt to seduce the world press with a bigger, better, juicier story.

"Senator, Senator." For what seemed like an eternity, Ayita patted her arms downward, asking for silence. God, what was she going to say? She needed perhaps another minute to locate her once brilliant self, but her muse munched on chocolates and couldn't be bothered.

"After I get well, I'm going to kick Arturo's butt." She waited for the raucous crowd to die down. Divine providence showed her the light at the end of the tunnel. Arturo bowed, encouraging her to respond seriously. He'd get his. She pointed to a Canadian correspondent. No matter the question from this meek reporter, she'd deliver only one answer.

"Dudley."

"Senator, will you consider the governor's proposal?" *Good.*

"I will, but only if the governor faces reality and realizes he'll be written in on the Democratic ticket as my vice-president. Folks, doesn't Ayita—Arturo sound better than Arturo—Ayita?" Their campaign chiefs cut their throats with their fingers, but she had one last thing to say. "Dudley."

"Yes, Senator."

"All of you here do not know the real reason Arturo suggested we crisscross our tickets." She waited a moment to build excitement. She winked at Arturo who started shriveling up into an invisible black hole. "Arturo just wants an excuse to hold my hand. We have to run." Zing.

Arturo smirked and whispered to Ayita, "Touché. Let's see the president." He turned to the crowd while Ayita settled into her wheelchair. "No more questions." Ayita guessed Arturo couldn't conjure up a comeback. But had she just made things worse?

* * *

By order of the president, the Marine guards stopped everybody from pursuing the nominees. Most politely filed out of the briefing room and downstairs to the press corps offices in the White House basement. But a couple of journalists gave chase, shouting. One somehow squirmed by the first set of guards.

The last to be stopped at the corner turn to the Oval Office was Buxom Elaine from Fox News who pressed her hooters against the crisscrossed arms and bayonets of two guards who didn't seem to mind but kept straight faces. Win-win.

"Governor, aren't you going to defend your honor against the senator's allegation?" Ayita—merely fifty feet ahead and stopped at a portrait of Lincoln—pushed her hair back over her ears.

Arturo shouted back, "Nothing to defend, Elaine. She meant we'd raise our hands clasped together in victory, nothing more."

"Oh come on, Governor."

He ignored her.

"I'll have to report something."

"You want an exclusive," Whatever happened to good 'olé fashioned journalism where reporters did their research? "Check out her talent competition when she won Miss Cherokee Nation. You had better retreat, Elaine, before the guards impale you." *And not with their swords.* He broke out his five-dollar smile. He heard Ayita laughing. She had eavesdropped. She'd also cultivated a wicked wit. Ayita had done standup comedy as her talent at the beauty pageant. Elaine would get her story.

"Thanks, boys. Thanks, Governor." Elaine beat a hasty retreat. He had handed her a fish, but, if granted time, he would have preferred she'd learn her craft properly instead of partially relying on her looks. Inside all that va va va voom was a brilliant mind just waiting to bust out.

22

"Ma'am," the guards responded politely. God only knew what passed through the guards minds as they watched her mini-skirted rear retreat. Arturo could almost hear Gypsy Rose Lee's band playing.

Arturo's nurse wheeled him completely into the corridor heading to the Oval Office. Ayita was still admiring President Lincoln's portrait. He caught up.

"Why didn't you say anything to rebut me at the press conference?" Ayita asked.

"The cat got my tongue." Ayita, as close to a tigress as a human could get, seemed skeptical, but from that twinkle in her eyes, he surmised she knew the cat he spoke of sat in a wheelchair.

The truth was her handholding allegation fell in with his plans. - If he felt the pulse of the country right, if he knew anything at all about news cycles, the two bombshells they'd dropped would dominate the bit more than four remaining weeks before the election. Every time someone spoke about the two of them, whether as running mates or illicit mates, more and more voters would write them in. The people of the United States would get both of them, which defeated the assassin's intent, and guaranteed both of them the job of a lifetime.

Sharp Ayita smiled. She must have caught on. He clasped her hand again.

"Stop taking liberties with my hand." He withdrew softly. She cocked her head and covered her mouth but couldn't hold in a gleeful snicker.

They rolled to a stop outside the dining room to the right of the Oval office where the Secret Service stood guard.

Arturo flexed his arms and popped himself out of his seat to impress his nurse. "I don't care what the doctor said."

"But, sir, you might fall down," the nurse retorted.

"You can take this contraption back to the hospital and thank everybody for me. I'm feeling great. Just get me a cane."

"Yes, sir."

"I'll be careful."

"Let me take your arm."

Ayita watched intently. The adorable Filipina nurse, hardly out of school, helped him into the dining room, quite strong for someone so petite. On a fishing boat, and if he were fishing, he'd throw this one back. He knew who he wanted for dinner, Ayita. The nurse was young enough to be the daughter he'd never had and looked a bit too much like the girl he'd married twenty years ago. The nurse's pageboy cut of thick, lustrous black hair, roundish face, cute nose, sensuous lips, winged eyes, brought a tear to his eye. God, he missed his Sheryl.

"Babalik ako," she said under her breath, but he caught the reference to General MacArthur's, *"I shall return."* Both nurses left.

He relished the opportunity to have a heart-to-heart with the opposition party's president, Dan, and his wife, Margie, and of course, Ayita. Since President Daniel Carthage had had a productive eight years, Arturo was lucky to be tied in the polls. He hoped that Carthage's wisdom would help the two nominees who had ventured onto very strange territory.

Margie, a slightly heavier and sixty-year-old version of Marilyn Monroe still wowed. The country loved her, for the most part, for her work with animal rescue groups and canine research. Today, she wore a simple autumn-colored dress with matching jacket. One hair, possibly wolf or dog, clung to her collar.

After some pleasantries among old friends, the president rose.

"Quite a performance, you two." The tall ex-basketball player raised a glass of Merlot. "Unfortunately, I have good and bad news. I've had every intelligence service give me their two cents on the assassination attempt. The CIA, Homeland Security, NSA, FBI, Secret Service and I all agree it is too dangerous just yet for you two to hit the road. We have good reason to believe they are hell bent on assassinating the both of you still. The good news is we now know who's behind the assassination attempt. A two-bit white supremacist group tired of non-whites running the country." The president was black. "At this point, they're under surveillance but we can't take any chances. We might not have identified all of them yet."

"And the bad news is?" Ayita asked.

"Give the Secret Service a week."

"We've been cooped up too long, Dan." Arturo said, offering sham resistance. Any lame or brilliant excuse for spending time with Ayita suited his plans just fine. He needed to get her out of his fantasy life or dive in deeper. Since they needed to plan a road trip…

"You both have a responsibility to the American people to stay safe. I don't want to preside over a constitutional crisis. If I have to put you two in shackles and throw you into our dungeons, I will." A funny man, the president conjured up imaginary rooms instead of adding on to the basement floor.

"What do you have in mind?" Ayita asked.

"You'll be our guests for one or two days, until our aforementioned security forces clear each location you two want to visit. Your estate in Virginia, Ayita, will be upgraded the moment you give permission to the service and staying there will round out your week in hiding. And then, you'll both be free, at last."

"Permission granted, but my home is already more secured than the White House. The NSA tries their experimental gadgets and systems at my place. Arturo might want to stay at a different undisclosed location, but he is certainly welcome. I have a huge estate."

"I accept your invitation, Ayita. We have a lot of planning to do if we are going to tour the country together." Her being an ex-NSA chief engineer, Arturo didn't doubt her home being secure for a moment. On the other hand, missile batteries, drones and boots on the ground protected today's White House. *What could she possible have better than this?* He'd take a chance.

"I'm not up on the technical, but apparently it's just integrating the needs of the Secret Service and getting them used to your beta testing of NSA novelties."

The First Lady spoke up. "Even so, we would love to have both of you as our special guests."

"We agree," Arturo said, knowing he'd figuratively just patted Ayita's hand—again, although her cute round bottom would be a more satisfying pat. Too bad dessert would be more prosaic.

"There he goes again, the presumptuous…" Ayita held her tongue. The two ladies shared a laugh. The president cleared his throat. Arturo shrugged and tossed his hands wide open, mugging his innocent boy look.

"What about our kids?" Ayita said with a barely held straight face, talk about presumption. She had to know the dinner conversation would likely now revolve around her handholding remark at the press conference. Good. Arturo tired of talk about the assassination, the funerals and services. The subject of the two of them as a pair would prove interesting. He'd anxiously wait to find out how this imaginary couple would end up.

"What about our cellphones?" Arturo asked. His had been partially destroyed and Ayita's confiscated, thus having separated them from their staffs and their soon-to-arrive kids.

The Secret Service's efforts bordered on paranoia.

"NSA is replacing and updating Ayita's phone, and if it's okay by you, Governor, they want to give you one as well. They think they can or already have retrieved your contacts."

"That would be great." A secure NSA phone sported far more bells and whistles than anything commercial, but did it play Angry Birds?

The president said grace. The food arrived and Ayita immediately forked a steamed carrot slice out of the serving bowl and downed it. Turning a bit red, she said, "Sorry, I'm so hungry."

* * *

Was Ayita's attitude toward him competitive or just a tease? Perhaps a little of both. He'd need to get to know her better, to disqualify her from being his soul mate so he could go about doing the nation's business and honor his father's prophesy that someday, he will become President of the United States.

Surely, Ayita had the same dream. Maybe she would show her true self to him and end his distractions over loving again. Or perhaps, she'd recognize a growing and someday mutual love too strong to dismiss. But her story, her modus operandi, as the world press and political circles speculated was that NSA had replaced her heart with one of their fantastic inventions. Not literally, of course. Simply put, driven by faith in God and science, she'd use the talents God gave her—to the max. Perhaps her hero husband, Pavan, who'd died in battle so many years ago, had taken her heart to the grave with him. Maybe her compassionate but sharp eyes hid some similar feelings for her opponent? *Fantasy.*

God blessed this stunning sexy enigma in so many ways. He might just go insane obsessing over the absurd notion he could have a woman like Ayita.

A carnal hunger overwhelmed him. But it wouldn't be prudent to rip off her clothes and make love to her on the plush carpet with the presidential seal in the dining room off the oval office with the president and first lady cheering them on. Still, it beat eating carrots.

He swore he smelled sex.

* * *

Blue point Maryland crabs were served with a savory pepper and vinegar sauce. Over dinner, the president discussed higher levels of top secret clearances for Arturo and Ayita. The president stressed that from a constitutional point of view the two nominees couldn't act in anything more than an advisory role. The wine steward kept filling everybody's glasses at the first lady's insistence. Normally, no one drank heavily, but Ayita played along and drank along, thankful to be alive and now at peace with Arturo's brilliant idea for their ticket. The room took on a red haze.

The reverie of friends came to a halt when the president, suddenly sullen, pushed his candied limes around his Dolly Madison plate and then stopped and winked at his guests. "Anybody notice the eight-hundred-pound gorilla in the room?"

Ayita's glance swept the room and she turned red again, too much wine and too gullible. Of course, she knew the president spoke allegorically. But of what? As usual, Arturo, with a wide grin, seemed ready to solve the puzzle, like a kid itching with the right answer. If presented with a buzzer, he would have pounded on it by now.

"My love affair with Ayita will soon be a figment of the world's imagination."

"I'll bet you The National Tattletaler will be disgraced and left in the dust by the normal press." Margie offered. NT made more stories up than Hollywood.

"If you love me, Arturo, why no roses, no chocolates?" Ayita jumped in. *Can anybody play?*

"My dearest Ayita, of great beauty and greater competence, which will it be, me or the presidency?"

"I'll take both, thank you very much." She broke out her wide smile.

His was wider. "I bet you will." My God, Arturo and Ayita *got* flirt. *Would this play on the campaign trail? Not likely.* Ayita displayed her congenial are-you-kidding scoff. Later, they'd talk.

"Seriously, you two," the president said.

"I don't know which end is up," Margie said.

"Are…ah, the kids here yet?" Ayita parked her tongue but somehow she couldn't resist caressing Arturo's hand, to get him back, of course.

He picked up her hand and planted a kiss that lasted a little too long. What had she done but lead him on? One tease too many? Okay, it was sweet.

"What did you put in this wine?"

"Truth serum," Margie said.

The wall intercom buzzed. The kids had arrived.

"Give them a little time to settle into the gym and game room," Margie said, obviously stalling, hoping for one of them to confess to something nasty.

"We better not mention our love affair—real or imagined—to them. Not even as a joke," Arturo said.

Anytime you tell college students anything, the whole world would know instantly via social media. Promoting speculation with the press to nurture the nominees' mystique and continue piling up write-in votes, differed from riling three kids who probably would love a new mom or dad, and as an afterthought would love to make their mom or dad happy. *Let them guess. Don't say a word.*

Bored by the truth that in the busy fishbowl in which they lived, neither she nor Arturo had a love life, and it would not be likely they'd ever find love again. *Sad, he's such a handsome Cuban American hunk who could too easily score home runs.* But not with her.

Through the drapes, Ayita caught the soft lights off trees and bushes, beyond which splattered the gathering gray of a day turning night. Would her life change? They met in a sort of twilight time, after assassination attempts, before the presidency and still under threat, and now by mutual agreement together on the campaign trial until an election do they part. Why it's almost like shacking up without the candy.

A time to lead the nation with new ideas. A time for love? She needed to understand Arturo and all the better to keep him close.

She had nothing to lose. She had awakened from a coma repulsed by his behavior then. She had suffered his slings and arrows during the campaign and primary season. If she ended up feeling the same distance between them, it would be no loss. If they ended up friends, it would bode well for when he'd work under her as vice-president. *Under her,* he was quite big, muscular, an ex-slugger for major league baseball's Marlins, she now recalled. He looked like he hadn't gained an ounce. The man had pride and/or maybe he was searching for a wife? Who was she kidding? She kept herself at her fighting weight for the same reasons. She had until now refused to recognize she wanted not needed a man—being too busy—the country needed her. The country needed them. Why was she even going there?

She had to stay focused because the good of the many far exceeded Arturo and Ayita's needs, if at all. What had Bogart said in Casablanca? Something like Ilsa, I'm no good at being noble, but...the problems of three little people don't amount to a hill of beans in this crazy world. Someday you'll understand. Now, now. ...Here's looking at you, kid."

Now, now. Here's looking at you, Arturo. Looking at him made her heart flutter, or was it the wine? The way he snuck glances at her legs made her feel like going to confession.

Chapter Three
Matchmaker, Matchmaker

The dinner and dessert nearly over, and the kids enjoying each other's company, Margie made one last point. A presidential nominee typically selected a VP to complement and not supplement the ticket. However, with Arturo and Ayita as the VP and presidential nominee and either being capable of running the country from day one, this would help the nominees' crisscross campaign. Her worry was centered on a revolt by the two parties. The parties could also play the write-in for president game. The president promised to apply his considerable influence to stop this nonsense. Ayita knew him to be a man of his word.

"The parties are one thing, but the American voter wants us," Arturo said.

The president moved away from the played-out subject. "I started my eight years with a double White House wedding. Perhaps one of you will do a single ceremony someday." The president referred to his daughter, the blinded Army General Rebekah Carthage, who on the lawn right outside these windows, married Professor James Boone in a double ceremony with the professor's mom, Margie and the president. It rivaled Camelot. The ratings had come second to the Super Bowl that year, which fueled talk shows and gossip magazines for months.

"I chose to marry the American people," Arturo said. "All kidding aside, and with all due deference to my lovely partner, I'll never love another woman like I did my Sheryl. So I'll likely join the list of bachelor and widower presidents." He nodded at his partner, Ayita. She said nothing, but tilted her chin down and frowned. It was obvious Arturo had to lose these two bloodhounds so his flirting could begin in earnest in more private times ahead. Because of what he'd said about Sheryl, perhaps Ayita would fall down a real rabbit hole, a hole built on a most dangerous game of flirting. And before she knew what hit her...

Ayita showed off, but this nonplussed crowd loved and knew their U.S. history. "Jefferson, Van Buren, Jackson, Buchanan and Arthur were widows, with Buchanan the only bachelor." Just like in college, she couldn't help herself, but then she spied her dinner mates' warming enthusiasm and relaxed.

"Yes. Tyler, Cleveland and Wilson remarried while in the White House. Harrison remarried after leaving here," Margie added.

"Once upon a time, I had thought I'd stay a widower too, but Margie drove me completely mad." Dan said.

Oh, the stories bandied about within the intelligence community, from their bodice-ripping first meeting in Margie's greenhouse and everywhere else in her home in Cherry Hill, New Jersey, to the noises heard some blocks away from the White House by those with overactive imaginations.

"What about you, Ayita?" Margie asked.

Ayita stole a glance of the Cuban American. "Someday, I suppose. I too haven't given it any thought since I lost my husband so long ago." Ever since she had awakened in that bunker after the assassination attempt, she had started drooling over men again. Must have had something to do with her brush with death or the truest meaning of life had come to pay her a visit— Love shall not be denied.

"Some say the ghosts of all the ex-presidents have nothing better to do than match make. So beware, you two, sleeping in the White House might be dangerous to your celibacy." The president focused on a portrait of Lincoln sitting with his war cabinet. "Slide Lincoln." The priceless artwork slid upward to reveal a monitor. "Your kids are on the third floor of our residence in the workout room. There they are. Go ahead, they can hear us but not see us."

Arturo's two handsome sons, Brian and Bill, were standing very close to Daya as if they had found their date for the winter formal and were about to fight over her. Brian was taller, maybe by an inch, but Bill was also tall and broader shouldered like his dad. Ayita figured Daya would like the huskier Bill better. She'd find out. Always her best friend, she couldn't wait for some alone time with her daughter.

"Aren't you three supposed to be studying?" Ayita asked.

"Mom, I miss you," Daya said, in a come to me voice. This, no doubt, was daughter speak for I miss you so much and would prefer to spend time with you instead of studying.

"Where are you guys?" Brian asked, looking around for cameras.

Ayita finished off the last bite of the scrumptious candied-lime dessert. The three college kids were testing gym equipment and each other. The two nominees would have a debriefing with the task force conducting the bombing investigation, and then the two families would treasure the rest of the night for catching up.

Everybody was set to stay on the second floor with the first family down the hall, probably just for the night. Ayita's Daya was given the anteroom off the Queen's bedroom in which her mom stayed. Arturo's two sons would be just off the Lincoln bedroom, also in an adjoining suite. Ayita gave thanks for three young people whose fate would now likely tangle, just like their parents. *Who will play a better Ken and Barbie game tonight, me or my baby?*

"Well, Arturo, it seems not only you and I are going to be friends, but your sons and my daughter are looking really chummy." She stopped talking, choking up over what could not be undone. The more she stared at her daughter the more she saw Pavan. A happy Daya, with a full and long life, would make up for her dad leaving this earth too early. It had to.

As she studied her daughter's face, her memories came flooding back. Someone had knocked at the door. She pulled up her nursing bra cup, held her infant close. Fearing the worst, she

33

peeped and then opened the door. Two Army officers festooned in medals sadly stared. She collapsed, sliding down against the wall. They helped her and the baby to the kitchen and made her soup.

But that was twenty years ago. Today, all she had in the world was her lovely Daya.

* * *

A tear dropped onto her lap and Margie, now up, hugged her. The men seemed to know and offered her their prayers.

"We have to run upstairs and say a quick hello," Arturo said.

"The security debrief needs to start in ten minutes, so they tell me," the president said but then promised to slow it down a little.

Ayita rushed upstairs to the Queen's room. Inside the famous room, she enjoyed her daughter's many hugs, tears and kisses, staccato requests for a couple of sharp outfits, the latest cell phone, promised stories of boys, yummy and otherwise. They'd comb out each other's long black hair and give and take back massages. Although the ever-studious Daya plowed into her pre-med, she had a perpetual fascination for the opposite sex, much like her mom in her college days. But Ayita had gotten pregnant and then married. Daya would not.

But all this girl stuff would have to wait. Arturo announced himself and knocked. *Time to wrestle with devils.* She'd have plenty of time for Daya in less than an hour.

Ayita stood and then bent over to kiss her daughter's forehead. "Study up, girl."

Chapter Four
You Only Live Twice

Ayita used a cane and her daughter Daya's arm to reach the bedroom door and greet Arturo. They'd make it to the basement situation room nearly on time.

"I am so glad to meet you, Daya. My sons want to challenge you to some video games if you have about an hour. I told them they'd have to study after that." What could Ayita do? The young people had a perfect excuse to offer their professors. Oh, what the heck, there was also no way she'd give up time with her daughter just so she could study. Perhaps they could pour over a book together. Organic Chemistry anyone?

"Thank you, Governor. I'm pleased to meet you too. Thank you for saving my mom's life." She hugged him. He hadn't actually saved her life. The two of them had gone flying together.

They said their goodbyes, but Daya lingered, holding the door open and watching her mom and the governor like an eagle. *Wonder what she's thinking.*

Ayita looked up and down the hall, confused. "Have you seen our wheelchairs and nurses?"

"I got our Secret Service teams to have them wait for us in the Red Room."

"But we're not going there."

"Exactly, now if I may have your arm, my lady." *The dirty old man.* If she had a soft pocketbook, she'd bop him. This guy was so damn charming.

Daya swallowed a giggle. Putting a hand on her mouth and crinkling her eyes, she waved goodbye. "See you later, Mom." and finally closed the door. Ayita thought she heard Daya mumble,

"And your date." *Daya, my little amateur sleuth, I love you to pieces.*

Out in the hall and with her daughter probably listening behind the bedroom door, Ayita said softly, "You just can't keep your hands off of me, can you?" She took his strong muscled arm and felt like fainting.

Arturo leaned on her for the shortest of moments. "You're so feisty perhaps you could hold me up." They walked down the hall slowly, intending to get to the west wing by a convoluted path east and down to avoid walking by the president's bedroom.

"I heard that the blast left you with slivers of wood, a pen and an umbrella stuck in your back."

"The umbrella fell out. I've got a thick back and a thicker backside," Arturo said.

"Oh, that paints a pretty picture. Seriously are you all right?"

"Nothing but my pride hurts when I sit down." He patted his rear and cringed. "I am so happy my body shielded yours. I really do like to think I saved you."

"By squashing me?"

"Yeah, sure." Perhaps he did. She was so thin an umbrella would have run her through and then open and off she'd float to heaven.

"Arturo, I thank you, really." He said nothing, so she filled the void. "I don't think the American people are ready for a steel-cage match with you pinning me, but it would be entertaining."

"Maybe we should switch bedroom suites," he said.

"Why?"

Arturo was warming her up for one of his zingers again.

"My bedroom, Lincoln's bedroom was merely his office when he was president. Do you know the story of Lincoln's ghost?"

"Are you making this up?" Of course he was.

"He died unexpectedly, as we all know. He was trying to resolve marital problems at the time, well, for a long time. Before his assassination, he used to pace back and forth in this very hall. He pondered a way back to his wife's heart. After he died, he paced for years trying to find his wife, but Mary Todd Lincoln had already moved on to her eternal reward, her afterlife. He became desperate. To this day, when female royalty and other famous or infamous women stay over in your room, his shy ghost appears, hoping for a fleeting chance at advice, and perhaps to experience passion eternally denied. At night, if you listen closely you can hear the indecisive and incessant knocking of his peg leg."

"That was Captain Ahab." If she had the strength to punch his arm, she would have.

"Oh, oh yeah, well, you could hear the tap of his heals."

"That was Bojangles."

"You could hear the clanking of chains."

"He was neither a slave nor criminal."

"Well...what you might hear—" he tickled her ear with his conspiratorial whisper, his lips so bite-my-neck close, "—is his desperate plea for your charms and advice." He let the words caress her.

"Do you do this all the time?"

"Only to goddesses." Broadly smiling, he raised and kissed her hand once again. For God's sake, there was only so much a girl could take. Something stirred her, awakened her, drove her a little nutty. Traveling with him across the country might prove more interesting than she could ever imagine.

* * *

A short time later, still laughing, they made it to the basement of the West Wing and headed over to a conference room adjoining the situation room. Their Secret Service teams had coalesced and were now run by Jason. He was busy arranging assorted tea bags. Strange, yes, but his little eccentricities helped him relax, so he had claimed.

"It's just me tonight, so I'll make it short and sweet. Colonel Petrovich couldn't show because he and his sidekick, Moon, are tracking one of the suspects.

"The assassins are a small group of four to maybe six or seven. We'll have the correct number pinned down soon. They're white supremacists or Nazis, if you will. They go by the abbreviation TONARTUS, meaning Tired of Non-Arians Running the United States." Jason lifted the towel off a wicker basket. "I made some scones."

"I'm stuffed," Arturo said, leaning over to inspect boysenberry scones. He seemed tempted. "Maybe one for later." Jason wrapped one in a napkin, dropped and sealed it in a zip baggie.

"Maybe one for Daya. Thanks, Jason."

"Would two more for my boys be okay, Jason?"

"It's my pleasure." Among other peccadillos, Jason obsessed over cooking and was hooked on the cooking channel. Arturo seemed to have a healthy appetite for sweet things.

Ayita turned to Arturo. "Carlos hates Nazis."

"I'd love to know what he's doing. Will we be debriefed?" Arturo asked.

"Not likely, but he does confide in me. I'll arrange for you to meet him and try to talk him into sharing with you."

"How'd he get his first name?" Arturo displayed a healthy curiosity.

"His mother was Basque, from the Spanish side of the French border, father Russian."

"He has a bad reputation at the Justice Department." Carlos, often suspected of eliminating Nazis and their ilk in hilarious ways, had never been tried in court for lack of evidence or as they say in the Black Ops community, 'you'd be cutting your own throat—*if you confronted Carlos.*'

"Don't worry." She would have loved to work in the field for NCS again as a spy one last time, something she'd spent too little time doing. She had had a couple of opportunities to play Mata Hari and missed the exhilaration that came from seeing the trap she set catch prey. She'd returned to Washington too cerebral, too geekish, too in love with creating gadgets to stay overseas for long. Besides, Carlos and his network of assassins had been eliminating counter threats to any NCS personnel involved. Europe and the Middle East were too hot. She opened her NSA phone Jason had just given them and texted Carlos. *"A penny for yours and Moon's thoughts."*

Carlos texted, *"I know you miss this. But it is just normal cloak-with-dagger work tonight. Give us no more than week and they will all be in jail or dead."* Carlos never failed to deliver on his promises.

* * *

Colonel Carlos Petrovich had defected from the now defunct Soviet Union to join the NCS which was the black ops arm of the CIA and later was promoted to director of OTTS, an agency started by Eisenhower devoted to unexplained phenomena.

He spotted his mark walking up 16th from the general direction of Lafayette Park, Washington D.C. He had expected the mark to park on the closest side-street because of the temporary no-parking signs Carlos and his sidekick had put up. His sidekick waited outside the mark's hotel apartment, which was just around the corner.

The cool night breeze picked up. He pulled up the flaps on his favorite gray wool long coat given him by the Commandant of West Point. Tomorrow, he'd likely need it dry-cleaned. He really didn't like getting dirty except when gardening.

Carlos had been in this situation too many times before. Kill or be killed. He was the best, not because he was built like a bear. Size really didn't matter. His sidekick was nicknamed Moon because of her somewhat unpronounceable last name and roundish face. Her full name, Sarantsatral, meant moonlight in Mongolian. Moon could handle anyone foolish enough to pick on her.

He took a swig from a pocket flask of Stolichnaya vodka to deaden the pain he was about to suffer.

With a few smart moves tonight, he would avoid killing this peace of shit walking toward him. Carlos hated white supremacists. Almost his entire family had been gassed by Nazis in World War II just because they were Jews. He had administered justice, one idiot at a time. But if all went as planned today, he'd have to delay or forego execution.

Yes, he had a penchant for bending or breaking the law, but no one had ever proved it. Such was life in and out of NCS. Being out in the field and working for his favorite spy and good friend Ayita, put a spring in his step. No one would ever hurt her.

His mark inspected each closed storefront as if window-shopping, as if he weren't in a rush to kill the nominees. Carlos surmised the mark was likely admiring his well-built frame and seemed to have a carefree or jocular manner. Perhaps susceptible to joking, if the smug GQ poses he mugged in the windows were any indication.

The shithead dressed in a thick black business suit with blue striped tie, playing the part of a D.C. businessman. Carlos hated ties, his neck too thick. A tie gave him neck wrinkles. Hey, even killers had vanities. What would his mark think if an old man beat the crap out of him...or took his life? The dead don't think and he liked it that way.

Carlos pushed off his immaculate Cadillac, slammed and locked the door, attracting attention. The car showed Louisiana plates—a nice touch when dealing with racists. The mark was only ten paces from the front of his car. Carlos picked up his pace, gave the man a quick worried glance and then tripped on the curb as planned. Carlos broke his fall with his hands. His left hand landed on the scattered remains of a broken bottle of Thunderbird wine he had placed earlier.

He shouted in pain, "Damn it, damn." He peered up at his mark, looking for approval. "Damn niggers leave their bottles of crap." He picked at the label. "Ouch. Whoa." Carlos hated saying racial slurs. It made him think of Nazi guards demeaning Jews outside the gas chambers—the screams, all the nightmares from the ghosts of his ancestors. He remained calm and hoped this would disarm the fuck-head.

"Need help, mister?" Got him. Carlos had laid out Hollywood fake glass but it still stung. The cut was also faked with real laboratory blood. He wore a skin-like and practically invisible sheath over his hands to accommodate the special effects and offer some protection against pain and DNA transfer.

"Yes, mister, just help me up. How do you stand living in this crap hole?"

"Visiting from L.A., sir."

Bullshit. Carlos wrapped his cut hand around the back of the mark's neck for support and lifted up with the stranger's help. He made a hole in the man's neck with a tiny sterilized scalpel attached between his fingers.

"Yo. Ouch." The mark grabbed the back of his neck, all according to plan.

"Oh my God, I am sorry, so sorry. I'll give you my card. I'll pay for your doctor." Carlos often thought he'd be perfect in some Hollywood movie like the Terminator, maybe.

"Shit." The mark felt his neck again, but of course nothing was there but a small incision and a little of his own blood.

Carlos picked out a piece of Hollywood glass from his palm, and grimaced with pain. "Me too. *Shit.* You are going to cut your hand rubbing your neck like that. I can see the glass stuck in your neck, let me pull the piece out under the light."

"No, that's all right. I'll check when I get to my hotel." The man moved his hand slowly over the back of his neck, now searching for the imaginary glass.

"I am Rusky doctor, best in field. You don't want infection there. Might have to amputate either head or body—" this received the hoped for laugh, "—and I have a little vodka that can be used for antiseptic."

The mark although under obvious agitation and in a rush to commit homicide turned his back to Carlos, moved under the street lamp and acquiesced to Doctor Carlos removing the glass.

"Make it quick, Doc, I have an appointment that can't wait."

"Okay, very quick, no problem." Carlos nudged into the cut a micro-transceiver-geo-tracker half the size of a grain of rice. The mechanical critter burrowed deep under the mark's skin. Carlos pretended to pull out a sliver of glass, which had been hidden earlier between his fingers.

"Look at this." Carlos displayed a nasty bloodstained sliver nearly a half-inch long.

The mark inspected the little spike with gaping amazement. Turning pale, he looked like it was his turn to fall. Carlos asked for the man's handkerchief and blotted the vodka into it.

"A shame to waste good vodka," the mark said, obviously recovered from the shock, and true to type, he made a little joke.

"Want a swig?"

"I really have to run." He started moving away. "Thank you, Doc."

Oh—a polite Nazi. "Take my card."

"It's okay," the mark said. "Take care of your hand. I promise you I'll drink later, drink a lot." God, they were practically brothers. It would be a shame to execute him *later*, if the mark survived his sidekick Moon tonight.

"The name is Dr. Mengele," Carlos said. "And thanks for saving an old man's life." Carlos was pushing fifty.

"You saved mine too. Call me Johann Bach."

Ha. Ha. Yeah, right, Mengele meet Bach. The mark picked up his pace, looked back once at a waving Carlos and turned the corner to go to the hotel apartment where Moon was waiting.

Carlos, ever fastidious, got out a pan and broom from the trunk of the Cadillac and cleaned up his mess and possible evidence. The mark would shower away any DNA transfers. In the meantime, Carlos treated his hands like a crime scene. He rolled off his supposedly wounded hand the small film of plastic and deposited it into an evidence bag and did the same to his other hand. The stranger's DNA was now captured.

Such tricks weren't legal. Americans were such pussies. They wanted their democracy, but were willing to fall prey to people who didn't play by the rules.

He drove to the next corner and parked on a side street in his very own no-parking area. He put on clear latex gloves, popped the trunk, dropped in the no-parking sign and lugged out a toolbox full of electronic goodies, including a universal electronic car door opener. After Carlos got done with the mark's car and modifying any weapons found, the man would be castrated.

* * *

Carlos's sidekick, Moon, had pasted a note on the secret service agent Jason's apartment door and waited in the walnut armchair at the end of the seventh floor. She held a *Glamour* magazine high. In its pages, she held and hid a .22 pistol, her favorite. She wore a short skirt, so the stranger would like her Mongolian farm-girl legs. Even Nazis were men with dicks and balls, but she didn't fuck them. She just killed them to please Carlos. Besides, Nazis were yak excrement.

The mark got out of the elevator about halfway down the hall and turned away from her. He rushed towards Jason's door but then stopped dead. He turned around. Moon stuck one hand above the magazine covering most of her face and waved. But he was still frozen, tongue tied.

"Hello, mister. I wait for my boyfriend. You not look at my legs, are you?"

"No, ah no, I wouldn't look."

"You know, I not a dirty street fucker. I like short skirts, everybody likes. You like?"

"I don't wear them, but I like them." When it came to sex, Nazis would screw anything pretty, no matter the color, or slinky eyes.

She was disappointed the reading lamp was behind her and the hall spotlights were weak, because her red panties with white happy faces were so cute. She re-crossed her legs, but the mark didn't notice.

"Ha. Ha. You funny."

"Sorry, I have to go."

"You go. Have nice life." She made a bubble-popping sound. At the door, he still kept his eyes on her.

She dropped the magazine just a little more to peek with both sloe eyes and waved with her free hand. He stopped gawking and started reading the note on the door.

Hey, Jason, my love, I got your message and headed over to Mom's. I tried to reach you to tell you I'd meet you there. I know you'll catch up with your cell phone messages and will never see this note, but you know me, better safe than sorry. I'm all packed and packed your stuff. We can go straight to the Poconos from Mom's. I'm so glad your employer gave you three days off. We need it.
Love you,
Jack

The mark hesitated, a look of disgust on his face. He peeked down the hallway at the occupied chair, the legs, and paced.

"You stop peeking at my legs, okay, mister?"

"Sorry, ma'am. I'm not looking, just thinking."

"Hey, you go in now or go think someplace else. You lose key?"

He had that look of someone wanting to kill an annoying girl. "No. Forgot it. I didn't want to go back down to the car. Thought she would answer the door." He knocked.

"Oh, he not she, leave with airport bag little while ago."

After some hesitation and more confused looks, he headed toward the elevator.

"I misspoke. I know where *he* went. Thanks, ma'am."

The mark didn't really know where Jason'd gone. Jason was debriefing the nominees. Too bad, the mark had nobody to try to kill. Nobody to impersonate. A very, very dumb and desperate plan. *Too bad, no hole in head tonight for you, mister.*

"Ding." The elevator opened and the dead man went in.

She looked down at her well-defined sexy legs and remembered how horny she felt.

Get a big-shot soon to satisfy me.

Chapter Five
Hot, Hot, Hot

Arturo caught up with his sons before the two boys retired to the adjoining bedroom off Lincoln's *so-called* bedroom, because Lincoln never slept here. They slumped in French provincial loveseats five feet from the stoked fireplace. His youngest one had his feet propped on a rather sturdy-looking latticed black-iron coffee table with a white marble top. Both boys immediately put down their hot chocolates with marshmallows to get up and hug their father.

"Are you feeling a little better, Dad?" they both asked.

Arturo then relaxed on the bed. It was nothing special. A queen-sized bed with drapes pulled to show off an enormous rounded wood backboard. Arturo smirked. The rounded carved wood could match an elephant's rear end in shape and shade. Well, Lincoln was a Republican. The elephant's rear would certainly not help him sleep. You never know when it would try to sit down in his imagination. Even worse, the drapes' top was held up by a gold leaf crown with red fringe. He vaguely remembered America getting rid of a king long ago. Right? Of course, they entertained heads of state here, so he'd stow his sense of irony and fear of huge behinds for the right dinner companion.

The boys went back to biting off, one-by-one, the hapless marshmallows from their cocoas.

"Take your feet off the table, Billy."

Arturo and Sheryl had enjoyed many a Scout camping trip with their boys. One of the most necessary supplies in being prepared for an adventure included packets of cocoa mix with tiny marshmallows. Tonight, the scones Secret Service agent Jason made would fit in nicely for these two chowhounds. He pulled out the baggie holding the scones from his suit pocket. The boys sprung up, grabbed the goodies and collapsed back down into slouches. Once again, Arturo, with the patience of a saint, asked his younger son to remove his stinking feet from the table.

"Sorry, Dad."

"Which one of you is going to date Daya?" He started the usual teasing.

Bill leaned forward. "She's a doll, but Brian is older and I'm swamped."

Brian, tapping his fingers on the loveseat's arm, had to chime in. "When you win, Dad, we'll all be here more often. I bet we'll both get dates, although I *am* better looking." His boys were practical, both going to Florida State and Daya at Catholic University here in Washington. He hoped the boys focused on their studies. The damn college wouldn't release their grades to parents, not even if he was governor. Somehow, in this upside down world, privacy rights usurped the sanctity of family and parental obligations. Some things were so wrong, but lest he alienate the youth vote, he wouldn't touch the issue. Or maybe he should be bold?

"She's plowing into pre-med anyway," Brian said.

Arturo kept the conversation going about girls. "Well, she is very pretty and smart." He loved watching the boys grow into men and wanted so much to be a grandpapa someday.

"Senator Starblanket is hot. Don't you think so, dad?" Brian was trying to turn the tables.

"Maybe we should talk about your studies."

"Dodge. Dodge." Billy moved his hips on the loveseat as an imaginary ball flew by.

"I'm surprised you guys would notice an old lady."

"Come on, Dad, she looks like Daya's older sister. Give us a break. She's hot, hot, hot," Billy said. Brian stood up and started dancing and waving his hands for them to join in. They all joined in the fun to dance to hot, hot, hot, a cha-cha-cha. A conga line formed as they circled around the two love seats. "Ah yita, yita, yita." Thank God, his boys had rhythm. Girls loved to dance, and Latin men were to them hot, hot, hot. All the better for his boys.

Brian gave up first and plopped back down as if it were musical chairs. Their happy faces revealed how much they missed this family thing—dancing and their father.

"Yes, boys. I'm not blind, but she's a freakin' Democrat." He raised his eyebrows. He marveled how easy it was to fall into college or boy speak around them.

"So are we, Dad, and you love us, we hope." They displayed big, ridiculous, sweet smiles. *But who would they vote for? Better not ask.* "Get with it, Pops. She's a slinky Cherokee princess who should raise money for her campaign by posing as Playboy's centerfold."

"I'd like that," Arturo said chuckling. Of course, he was thinking of the fallout and loss of votes for her, but one could never know these days. Still, his boys tagged him with an image of Ayita in her birthday suit and a slim strip of thin see-thru silk running from her ankle to her lips. The image now became like the song "It's a Small World After All", so hard to get out of his head. So, he'd keep it, maybe cultivate it.

No woman running for president should look that good.

But unless he peeled her down to nada, he'd never know for sure just how disqualified she was to be president.

"Maybe *Sports Illustrated* swimsuits," Brian offered sarcastically, staring at the high ceiling, "to hide stretch marks." Now Arturo pictured her scuba diving with him off the Florida Keys' coral reefs.

Arturo decided to let the stretch-mark comment pass. What did they know? Not much. "Have you two seen *my* nurse? Hmm?"

"No way," Billy said. "She and the other nurse were joking in the Blue Room downstairs."

"She looks too much like Mom in your wedding album. Never, Dad. Too young for you. I miss my mom," Brian's lips trembled, still the little boy lost without his mother's hugs. Bill caught the emotion. They both looked like they were going to bawl. Arturo would follow them if they didn't compose themselves. *Oh Sheryl, your boys are so beautiful.*

"We all do." Under his breath, he murmured. "Yeah, it's like hell without you here, honey." He hugged both of them in turn. "Listen, sons. I love, that is, I am dedicated to the American people and the memory of your mom. Can you understand this?" It would have been fantastic to have seen his Filipina sweetheart as first lady.

"Of course," they both answered. "Even if you are a Republican."

"It's been more than two full years, Dad. It's okay. Mom would want you to be happy," Billy said. These kids were relentless.

"You know nobody could replace your loving mom, my sweet wife."

"Love is limitless, Governor," Brian the sophomore philosophy student said.

"Listen up, boys. No matter what happens in the press, don't listen to all the gossip. Ayita and I are just trying to raise write-in vote totals."

"This is so freaked-out political cynical." Billy appeared ready to burst.

"Hanging with her *all the time* might change that. And this's okay, Dad. We give you permission. Mom would want you to find somebody nice, and Ayita, well, she could be president. People love her. She's got a great heart and we like her," Brain said, like he was trying to win a debate.

People loved her. That was the real problem with this election. Yep, people loved her, only liked him, except for women. But lust by legions of women voters wouldn't get him the top job. He'd have to build up his *love* numbers. If this didn't work or even if it did, he wanted one very lovely and brilliant woman to fall in love with him. *I am ready to move on, Sheryl.* This stunning girl, his double-running mate, was slipping into a nightie just down the hall and probably having a similar conversation with her baby.

Or maybe she slept *au natural*. He went back to the centerfold in his head and decided the silk had a light pink hue.

After his boys left, he scrolled through a myriad of calls, emails and texts. He texted his secretary.

> *Dear Matti,*
> *Please send a broadcast message to everybody thanking them for their thoughts and prayers whether they prayed or not. Cite the wishes of the Secret Service. I'll be responding soon on Facebook and Twitter and will get back individually to some of them as soon as I can. Tell the RNC chair and my campaign chair to hang in there. We'll have conversations at length tomorrow or the next day.*
> *Thanks, you are a blessing,*
> *Arturo*

Although not entirely sure, Arturo guessed he had just turned a corner in the direction of Ayita's heart, thanks to his boys' overwhelming approval of her, stretch marks or not. He cocked an eye and then closed them.

Doubly tough work ahead.

Chapter Six
Diamonds are a Girl's Best Friend

Ayita and Daya basked in the warm glow of the crackling hearth. A beige flat fabric with pink carnation brocade formed the canopy and dust cover on the king-sized four-poster colonial in the Queen's suite of the White House. They relaxed cross-legged on the firm mattress as they brushed out each other's long raven hair.

"Momma, I'd like you to do something for me."

"Sweetie?"

"Be nice to the governor."

Would Arturo's boys be putting him on the spot too? Had they developed a strategy to marry them off? *Terribly romantic, terribly ridiculous.* The only reason she'd ever kiss a Republican super star on the lips would be to change him into a frog. Surely some potion or charm could win this election. If she had time before Election Day, she'd visit her medicine-man grandfather, Viho, whose name meant chief in Cherokee.

"I heard you say you'd kick his butt and I know the faces you make, Momma. You're disgusted with him."

"*No*, I, I just worry about those just assassinated, the election, his ideas for the country."

"Get real. He's so much like you."

"Oh, how astute you are, little one."

"Can't we all just get along?"

"What are they teaching in pre-med?" Daya, a freshman at Catholic University enjoyed a healthy sprinkling of sociology and philosophy to go with the traditional sciences.

"They're teaching liberal, very liberal arts."

"I'm getting to appreciate him. Why are you concerned, my little matchmaker? Arturo and I are both grownups. We're playing the same game, with one winner and one loser."

"I think he likes you."

"Did you sign up for a class in body language too?"

"A girl knows when a boy likes her."

"Like Brian and Billy?"

"They both like me, more for my looks than for my brain. I don't think they noticed my brain, but I'll overcome that male silliness if they transfer to a local school. They're just being boys."

Daya looked much more like her handsome father than her mom. Daya dazzled with her dad's green eyes, broader face and more athletic build. Both stood five-foot seven wet, hair tickling butt, high cheeks—front and rear—small breasts, Cherokee slight hooknoses and clear bronze skin. Ayita did not consider herself beautiful, just exotic. With Daya's personality and looks, she would have no problem when *or if* the time came for her to attract a husband.

"Have you three been doing some planning?"

"No, not us. You can't hear us, can you?"

"No, baby. Which one do you like?"

"Both are good looking. I've got school. I've got dreams, Mamma. Marriage is way off, and when the time comes I'm going to make sure I get it right."

Great, this was the lesson she had drummed into Daya's head since the eight-year-old had put Ken and Barbie together in bed, one set of toes upside down, and asked them to make a baby. Lessons continued through prep school until they were engrained. Stopping her from being the star quarterback's play toy had been the closest call, but Mom's finest hour. She'd squashed that romance by arranging a seemingly chance get together between a neighbor's pretty, blonde daughter and Mr. Footballs-out. Although Joe wannabe Montana might have been a very nice boy, her Daya wasn't ready for a guy with too much easy at the end of his touch.

She steered Daya to chess club nerds and the idea that brilliance was attractive. Daya learned to play a mean game of chess but claimed she needed chemistry of the most flaming kind. Well, like mother like daughter. Her daddy had rammed her mother like a runaway express train and gotten her pregnant before marriage.

"I'm glad you'll put your studies first. I'm so proud of you."

"Always, Momma. You raised me right."

Daya left after sweet kisses and a long hug.

Ayita tried to fall asleep but tossed and turned worried about Lincoln's ghost hopping into bed with her. To make it worse, images of Abe kept morphing back and forth into the governor of Florida who dared get into her bed wearing his Marlin's baseball uniform, cleats and all. She could smell the chaw and grass. She cursed CNN for putting on TV the nominees' bios practically twenty-four seven. What a hunk. Even when he was a kid, he posed in a Star Trek captain's uniform raising his arms to show off non-existent muscles. Too cute.

The next President of the United States, as she liked to think of herself, tried to sleep.

Madam President.

This dreamy guy, Arturo not Abe, was her worst nightmare, likely to scar her for the rest of her life and then some. Life now had already changed. She had fallen down a rabbit hole to a world of someone else's brilliant musings and/or machinations.

She wrestled with ghosts a while longer and then sat up, leaned to the end table and grabbed her cell phone. She had put off her campaign manager for too long.

"I'm sorry, Grant, about the late call."

Grant Barrymore launched right into her like a mother berating a child but finally got around to asking her how she felt and what was happening with the Secret Service investigation.

"I understand, but what are you going to do about Arturo's suggestion to crisscross the tickets?" Hadn't this already been asked and answered? The best reason was that both of them would serve. The second best reason, both of them were the best both parties had to offer. And third, they thumbed their noses at the assassins. But dense Grant couldn't see any of it. Yet.

Replacing a vice president in the middle of the campaign was rare. It had happened in the case of Senator Thomas Eagleton stepping down. Also rare was having a president from one party and a vice-president from another. Adams and Jefferson, followed by Jefferson and Burr, and later Lincoln and Johnson were the only instances.

Grant offered a concrete alternative. "Well, I thought about flanking Arturo by taking in the Governor of Mississippi—"

Ayita interrupted. "But then he'd withdraw his offer and consider the senator of Connecticut or worse the governor of New Jersey."

Okay, just where was Grant's head? Maybe he was sleepy, so she decided to try pinning him down. Before sleepy head could speak—

"Right. I'm so glad you see this the way I do, Grant. It's a loser for us if we don't embrace his idea wholeheartedly."

Daya knocked. "Are you all right, Momma?"

"Fine, sweetheart, just talkin' politics." She looked over at the clock, 12:16 AM, and remembered the countless times her baby had asked her if she were all right, more to get warm milk. She knew Daya was displaying her own mothering instincts now.

"Nighty night."

"I love you, honey."

"I love you too," Grant said.

"No, not you. Well, of course I love you in a platonic sort of way. You big goof."

"Hmm, too bad. We could really *screw* up this election if the tabloids even thought I bagged you."

"Bagged?" She held her temper. Men. "Don't go there." Grant was—well—more handsome than Cary Grant, as if possible. But she never saw him dating or with women other than his sisters and mom. At the very least, this Glee Club Yale boy and a project

Runway fan, was in touch with his feminine side. Maybe she'd ask Jason for a read on which side of the fence Grant grazed.

"What can I do for you?" Grant asked.

"Please draft a press release saying I'm completely sold on the idea. The governor is a great asset to our country and I could not think of a better team. Take the high road, the good of the country, time for civility, etc. Call the DNC chair and put her off a couple days. That's it for now."

"It's as good as done. Just don't be a stranger, even though you're not going to debate next week, we still need to strategize and talk tactics every day. Arturo is not going to be able and probably does not want to cancel the ads. *And* I have 623 activities until November second now all up in the air."

She yawned. "Oh, I promise. Just a week until the Secret Service lets us out of hiding—but you didn't hear it from me. Would you be a dear and work with Colleen what's-her-name, Arturo's—."

"Yes, I know the b— I know Ms. O'Hara."

"Right, the brilliant but not as brilliant as you, Ms. O'Hara."

"I understand. I love you, Ayita. You know this. Now get some sleep."

"We better stop saying those three little words for the next month. Just know I care for you too. Goodnight."

Arturo with his Latin looks and a great body could rival her younger campaign manager. She laughed herself to sleep by counting diamonds delivered by adoring men in top hats, spats and tails, with every girl's lullaby as background. The men looked suspiciously like Grant and Arturo and a few Hollywood leading men thrown in to complete the dance team. "Diamonds are a Girl's Best Friend" played. She was forwarded to front stage on a bed of men's hands. The last man, Arturo pinched her lovely wanton ass.

Surprised and wet, she rubbed her upper thighs and rock 'n rolled to fall asleep.

She preferred dogs, as friends, in real life, not that she'd turn down a diamond on a ring by the right man at the right time. She was driven. Hopefully, she'd have eight blessed years to lead this country. She could see Arturo as vice president or president of vice. When was the last time she went to confession? She needed a reason. Hmm?

Arturo's eyes had blossomed when he took her in as if he could clearly see her heart and soul. She slipped her hand down her toned tummy and under her laced red panties, knowing what a weak substitute this was for the beautiful explosive feeling shared with someone who loved her. Arturo, although flirty, had to be focused on the world's best job, no less so for Ayita.

The truth was Arturo liked her. The way he stared at her, he wanted to do—things—to her. Would she be a conquest like the presidency, or could the impossible happen? In the meantime, she didn't mind—at all—beholding him.

Chapter Seven
You're Getting to be a Habit with Me

The next morning Arturo called Ayita and warned her they wouldn't have much time to hobble off the elevator before the nurses would catch up with them. So, grabbing Ayita's hand and taking both canes, he slowly ran when the two nurses spotted them exiting the elevator. Not so fast that his Native princess would stumble though.

"Feels good to run again," he said after they'd eluded the nurses by making it to the now restricted, to nurses, hallway near the Oval Office.

Ayita smiled broadly. "Those poor young things can't keep up."

"We're required to be with you two until the end of today," The exasperated nurses shouted from the end of the hall, up against but not touching two Marine guards.

Ayita raised her cane and waved them off. "You need those wheelchairs more than we do." Their angels of mercy left, probably to call and complain to their doctor.

The nominees snuck outside, through the rose garden, intending to come in again through the main entrance. Arm in arm like a couple, they allowed the sun to warm them in spite of the brisk day. Ayita stopped in the rose garden and turned to Arturo. "Did you get the why-don't-the-two-of-us-date treatment from your sons like I did from Daya?"

"Sure did, but you wouldn't pose for Playboy would you?"

She mumbled, perhaps loud enough for him to catch her meaning. "I'd pose for an ex-playboy governor."

He heard if his broad smile meant anything. "I've been true to the concept of love and my wife my whole life. Those tabloid stories about naked women climbing my hotel walls to get into my room are vastly exaggerated."

"Which part? The scaling, the nakedness or getting into your room?"

"They didn't use grappling hooks." The nominees made their way back into the White House through the main entrance.

"Have you turned on the TV yet?" Ayita asked. The press, legitimate and otherwise, had them shacking up at the Watergate Hotel. Reliable sources had revealed the tryst to reliable reporters.

The two nurses nursed huge grins when they waylaid them outside the Green Room. "Sit, both of you," said his deceased wife's doppleganger in a slight but effective voice.

"Do you want us to get fired?" the other added.

"We better sit before these two vote for crazy Edgar," Arturo said.

They sat, victims of their greatest weakness and strength, the will of the people. Arturo smiled at his rolling mate. "Please summon the doctor. As much as we love you two, Ayita and I are obviously healthy enough to walk. It only hurts when I sit down on this hard chair." He cleared his throat. Saying hard-assed chair might shock these two fresh-faced girls.

The nurses assured the nominees the doctor would see them before they left. They also offered embroidered maple leaf pillows for the nominees' behinds, which the nurses had pilfered from a colonial sofa outside the Green Room. Probably one way the White House used to get stripped of its accoutrements over bygone years.

All four waited a moment outside the now opened double doors. A tall, latticed window framed trees with withering red, yellow and orange leaves. The sun and clouds danced across the not-far-off Washington Monument, mixing gray and promising showers on this cold early October morning. Ayita's outfit was more interesting. She wore some sort of stretch black exercise pants, which accentuated her rounded bottom and long shapely legs. Her top was a Catholic University long-sleeved sweatshirt.

Arturo's stomach groaned as much from Ayita's looks as from the wafting smells of ham and eggs, English muffins, orange juice and Cuban coffee. He could drink three cups of his ancestors' native brew when it was done right. The aroma transported him to the street vendors of Havana. Even though he was born in Pittsburg, Havana coursed his veins.

He needed to be elected president to push for Cuban freedom using opened doors and trade instead of bullets and boycotts. Although Ayita also had a decent agenda, he'd be better for the American people. Besides, the Dems had controlled the White House for too long. Ayita and others had come around to his idea, but it was his idea and the voters would recognize his proactive nature.

Now for round two with Dan and Margie.

Chapter Eight
Que Sera, Sera

"We've got to get out of this place," Ayita said to Arturo, a bittersweet song swirling in her heart. She downed the last of great Cuban coffee from breakfast. Although wanting to go home, she enjoyed the feel of the future for her and Arturo. Her intuition wrestled with logic. She couldn't dismiss the crazy idea that both would realize their dreams. Had she graduated from Alice in Wonderland to Pollyanna?

Braced for the cold in a gray wool coat with huge black buttons and a pink knit beret, she stood on the south side at the carport admiring the strong white lines of the people's house. Her people once revered and feared the great white chief who lived here. It was past time for the final healing. In homage to Sky Father and Earth Mother, she enjoyed the natural scene as well, the soil, grass, fallow roses bushes and great deciduous trees.

The first lady came running out of the White House in three-inch heels and a house coat, her hair a bit wild. Although she administered to wild wolves and one wilder president, she was not considered a tomboy. Something gray and furry nestled in her arms. So very cute. Oh, Ayita had to have and hold the legendary protector of Cherokee women.

Margie ran up and out of breath said, "Before you two leave, I want you to meet my wolf pup. I named him, Idaho." Arturo put his hands out. Ayita would wait, her ties to nature closer. The pup did evoke the raw beauty of Idaho.

"So this is a wolf," Arturo said, raising the pup high over his head and smiling broadly. Taking the pup back down, the fur ball nestled his face into Arturo's athletic neck, the pup's body over the

60

man's heart. Arturo dropped his jaw to his neck and the pup licked him.

"Not so tough are you?" He gently cupped the pup and handed him over to Ayita, who took him to her shoulder and patted his head gently. She closed her eyes and hiked the Sawtooth Mountains in a sweet interlude of pure devotion. She dressed in moccasins, form-fitting deerskin and a modest feathered headdress. She avoided snapping twigs as she moved like a whisper. The forest mist hid the stealthy hunter, the air was clean and heavy and the leaves fell about her like large confetti twisting around rays of a winking sun. The wolf at her side alerted her. Hordes of buffalo grazed in a clearing just over the ridge.

Arturo patted the pup and Ayita's hand. "Since you two have been in the White House, wolves have made a huge comeback. As you know, it has irritated my base and almost lost me the primaries. Perhaps I should bring this little ambassador to some of my meetings." Hearts and minds, an eternal struggle. The two parties divided by philosophy, Republicans more pragmatic and Democrats more idealistic. The country probably stayed healthily balanced by these eternal questions...and a few others.

"I know you two differ on this because of your platforms. In the end, we are of, for and by the people. I respect—no, I revel in our democracy. But I must say my heart would be broken if we go back to delisting these wild dogs and allow open season once again," Margie pleaded, cocking her head and smiling sweetly at Arturo.

"These ears are huge," Arturo said, not answering. He ran his fingers to the ear tips and accidently brushed Ayita's cheek, or was it accidental? No, this man apparently was running two campaigns, one for her heart and one for the presidency. He might win one. Probably lose both.

Arturo smiled at the sun. "I'll do what I can. Know that an Arnez-Starblanket administration will not revisit your husband's executive orders." Although he accented the negative, his heart was in the right place.

"I've got to bring this baby back to Cherry Hill, New Jersey, today with my hubby in tow. I miss my furry friends, my research facilities. Dan wants to visit his home too. Visit us sometime. I'll give you both a tour and we'll have tea at his place."

* * *

Arturo moved closer again, his eyes twinkling, and lavished the pup with more pets, just inches away from Ayita's breast, her heart. He felt a strange thrill and noticed a telltale swoon from the girl he'd hunt. Hunting Cherokee beauties was not allowed, they too were protected species. But every rule had its exception.

They said their goodbyes and thanked the first lady for her and her husband's hospitality while the Secret Service downgraded the threat to their lives. Maybe five more days and they'd be free.

Ayita clicked on her car keys. A cherry-red Shelby Mustang pulled forward with no driver.

"What the…" Arturo should have known Ayita would start displaying her engineering genius, but such a pretty package deceived the beholder. Was it just a girl before a boy, showing off? Nope, it was transportation.

"I've never gotten my inner geek out of me. Detroit has developed driverless cars, but I, through my own invention, have one special honey." She leaned into the front window, which presented a hug-from-behind moment he'd avoid. *Wouldn't be prudent.* He was in a bad way. She pulled up a dummy, strapped him in, slipped sunglasses and a Redskins cap on him, and pushed something on his neck. The dummy smiled.

"Our driver, Jeeves."

Arturo didn't care if he sounded like an awestruck kid. "This is so cool."

"You ain't seen nothin' yet." Ayita explained how the car's on-board computer was voice activated and had an attitude she and other NSA engineers had programmed. She'd created something a bit funny, sassy, smart, conversational and irreverent, something that felt human with an attitude.

"Welcome, my lady," said the on-board computer.

"He can morph into any character you so desire. He, or sometimes she, can pick off what rambles about your eardrums and/or larynx. Just things on the tip of your tongue. Perhaps things you'll reject saying. So mind your tongue." She cocked her head and twisted her lips into a smirk.

Perhaps something strange was about to happen to Arturo. No matter how hard he tried, his mind leapt to the one most embarrassing image he'd enjoyed over the last two days, thanks to his boys, Ayita in various poses as a *Playboy* centerfold. He tried to hide the image and think of something else, an elephant watering his garden. As outlandish and as fun as the elephant image was, it just couldn't replace Ayita on her tummy, calves in the air and toes pointed skyward, on a beach blanket on a nude beach.

"So I take it you fancy Ayita naked?" the computer said.

I'm so busted.

Arturo rolled down his window, hoping the airflow would interfere with the electronic monster's ability to hear him. "I'm thinking the new administration should recognize Cuba."

"So you'd like to see me naked?"

Ayita was having entirely too much fun. *Just you wait, girl.* She wouldn't be taken off track, even though Cuba was a hot button in the Republican primaries and one of the questions sure to be asked at the debates if they had any.

"I hope your home isn't wired like this."

"The home has even more bells and whistles. Believe me; you'll want this too after you get used to it."

"What do you call him?"

"I call him or her, Topper, because he's like a funny ghost who knows all."

"It's not fair, Ayita."

As if on cue, Topper came to Arturo's defense. "Ayita thinks you're one of the most handsome men she has ever seen and would like a kiss from you. The rest I will not repeat, because she's my boss."

Ayita turned red. "Topper has never done this before—to me. Where'd I put my wire snippers, Topper?"

"I don't remember. Listen, I won't repeat sexy stuff, okay?" Topper said, in mock horror.

"Deal." Ayita nudged Arturo. "I've created a monster."

"I agree, and thanks, Topper."

"Quite all right, but I'm not a monster, unless Doctor Frankenstein here used a bad circuit board."

"Is your home like a geek heaven?"

"It's my playground."

The car pulled into a parking garage, still in D.C., leaving the undercover Secret Service vehicles for the moment. Before he could say anything, Ayita took his hand. "Not to worry." The car changed color from red to blue and the Shelby scoop disappeared into the hood. "Just some added precautions. The license plate changed too."

They zipped out onto the road again, the dummy on the floor. This time, Ayita, in a blonde wig took over driving and Arturo stayed hidden in the backseat behind smoked glass side and back windows.

"I'm thinking…on the tip of my tongue, I have a cute blonde driver."

"I know." In the rearview mirror, he caught Ayita's wicked smile. What other tricks did she have up her sleeve? Someday he'd peel off her layers one by one, God willing.

"I won't say a word," Topper said.

"Nasty thoughts back there?"

"No teasing, Topper."

"Oh, all right."

Arturo leaned over the front seat with his lips so close to her delicate neck he could see her tiny hairs stand to greet him. "I like your raven hair better, Princess."

She let out a soft purr. "If you saw me naked you'd run away screaming for your mamma."

Somehow, he didn't think so. He just smiled as he slipped back into the seat. She seemed to like his advances. Well, there'd be more. Her sense of humor would prove interesting over the next month, and if they did a great job for the American people, she'd be easy to take as part of the new administration. But what of forever?

They both wanted to change the subject, which bordered on embarrassing.

They discussed town-hall meetings, doing the two remaining debates in earnest—somebody had to win the presidency—and other ideas. They were hung up for a while on which States to visit because they had different needs but settled on coin flips. Something nagged at him. Once the party loyalists and their campaign managers got a hold of them, they'd struggle to stay together.

They could hole up, not go out at all, these days so much could be accomplished using social media. But it was in neither of their natures to hide indefinitely. They agreed that after the Secret Service gave a green light next week, they'd hit the road and see the country and weather their parties' storms. They rolled by the nearly endless Dulles Airport heading west into the beautiful Virginia countryside.

There came a quiet to their conversation until Ayita said, "The National Enquirer has me pregnant with our love child."

"Are you old enough to get pregnant?" He patted himself on the back for the cute way he put it. Ayita, forty-two, was perhaps too old to have children. Maybe he should buy Trojans. If only in his dreams.

She sputtered, seeming amused, so he filled the void. "I'm part Native American, most Cuban Americans are."

"And part Republican, just like our baby."

"A Republicat."

"Or a Demoplican."

She had come to enjoy his company. Very much indeed.

"I want you to know, I'm not a racist." This charge had been leveled at her during the primary season. "It just worked out that way for many generations of Cherokee." She couldn't believe she was discussing marriage under the veil of chit-chat with Arturo. But the sexual tension between them could drive the car without gas.

"I like you Ayita, but I'm focused on beating the *pants* off you...in the election." *Seeing Arturo without pants might be worth a vote or two, but that's it.* It was a tough choice, but she'd probably vote for herself.

She slanted her head, eyes still on the road. "You're funny."

"I mean no disrespect. You know me better now."

"Think you could work under me?" She tried a double entendre.

He stumbled. "I'm glad Topper isn't repeating just now. Of course I can."

"You two are destined to—" Topper said.

"Destined to win the election," Ayita said.

It became quiet for a while.

"I miss my husband."

"I know you do. I miss my wife."

"We're so busy—"

"Doing the people's business."

"Right."

"You two are so full of shit."

"Mind your tongue, Topper," Ayita ordered.

Topper said nothing.

"Do you hear me?"

A little girl's voice said, "Yes, ma'am, *sorry.*"

They neared the end of the Dulles Greenway, Leesburg, Virginia. The outskirts of the town were spotted with large estates, deciduous forests, deer, fox and her home.

Chapter Nine
Fallin'

Ayita owned a beautiful stone-front and slate-roofed mansion that reminded Arturo of Scottish country estates. He wondered how she survived without fences, but he suspected the answer would be interesting. The car pulled up a small hill, which sloped down to the street on both entrance and exit. Ayita said the car would park itself in the six-car garage off to the side. She offered him a large brimmed straw hat with droopy sides to keep his identity secret from the one neighbor who could see the front. Arturo stepped out, adjusted the hat, noted the time 11:07 AM, not a long trip. He gaped at the spotted deer that grazed unperturbed on the neighbor's lawn across the street.

They entered into the foyer through double mahogany doors with stained-glass trim. Off to one side was a "Gone with the Wind" staircase with cherry-wood steps and rails that presented the first impression of an appealing well-appointed and cared-for home.

"You'll have the second master bedroom, Daya's room, which is up and then to the left," Ayita said.

"Won't Daya be visiting?"

"No, she lives on campus and needs to catch up on her studies. Besides, she has a big test tomorrow. She's neat like her mother, but please forgive her. She may have left a thing or two lying around."

"No problem."

"Leave your bag in the kitchen for now. There's plenty of closet room with an empty dresser. Come with me."

Ayita led him through to the back of the home into the sprawling kitchen with a huge pink marble island and a horseshoe breakfast bar. Long hallways went right and left from the kitchen with rooms to the back and front of the home.

"Come to this window."

Peering out the back of the home, he loved the view of mostly flat to slightly rolling lawns mixed with stands of oaks, maples, some pines and full forests close by. He stepped out onto the twenty-foot-wide deck, which ran most of the length of the back of the home. Walking to its edge with Ayita beside him, he then leaned over to look down at the hidden from the front first story and its windows and doors.

The neighbors were off at a distance. A large shaggy dog, a Saint Bernard mix, chased a reddish whirl of something very fast which found refuge in the undergrowth of a rolling hill.

"How do you stay safe with no fences?"

She pointed at the berm. "That whirling dervish out there you might have glimpsed was a red female fox and my dog, Churchill, who will never catch her. He pays regular homage to that berm, hoping the fox will come out and let him eat her."

"Howard Huge would work better for a name."

"About being safe, besides the Secret Service I have ground and air drones that can stop anything."

"Ground drones?" Arturo wasn't up on all the advances over at NSA.

"Move back from the ledge."

A hawk landed and a red fox climbed up and sat next to the hawk. "NSA and its contractors have been experimenting with all kinds of critters, from a fly on the wall to a field mouse."

"Explosives."

"Yes, or something to temporarily paralyze the attacker. What you see are basically dressed up smart grenades, or venomous critters with cameras and GPS. We also have an IFF grid and satellite surveillance. More later."

"Very realistic," Arturo said.

The hawk screamed in seeming agreement.

Inside again and in the kitchen/dining room area, the Secret Service agents were rummaging through the sub-zero refrigerator freezer, the breadbox, making sandwiches, spreading mayonnaise, skewering pickles and asking Topper if he could make coffee. The nominees Secret Service team leader, Jason, didn't wait for Topper. He ground coffee for the group.

"*Mi casa, es su casa*," she said, turning on her charm with a broad smile. He grinned in appreciation, opened the fridge and grabbed a cola.

Pulling the tab. "Thank you, my worthy opponent." He toasted her.

"Silly Arturo, you can just call me Madam President." The sandwich munchers seemed to think this was a good joke. She grabbed a yogurt, a spoon and then they relaxed on the bar stools at the breakfast bar.

After lunch, they went down to the first story past the pool table and through a metal door with a safe lock on it.

"You remember Packman?" She showed off a flat TV display about half the size of a Ping-Pong table. The Secret Service agent studying it looked up for a moment and said hi. Little dots showed on separate maps.

"Guess."

A worrisome idea formed. "Somehow you're keeping tabs on your neighbors. Not legal."

"Nope. Most of these maps today are of the assassins moving around in various areas of the country. We also track all creatures human or otherwise that come close to the home, or we can pinch the screens to become one screen, or take in the entire world." She went on to explain how this system was similar to ones in place in the White House and elsewhere.

"We have a secret retreat, tunnel and some top-secret systems that I can't disclose yet. Don't worry. Nobody ever bothers me."

Although she couldn't divulge what the remaining equipment was or did, he rested more easily, except for diminishing back and butt pain from the assassination attempt. He left all his worries behind as they ascended back up to the kitchen area.

They retired for a while to offices down the hall to catch up on calls, emails, texts, etc.

They chatted over dinner about whether they should put off the weekend's interviews on Meet the Press, Face the Nation, and Sixty Minutes to next week.

They agreed it would be best to delay.

TV was by far the most effective way to campaign and the least dangerous. Tomorrow, Saturday, they'd invited their campaign chairs to visit Ayita's estate. Not without a small bit of trepidation did they look forward to seeing them. Both Ayita and Arturo's campaign chairpersons were strong willed and brilliant, but in the end they'd serve the needs of the nominees.

After supper they went back and made themselves comfortable in the same adjoining offices. They could see each other through a full glass wall. They waved and smiled occasionally. Was this more flirting or just being civil? Trying to agree with other politicians reminded him to pray to Our Lady of Perpetual Futility. Oddly, right now, the most reasonable person on the planet was a Democrat named Mary Ayita Starblanket.

Next, they settled in the TV room across from the offices. Another TV room off the dining area was packed with Secret Service smack talking and shouting over the Friday night fights. He was shocked to see betting going on in this establishment. They closed the door and the noise disappeared. She patted the love seat, her lips pursed, as if to kiss.

"How'd you get your names?" He had watched her bios on TV but with constant interruptions, he'd missed the early history.

"Mary is my Christian name. Ayita is Cherokee for 'first to dance'." That's all he needed to know. "And in 1883 my family was forced to choose a last name while sitting in front of missionaries who worked for the U.S. government census getting my family registered. The missionaries argued for English names like Smith or Jones. But my family wanted to honor the nomadic life of the tribe when they sometimes chose nothing more than a blanket of stars for the night. Sometimes being chased to oblivion by Europeans meant running without teepees and other supplies. So the name became a private protest joke. The missionaries didn't get it and bought into the story they wanted to keep a piece of their heritage, which of course was also true. The name was—is beautiful."

"I love it." He dared not add, *just like I love you.* Still uncertain of the depth of his feelings and the craziness this election would bring out in both of them, he held his tongue. She'd only think he was trying to manipulate her or get her into bed, or under a blanket of stars to touch her soft sweet skin.

"I've programmed this huge screen to record and play back political shows and a bit of political humor that can be our dessert." She handed the controller to Arturo, who promptly asked for help. The controller, more like a tablet, illuminated its screen and showed eight quadrants, each with labels identifying the shows.

"This is a good sign. Men don't ask for directions."

"I'm sure, Ayita, we'll help each other navigate our journey together no matter what Grant and Colleen try to do to us tomorrow. I've come to sense your heart beats with the same purpose as mine."

Ayita seemed about ready to laugh or cry. "I feel your heart, sweetie, but what's about to happen to us will test a saint." She must have sensed some power plays would be coming their way via the DNC and RNC through their campaign managers.

"Instead of either of us winning the presidency, perhaps they'll try to canonize us in consolation."

"No, they won't. They'll build a statue of the two of us kissing like the VJ day nurse and sailor."

"And pigeons will leave their opinions."

He wanted to blurt out how lovely her laugh was, how much he wanted her right now. No. No. No. Hot, hot, hot rambled through his feverish brain.

As always, their passion for all things political led them to actually watch TV.

They sampled Chris O'Reilly, Bill Matthews, the CNN newsroom, various talk and comedy shows. Smart headphones were also available. Voice commands could change the channels and increase or decrease volume. Tickers with words ran across the bottom of the boxes within the larger screen. It was only necessary to see what the shows were promoting at any given time, because their marketing departments typically had an agenda and always an appetite for ratings. Fox catered to the worries of Republicans and MSNBC did the same for the Dems. CNN marched down the middle.

Chris O'Reilly of Fox was talking, "Governor Arnez is courting the middle. You know what that means folks? This is the subject of tonight's last word. What is the governor to do without his conservative VP? Fail? Perhaps. Good riddance. I don't think so. Will a welfare-state Democrat help him or hinder him? You decide.

"I would be remiss and dealing in abstrusity, today's word folks, if I didn't at least mention a certain popular myth. Come on, Arturo and Ms. Ayita getting it on? Get with it folks. We have important matters before us and so do they. The future of our country is at stake. Do you want the ever-increasing menace of socialism to take your last right away? I doubt anyone with a modicum of sanity would say yes. Yes, please take our freedoms away." After a dramatic pause, Chris spoke again with his eyebrows raised and that signature Irish smirk on full display. "I'll grant you Ayita is easy on the eyes."

Arturo and Ayita agreed to switch next to MSNBC's Bill Matthews show. Bill spoke. "The middle, the great unwashed, the undeclared. Kind of like between the forty-five and fifty-five yard line. No man's land, or should I say no woman's land? It is unlikely you can score a touchdown from there. Try it. Will Edgar Rice pick up the far right and the just plain wrong thirty-five percent of the country? And what is all this about romance? Come

72

on, folks. The gossip bloggers, tweeters and other wannabes started this from zilch, nada. Is that all the American people can talk about? Is this election a reality show to beat all reality shows? The Bachelor meets the Bachelorette. I think not. This is about our great country. Wake up, America."

CNN's Blitz Wolfer had this to say. "We can report that the Watergate Hotel sighting of Governor Arnez and Senator Starblanket taking a room together is untrue. Here's our interview with those who know at the hotel." After the hotel interviews Blitz switched to the Paris bureau. "And now we are going to Paris to show you impressions from ordinary people on the street of what they think about the American election." The Eiffel Tower was centered in the background.

Evette said, "they should make love not war. These two beautiful people belong together. In this way they will stop meddling in world affairs and have one of their own."

Francois said, "no, no, Evette. The Americans will stab each other in the back before they make love or while they make love. They should come to Paris and learn how to live." He broke off a piece of baguette and offered it to her.

Arturo chuckled and caught Ayita's merry eyes, deep and wide wells of glistening black. He sipped a lot more cherry brandy than usual, his third goblet. He needed to deaden the pain from the assassination attempt, a decent excuse. Listening to O'Reilly, you'd think Ayita was Arturo's pain in the ass and everywhere else too. No. She was a living doll, too cute to be president. That was Arturo's last word.

They were awfully close on the loveseat. She showed off delectable thighs he could kiss all night long. If he accidently stretched, he'd knock into her pumpkin-colored country dress. Her knees called for his kisses, or was it the brandy asking him to bend over? How many couples would vote instead of sitting out because of all this gossip about the two of them? Something to research. Right now, he had an embarrassing urge to get on his knees, lift her dress and bury his head. The brandy and the woman made him crazy. Her long legs were beyond perfect, his brain stepped beyond reason.

CNN was doing a special on well-known romances over the years. Where's the popcorn? Arnold and Maria, King Edward and the Mrs. Wallis Simpson, were maybe not good examples. All the channels and legit papers seemed focused on Arturo and Ayita as a couple rather than nominees, which got him belly laughing. At one point, she patted his knee. Why did women do that kind of thing to guys when they had no intentions? Or did she want him? He wouldn't dare pat her knee. Although if she patted him, he could do the same. Fair game, right? Not tonight. He was chicken shit, really. Afraid of the not-so-big, not-so-bad she wolf.

Most of the country wanted them on the same ticket and apparently in the same bed. Nearly every man or woman-in-the-street interview expressed these emotions.

Their nightcap was Stewart and then Colbert. Colbert took a different tack. "Ayita is a full-blooded Cherokee. She was born on a reservation in the sovereign territory of the Cherokee nation. Where's *her* American birth certificate? Was she born on the hallowed ground of the U.S.A.?" He waved a huge flag and Ayita looked a bit pink in the gills. He'd catch her if she passed out from the brandy.

Ayita had not yet talked to him about her younger days. He'd ask her sometime about what it was like to win Miss Cherokee Nation. He could have won Mr. Cuban-American if there were such a thing. His thoughts were beginning to make no sense. He was so definitely drunk.

Colbert ranted on with his comedy routine. "She's not a real American. I don't want to be scalped? If she became president, an illegitimate president mind you, she'd make all us white folks move onto reservations, but she'd construct plenty of liquor stores. You betcha. Where's that old-fashioned white guy running when you want one? We need a cowboy like Edgar Rice to ride his high horse to our rescue. Don't you want to homeschool your children, close the schools, libraries. Hell, who needs traffic lights, they just slow you down."

Arturo had heard enough. They shared many a chuckle, all in good fun. He shook her hand, complained without whining or being specific about his pains. She knew. He excused himself. He needed to get upstairs before he fell down.

"Let's talk about our next moves tomorrow. I'm exhausted," he said.

"I've got a lot more catching up to do. I'm going back to my office down the hall. See you tomorrow. Good night, Arturo." Odd, she didn't need to share a reason. It wasn't like they were going to hop into the same bed. They weren't married—yet. Hmm.

"Goodnight." *My gorgeous, slap-me-silly, you-drive-me-out-of-my-mind princess.*

He walked back to the kitchen to pick up the brandy bottle to take with him, grabbed a fresh goblet and his suitcase. He slowly took the back steps and paused when he got to the top. *She said take a left to the master suite. So I will.*

He entered the suite. His butt still hurt and he wanted to soak in a nice bath. Ayita's second master suite had a huge tub nearly big enough to do laps in, he joked to himself. At least he hadn't slurred his goodnight. He poured another brandy and set the goblet on the ledge of the sink. He hadn't gotten drunk in ages.

Somehow, all the pressure to carry out his outrageous plan to win the presidency and her heart deserved one crazy night. Right? He wouldn't drink again after this, at least not this much. But she had kept up with him somehow. Her thin body had to be in worse shape. Not since college had he even come close to taking advantage of a drunken girl. Even then, his conscience had forced him to treat the girl with respect whether she had really wanted sex or not.

He was confused. He drew the water, noticed the full-ceiling moonlit skylight with fake and real stars, and turned off the lights. The stars twinkled, the lighting perfect. Soothing. He sipped some more brandy. Then he put his goblet and bottle down on flat marble surrounding the tub. He headed back into the master bedroom. A mini-gym complete with mats, treadmill and all-in-one weight machine filled a corner by the far picture window. He inspected portraits of mother and daughter, daughter cute, mom beautiful, so loving these two. He checked out the walk-in closets. Plenty of chic clothes, designer jeans, a gorgeous headdress fit for a chief or for a girl playing cowboys and Indians, moccasins and a leather-and-feathered breast plate.

He thought about Ayita's invitation to visit her childhood home someday. He'd love to go. He stripped, tossed his clothes on the floor in the vacant portion of the second closet behind two lacquered pine chests of drawers. He opened the overnight suitcase he'd lugged in from the hallway and decided to organize it later, because he suffered too much pain and needed to relax. He made one last run through the room. On a table, an attractive tiny Cherokee village with teepees and soldiers and braves on horseback took him back into the nineteenth century. The artwork was lovingly rendered in realistic detail, from Winchester rifles, papooses and dogs barking at plump ravens. The whole display reminded him of an elaborate Christmas train set about the same size. Oh my God, he had forgotten the bath water. Stiff in the back but with little pain in his legs, the ex-outfielder ran, but the tub wasn't quite full.

After a while, he turned the water off and carefully eased into the tub, let out a sigh and just relaxed for a while. He swirled bubbles and sipped more brandy when he noticed the glass-encased shower come on automatically on the other side of the tub. The room began fluffing full with steam. With so many controls on the sides of the tub, he wondered if he'd accidently elbowed a button or two. That lovely geeky opponent of his must have designed the bathroom.

He stilled at the short, tiny sound of the door moving and then a vision appeared before him. A Cherokee princess floated into the bathroom, hooking her white terrycloth bathrobe on the door, forming just one more cloud puff. The Earth Goddess in all her natural glory, thin and perfect, long flowing raven hair, moved with the mist caressing her like a painting of Eve in an early morning paradise. God's glory had never been more in evidence.

He didn't need cherry brandy to know this euphoria. He remained quiet and unmoving except for a pounding erection and heart.

He didn't feel guilty about cheating on his lovely deceased wife. She'd made him promise to live life but never forget her. He'd never forget her. But he needed and wanted Ayita now. Perhaps this naked woman was his soul mate. Ayita as Eve clasped no apple, but he devoured her fruit with his eyes.

She stepped in the glass-enclosed shower. Ridiculous as it might seem, he felt embarrassed now, worried about being caught gawking, eyes bulging like some cartoon character. He slowly, quietly heaped bubbles up his chest. He needed a plan. He used to prosecute peeping Toms.

Her long black hair tickled her rounded behind. She hummed some Cherokee lullaby that he would someday want her to teach him. She strung beads of shampoo and smoothed it into her hair in some kind of feminine ritual. Hot water struck her smooth skin, peaking her dark-red nipples on perky small breasts.

Oh God, if the press ever got a hold of this, they'd both be tarred and feathered. Maybe not. Everybody was talking romance, something to take the public's mind off all the troubles of a world gone mad. Allowing this to grow into a real romance might play well in Peoria. If everybody thought they were making love, why shouldn't he and she? Nobody would know for sure anyway.

She pirouetted again in his direction and then she saw him through the fog and his bubble defense. Her eyes flicked wide. She dropped in a flash behind the pink travertine lower wall. Only the top of her perfect bottom remained. Unfortunately it disappeared and then she raised one eye high enough to see him. She squealed like a cornered rabbit and then said in a soft, controlled voice, "What are you doing here? You're in my room, you, you…" At least she didn't say *pervert.*

* * *

Ayita had surprised herself. Arturo and she sat on the loveseat like a married couple watching the TV. At something funny Colbert said, she grabbed Arturo's knee. Would she pay for this? She knew you should never, never touch a man. They always got the wrong idea. Yet she felt something. Who was she kidding? For the first time in twenty years, she ached to have a man, this man. So virile, so smart, so fucking Republican. Damn it, what had she gotten herself into?

Arturo started in on his goodnights. "I'm aching from the assassination attempt. Just exhausted."

"There's a large tub up there with Jacuzzi jets," she said. Her daughter and she had identical suites.

"I'll just soak. Do you mind if I grab the brandy bottle?" He had been drinking too much, but she understood. The brandy was an excellent substitute for the pills he had stopped taking. Her face felt red from too much brandy. She had tried to keep up with him.

"You're not a drinker, are you, Arturo?"

"No, but I can hold it. How do you feel?"

Her pain had subsided and now only the pleasure from being almost drunk tickled her imagination. She fantasized about squeezing his buttocks as he thrust deep inside her. Oops. A slugger for the Marlins had to have beautiful muscles.

"I'm fine. I tried to keep up with you. If I drink too much I tend to rain dance naked under a rustling tree to the beat of a drum." *Oops again. Had some spirit grabbed her tongue?*

"A nice image. What kind of Indian ceremonies have I been missing and when can we go?" He got up, crinkled his mischievous eyes, shook her hand and said goodnight.

"I-I was just teasing you," she shouted down the hall. Lame, so lame. She was acting like a co-ed. She needed practice. *Stay cool, calm and collected, more like frigid, arrogant and neglected.*

"Keep up the good work," he shouted back.

She made a couple of calls and then went up to her bedroom.

She wiggled out of or stripped and tossed her clothes on the bed. She grabbed her terrycloth robe from the closet, picked up the bathroom controller off the bed's end table and pressed STEAM AND SHOWER.

The pampering warm rain of a natural shower relaxed her. She wanted to keep her thick lustrous hair clean for Arturo. *Oh my God, repeat after me, clean your hair for yourself, you always have. Pride, girl, pride.* Still, she liked the way he looked at her. She had seen that look too many times before. All of them wanted her body. Flattery. She was tired of flattery. How about love?

She pirouetted in the shower like a ballerina. She could still dance, still sing.

It was about time a woman became president. If women had ruled the world since the first human hungered for love and family huddled in some cave, there would have been no wars. Men were hunters, but why did they have to hunt each other? They needed to talk out their problems, solve them together, not measure who had the biggest penis, army or country.

It was then she saw him, that...that man, Arturo, soaking in a mountain of bubbles, hiding in her tub.

In my tub.

What an idiot she was. Of course, the silent peeking Tom wouldn't protest her presence. Men. He wouldn't save her the embarrassment, try to protect her dignity. Men. What man could resist the show she must have put on, dancing like a sprite, humming, singing?

Limber, she dropped like a humming bird to the bottom of the shower. Oh shit, her butt was up a little too high. She relaxed and spread her knees. Her butt dropped down a little more. She scouted above the travertine with one eye. He was still there. Duh. She'd swear off cherry brandy.

Softening her voice, she asked, "What are you doing here? You're in my room, you, you..."

"I am so sorry. I didn't know you were here," he said with a relaxed, low tone.

"How could you not…"

"I've had my eyes closed. I was lamenting the deaths of our VPs."

He's lying.

"You should leave."

"You asked me to take your daughter's bedroom with the bath attached?"

"No, she has a duplicate room in a lighter shade of pink. You just made a wrong turn."

"I'm so sorry, too much brandy."

"I forgive you, but you should leave."

"I can't. I am hurting really bad. I can't get up." Yeah, right, he had a boner.

"I'll call an ambulance."

"No, Ayita, I don't want to go back. I can't bear the thought of seeing her again."

"Who?"

"My nurse looks like my wife's ghost."

She hesitated. "Turn around, Arturo."

He sobbed. God, he was a good actor. Taking her off her point just as if it were nothing. She abandoned her attempt to shower. She slipped on her bathrobe and was content to go to her daughter's bathroom and bedroom. She had to continue the shampoo and conditioner treatments, otherwise her hair would be left…well, goopy. She'd survive. Her heart yearned and pattered as she paced the tiled floor, wondering whether to call an ambulance or jump his bones. He had to be lying.

But he was hurting. It had to hurt. Just how much? He had obediently turned around so he couldn't see her, a sweet gesture. His back had huge black and blue marks mixed with mountains of suds.

"But you probably wouldn't get the same nurse," she said, hesitating at the door. She was so screwed.

The man obviously loved his wife. She remembered her war-hero husband, Pavan, how much she missed him, how much she missed his tender caresses, the way he showed her he loved her. On one dangerous mission, Pavan had called to ask her to someday marry again if he didn't come back. Pavan, like the meaning of his name, the wind, had blown out her flame when he joined the spirit wind. He didn't come back. She didn't marry again. No man had ever come close, until she met Arturo. Confused by his physical pain and her needs, she stopped pacing and took a step toward him.

Tonight, her life would change forever. Tonight, she might find love again.

Chapter Ten
Who Let the Dogs Out?

He had politely turned away from her, keeping his eyes focused on a hair dryer and other fascinating beauty products on the marble counter. For some reason, she didn't leave the bathroom. Through a foggy set of mirrors above the counter, partial images of what was behind him tantalized. He made out her stepping hesitantly in his direction. Her motion drove his anticipation to the breaking point. Possibly, she felt torn as much as he did. God made men and women, and maybe she felt what he felt in an upside down sort of way. All his senses came alive and twisted his heart. He could hardly take a breath. She took another step. Men knew of these small surrenders. Their bodies alerted by some primal instinct. He spotted her hand trembling. She had to be conflicted about what she was about to do, whatever that would be. He could only hope it would include him.

In his peripheral vision, he saw her kneel just behind and to the side of him—as if praying. *Hey, there's room in this tub for me and you and half the electorate.*

The smell of tart apple wafted from her shampoo. Kneeling was not a good sign unless she was about to propose. Jumping into the tub would have been more practical. He could have sex with any political groupie he wanted, almost anytime he wanted. But because of the potent mix of bad press, bad girls and the memory of Sheryl, he had not dared. Also, old fashioned, he assumed sex without love would be shallow. Each encounter would have been a bogus remedy for loneliness and a recipe for disaster. Meanwhile, Ayita seemed to be gathering her resolve with asking eyes.

He had wanted to seduce Ayita. All he had to do was tell her she was stinky and needed a bath. But he wanted more. How could he tell her they had an election to play out and he had an erection harder than Mount Rushmore? One of them would lose and one would win. Sad. How would she feel taking second place? How much would she love him then?

She placed her hand on his shoulder. "Earth to Arturo."

"I was thinking. You and I are destined for each other."

"I was thinking I could rub your back instead of calling the hospital."

There'd be no rub-a-dub-dub tonight. But why should he give up? Giving up wasn't in his nature once he decided on what he wanted. In his imagination, he carried the memory of his deceased wife with him in the form of a dialogue and sometimes in visions. This embarrassed him because half the time he wanted his little conversations to be real. During those times, he had wanted to reach out and take Sheryl into his arms. Now he felt embarrassed to think Sheryl was watching them. His future wife caressed his shoulder gently.

"Just avoid the black and blue areas. I ache for you, my Cherokee goddess."

Her touch, so soft, so sweet washed his soul.

"Come on in here with me. Touch me with your body."

"I love the beef."

"Me?"

"You're so much more than a perfect body and handsome face. You have more than any man in the world to offer a lucky girl. But why me?"

Ayita had just stolen his heart. Done deal.

Sheryl had once asked the same question many years ago when she'd given him a greeting card full of cute sayings and a big yellow question mark matching the questioning look on her impish Filipina face. *Maybe we'll hold hands, maybe we'll fight, maybe you'll win, maybe I'll win, maybe we'll make up, maybe we'll kiss... Maybe, I'll say yes.*

"A long time ago in a Miami bar, I played wingman for my friends. You, with your girlfriends and a few drinks, came over to me…"

"Oh my God. That was you." Even though drunk, the kiss still stained her memory.

"I didn't think you'd remember."

"No, baby, I remembered, but the lighting wasn't good. You looked like a Latin James Bond with that white panama hat partially hiding your beautiful hair and your perfectly tailored white linen suit. I didn't know who you were, but I wanted you as if my whole body were bursting. No guy before or since has done that to me." She muttered. "Not even close."

"You were drunk."

"So deduct ten IQ points. I still had enough noodles to know what I wanted."

"Come in the tub, sweetheart."

But she didn't. He lamented his pickled brain, his feeble attempts as an out of practice bachelor-seduce-a-girl. On the other hand he likely exuded that married man type, loving supportive, and with this gal, very attentive. Perhaps she felt comfortable with him because she felt his utter sincerity. She felt like a cherished wife. Sincerity was his strong point with the American people. Although this woman wouldn't vote for him she would love him.

"No, not yet. We have an election," she said.

"I have an election right now." Hey, a little humor.

She chuckled. Impishly, she dropped her hand down his chest, lower still until she wrapped it around his bulging shaft. He gasped and the bubbles flew every which way.

"I can't get into the tub tonight, honey, but I can relieve you."

"Why not?" he moaned as she stroked and squeezed him. It would be embarrassing if he came too quickly. But the erotic setting, her great beauty, her striving to understand what was happening to both of them would lead to the inevitable. He had to hold on. She had that demure faraway look that told him what every man wanted to know. She loved the feel of his manhood. She wanted him bad.

"We're a widow and widower. The whole world wants us together. To write another great love story."

"We're too drunk tonight to know what we're doing," she suggested.

"All the more reason to make love. We'll have nobody to blame."

"I don't know." Her grip on his penis loosened, and just in time. He slipped his arm under hers and around her satin-smooth back. He lifted a little, encouraging her up and into the tub.

"I don't know. I don't know." Her legs wobbled as she stood. Perhaps she was scared.

He blurted. "I'm in love with you."

"What a silly thing to say." She let her robe drop, revealing heaven and stepped over the tub rim, one gorgeous leg after the other. She leaned into him. Smothering his face with her pussy. He kissed her, licked her. He raised his hands to her shoulders and slowly pulled her down toward his waiting shaft. They would be one.

She hesitated and shook just above his penis. "Crazy, huh? But there could be a backlash, you know, by the people against premarital sex."

Good, she's thinking sex.

"We might lose two or three votes, total. One of them being my mother," he said. Her conflicted look told him he shouldn't thrust up taking her easily. He needed to give her time to make the decision on her own. He was certainly ready. His best action was to talk while she pondered a huge step. If only he could rein in his tremendous urges. Was he a cad?

"People don't fantasize about what their parents do in bed. Doesn't the President of the United States strike you the same way?" It seems she too used words to forestall what he now knew as inevitable. They were destined for each other. What was it about politicians and words, anyway? He remained ram hard and felt incredibly selfish, to take her, to make her his. But he had to have her.

"No presidential nominee ever looked like you, princess."

Finally, she surrendered to him and slipped down of her own accord. *Thank God.* Mea culpa. She started an exquisite slow dance grinding him with undulating hips and back, her head tossed languidly to a beat all her own. Minutes later, she probably could no longer wait, because she quickened to a frenzy. He matched her trying to hold back exploding inside her, their bodies a perfect fit, but then she stopped, he guessed to rest because her injuries bothered her. She gently nestled her head to his chest. He bent to kiss her. Her eyes were closed. "Ayita. Sweetheart?"

She had passed out, probably drunk. She was certainly stable in his arms. He was inside her. My God, he couldn't do this. As much as he ached, he couldn't take advantage of her. Just a couple thrusts and he'd fill her with his seed. He had been right about her. They were a perfect fit, mentally, spiritually and now physically. She was that mystical soul mate he had dreamed about. Her kiss many years ago had been no accident. Life had put them together. Whether they had run for dogcatcher or president, they were meant to find each other, to be together. Nothing would stop them now. He'd only have to weather the storm of political pressure, their own drives to succeed and he'd have a new wife. Two families would become one.

He was no cad. He took what was his and he was hers. Now he had to consider her feelings in everything he did politically. An interesting problem.

How beautiful to behold. Her silken skin, lustrous hair. Her hair had some sort of gloppy stuff in it. She had not fully rinsed. One palm of bath water at a time, he rinsed her hair. Lovingly with every stroke he cleaned her. He kissed her forehead a thousand times. His tears of joy mixed with the bath water. He bent farther and kissed her nose. Bending farther still, he stole a kiss on her bowed lips.

He lifted her off him enough to free their union. If he didn't, he would not be able to stop himself. He still didn't know if she was fertile. Someday, someday soon when both sober, they'd try again. He'd say he loved her and ask her to be his wife. She'd say yes. She'd loved him too. Fairy tale? Was he a schmuck to think the woman made of steel could melt for him?

But Ayita had lost her husband and became dedicated to public service. Would she deny herself a new chance at love, confusing dedication to America without understanding that a whole woman or man, a loved person, is a stronger person who could serve her or his country better? He'd make this argument when the time was right.

Yet she is a woman, she has needs like every other woman.

She stirred. He quickly wiped suds off her forehead before they ran into her eyes.

"How's that?" She feebly started to rub his shoulder with one hand as if she were still on the outside of the tub. She seemed disoriented, still in a stupor, but she was sharp enough to cover her breasts with her other arm. Perhaps she didn't know what just happened. He needed to tread delicately here. To protect his woman and their fledgling relationship.

He groaned approval.

She purred. "I, ah, I'm wet." Now that was funny. "Am I just another pretty face?" She said, obviously trying to come to terms with where she found herself.

Her eyes went wide and big. "Oh my God. Did? What just happened…did it really happen or didn't it happen?" She squirmed on his lap. Think she'd notice his equipment?

"Nothing happened. You were getting me a towel, fainted, and I caught you."

"Conveniently naked."

"I saved your life again."

She put her head back on his chest. "I'm going to like this too much."

"Hope so." Oh God, he hoped so.

"You're too much man... And I, I'm too much embarrassed." She tried to stand.

"Easy now."

She fell back into his embrace. "Please go easy on me with your devilish charm. Let's just chat." *Oh no. Not chatting. Women love to chat. Chat and shop. Let's buy more soap.* The bubbles were slowly disappearing where they sat. All she had to do was look down to get an eye full.

"Do you love me, Arturo?" She must not have remembered their conversation before she passed out.

"With all my heart."

Ayita sobbed and dropped her hands to his waist. "I'll tell you this..."

"Hmm?"

"If you play your cards right, you'll sleep in the White House." She pulled his ear.

He squeezed her glorious bottom. "After I win the election, I'll invite you over once in a while too. We could discuss the role of the vice president."

Her face soured. "I shouldn't be in your arms."

"No, my sweet. I don't think we are doing anything wrong. We are two unmarried adults who have a right to love."

"I'm not giving up fighting you."

He kissed her ear and whispered, "Neither am I." He knew he lied, but he'd still show fight, well for show.

She listened to his heart.

"You still have some gobs of conditioner in your hair. Maybe I should..."

"Maybe I should slide out of here. Me and you, Arturo. We're not ready yet."

The bathroom door banged opened.

"Oh no," she said. "Not now, Churchill." But it was too late. Her Saint Bernard mix took a flying leap and disappeared under the remaining suds. The force of his body sliding into the far bath wall caused a tidal wave in all directions. Suds flew onto every fabric, knick-knack and stray towel, leaving the bath a national disaster.

"Oh my God."

Ayita grabbed Churchill's neck and rode him like Shamu to the surface. Up and laughing, she now wore a glob of suds for a headdress. She grabbed a pile and plopped it on Arturo's head. Churchill suddenly noticed Arturo and it was every man, woman and dog for themselves. A huge face gave Arturo a kiss to end all kisses and remove all bubbles.

Ayita wanted a kiss. "Me too." With her elbow and the side of the tub for support, she slid Churchill out of the way and kissed Arturo long and hard. The dog made his way back and had to sniff why his mommy's face was locked to this stranger.

"Maybe we should bathe him."

"Down boy."

"Woof."

Apparently Churchill didn't speak English. He made up for his lack of elocution with more licks for both humans.

"Once in a while, when he gets dirty, I hop into the bath with him."

"Somehow I didn't picture our first intimacy this way."

"I think we need to laugh at ourselves. I love you too, Arturo." She may have forgotten she said this before, but she hadn't forgotten how she felt deep within her heart. This was beyond good. His plans were becoming true much more quickly than he had hoped. He reminded her about the Miami bar incident again just in case she had no memory of their first conversation. She remembered.

A most pleasant smile overwhelmed him. He might have to go through life wearing this grin. His soul mate was playing ball with him.

They lathered the dog. Ayita's dark cherry nipples and broad areolas filled him with desire anew. But Churchill literally got in the way.

"Your breasts are perfect. You're perfect." He leaned around Churchill's big head.

"You too. You should pose for *Playgirl*." She ran her hands up and down his hairy washboard stomach.

"Maybe our new administration could put out a calendar with me and you splitting up the months."

She caressed his stubbly face, which felt so manly. It had been too long. "They'd impeach both of us and exile us to France."

Arturo leaned forward and pecked her lips. "I've got to get out of here before I completely lose my dignity."

"You devil. You don't know how handsome you are. Do you?" She poked his chest and then twined a bit of his curly black chest hairs. He knew. Somewhere along the way, someone had mentioned it to him in passing. A few years before, he had beaten out a bunch of younger men for the sexiest man alive, but he'd never brag. Nope.

"I've never seen a more beautiful woman."

She leaned in once again, kissed his cheek, jumped out of the tub laughing and ran out of the room. She shouted back to him. "He likes the towel with ducks on it."

"One towel?" But she was gone.

* * *

Needless to say, he didn't sleep much that night.

She could someday be his wife. He was alive again. If she'd have him. He mulled over every word, every move, her graceful lithe body, the way she crinkled her nose, her soulful eyes, her upturned lips, her impossible legs…

It was around 2 AM when he heard the door adjoining the two master bedrooms creak open. Maybe later had become sooner. Maybe she was still as horny as he was. His dick stood to attention. Maybe she had to run in and tell him she wanted his love child. Maybe they'd make delirious love all night. He'd kiss her everywhere. A very uninhibited lady would do things to him too. He'd start with those dark-cherry tips, the nape of her neck, her ear lobes. Make sure to kiss up and down her Cherokee nose. Those lips, my God, those lips. He felt like a schoolboy again.

It was then she playfully jumped on the bed and slammed her body into his. Oh, a tomboy now is it? Native Americans were so primitive. He got his face licked, not what he was expecting, by a tongue too big. She must not have brushed her teeth or seen a dentist, because her breath smelled like dog kibble.

Churchill slobbered his way into Arturo's heart. He heard Ayita giggle and then the door closed.

Guess not.

The huge but dry dog flipped upside down, legs now up, leaning on him, and let out a guttural sound of satisfaction.

Arturo rubbed his chest. "How do you feel about Germany, Mr. Churchill?"

The dog grunted. Obviously, Churchill demanded quiet, a large portion of the bed and couldn't give a damn about Germany. Interesting philosophy.

Chapter Eleven
The Days of Wine and Roses

Ayita awoke confused. Had she told Arturo she loved him amidst a mountain of bubbles? Yes. How did she end up in the tub with him, both naked? She brushed her teeth while admiring her body. She still had *it*. She applied a little lip-gloss, a slight red almost raw umber. She brushed her hair the required one-hundred strokes and pranced with it like a nightgown, wondering how enticing the swinging locks would look to a certain gentleman.

Did she really love him? Yes, but what kind of love was it? She certainly wouldn't let it interfere with the race ahead for both of them. The people loved her. She'd have ample opportunity over many a coffee or tea to discuss what was now between them. She couldn't trust a Republican. Not yet, although both as centrists would never steer the ship of state of the edge of the earth.

Her body had gone wild last night. Not even her young deceased husband had turned her on this much. Pavan hadn't been able to hold back his orgasm. He had blamed a younger version of the lady in the mirror for being too beautiful, too much for him to handle. Praise like that was nice, even though he'd taken one to three minutes, tops. At least he had adored her, which had made her feel like an Earth Goddess. The calmer and older Arturo was better looking, a genius, and one way or another was about to be part of the most powerful team on the planet. They could accomplish great things. They could make beautiful love, hopefully. Perhaps they could have a baby.

Had she grabbed and squeezed his hothouse cucumber? It had been huge and hard and had to be a dream. She'd fallen into the tub and passed out according to him. He'd saved her life again.

Well, maybe, but he did have a sort of Latin version of blarney coursing his veins.

But where were her clothes? She walked over to her bathrobe tucked into a towel rack. It was nearly dry except for one sleeve that was still drenched. She had to stop thinking about it. Colleen O'Hara, his campaign manager and Grant Barrymore—hers— would be here soon. They'd both be foaming at the mouth because the nominees under the auspices of the Secret Service had ignored all their support people as if they had contracted the plague.

She left the bathroom in a rush and rummaged in the closet to find a pair of her daughter's low-cut maroon corduroy jeans, snapped on her bra from the night before and found a lacey blouse with V ribbing pointing to her belly button. It was all the rage with college kids. Arturo and she would switch bedrooms so she could get her more conservative clothes back.

She addressed her computer, Topper, by talking to the wall. "Topper, please prepare a dossier of Grant Barrymore for me and show me a chronological summary page. Thanks, Topper."

"It's ready for display," Topper replied.

A screen, one of many throughout the home, turned on.

"Would you expand his Yale years and match to Colleen O'Hara's years?" Just as she'd suspected, they overlapped at Yale sharing three undergraduate years.

"I'm going down for breakfast now. Investigate any connections they had at Yale, and if you find any, continue to before and after. Can you brew some Cuban coffee on the spare?"

"I already started it. Arturo figured out how to ask me."

"He's a quick study."

"I'm not saying anything."

"Fill me in on what happened last night."

"I can't. I made a promise to Arturo, remember? It wouldn't be fair to him."

"*Topper*, who's the boss?"

"You took off your robe, grabbed his penis, stroked and squeezed it, passed out, later declared your love and kissed him. All while cleaning that filthy dog."

Yes, this much she felt she remembered and fantasized about a few times already. Just hearing it again from Topper made her wet.

But her rational brain could not be stopped. It dawned on her Topper had to know, she had programmed him, that she remembered these details. He was giving her nothing. Not even threatening him with wire snips would make him tell, in her humble opinion. She'd try him later nonetheless. She'd never give up.

She also knew better than to try to change Topper. He seemed to think he had a mind of his own. Since he was connected to the NSA super computers Ayita had designed, he was definitely sentient if not alive. Yet for some irrational reason, Topper didn't like Churchill. Go figure. Churchill was a baby doll, a big lug, a goofy pup. A wondrous creation.

"I'm only worried about the two of you staying clean. There could have been ticks, fleas and stinky debris floating around."

"Topper, clean and then sanitize the tub, please. I'll go get Arturo and force him to shower with me."

"That's a good one." But it wasn't a good one, she yearned for Arturo.

Chapter Twelve
All of Me

Topper's laugh could be heard as Ayita walked from the bedroom to the top of the steps leading to the kitchen, because he abused the abundantly placed speakers. His echoing laugh had a funhouse-clown quality, which made her skin crawl.

"Topper, a little decorum, please." Topper shut up.

The strong smell and sounds of sizzling bacon and Arturo's heady Cuban coffee enticed her down the steps to the kitchen. Arturo was leaning forward onto the middle sill of the picture window, a White House imprinted coffee mug in hand.

"I cooked bacon and eggs for us and our company," he announced as he put down two full plates.

She sauntered over to him. "I've never experienced a more ridiculous, crazy, romantic interlude than we had last night."

"It's just the beginning for us, Princess." He smiled kindly, a regular sweetheart.

"I hope so."

Jason came into the kitchen and refilled his coffee mug.

"Top your coffees?" Jason poured and left.

"Thanks," both nominees said to the swinging door that led out to the library.

Arturo swiveled to face her. "If we survive the debates and all the other slings and arrows, maybe it will be because we were meant to be."

"I remember, I think, talking about a bar in Miami."

"We did."

She smiled. "Topper, orange juice and grits." They both helped themselves to bacon and eggs.

"How does Topper do all this?"

She took up her plate and forked half of it onto his plate. "You're a growing boy."

"I'm still my rookie weight."

"We humans, not Topper, stock the shoots or funnels with a limited amount of choices like grits or oatmeal. If I want something different, I'm happy to do it the old-fashion way. On another subject, we have the first of our big problems arriving here shortly."

"You're the most beautiful—"

She slipped off her stool, leaned into him and pressed her luscious bow lips to his. "That should shut you up. Forget our beauty. The American people are beautiful."

"For as long as I can stand it."

Arturo wore a blissful grin. He had a bad case of Ayita-itis. And she wasn't far behind with her feelings. Just think, they'd travel everywhere together over the next month. They could make love like rabbits and no one except the Secret Service would be the wiser. He'd have them wear blindfolds, just like the boys in the band in that classic Marilyn Monroe movie, *Some Like It Hot*. The nominees would have a chance to develop a lasting relationship, if it were meant to be. Or they'd kill each other.

First to arrive was his campaign manager, Colleen O'Hara. She took a seat at the breakfast bar stool and swiveled. Dressed right, she wore an orange and light-brown wool business suit that crept up her shapely legs because of the height of the stool. Her curly red hair could have been afire. What a scourge, but then again, Arturo had put up with her unintended sexiness for years. Her cross expression changed his mood to a little boy about to be admonished.

After a couple quick munches of bacon and eggs she had served herself, Colleen stuck an imaginary fork into Arturo. "Okay, I'll admit it. I'm jealous," Colleen mocked, glancing at Ayita and then pointing a fork at Arturo. So this would be her opening salvo. Jealousy? Nothing of the sort. This girl was all business. She had to want something.

"Oh, but honey bunny," he mocked her back. Then he poured her some orange juice.

"Don't give me that crap. You have a choice to make." She sipped and nodded her appreciation.

"I thought we went through this already."

"Yes, but fifty million dollars of PAC money would bring you level or ahead of Ayita," she said it as if Ayita weren't sitting next to her.

"Just temporary ups and downs." Private donors and PAC money were the bane of rational national discourse, but without money they might as well read poetry on a local college cable TV show at 2 AM.

"Don't get me wrong. Somebody has to win this thing. I'm sure that squirrel Grant feels the same way."

Ayita's campaign chair, a squirrel?

"By the way, you two, if you are both serious about a unified ticket, I have more experience than Grant. I'd like to take over for both of you. Grant has quite a few opportunities waiting for him." True, Colleen had worked for Democratic candidates and had a perfect track record. The most stunning of which was coming from fifteen points behind in an upset win of the Virginia governorship.

Still hungry Colleen spied what Ayita had just munched on and asked her to pass the serving bowl. Ayita handed her the seeds & grains toast bowl and a jar of grape jam. "We can afford Grant too. Neither Arturo nor I want to worry about conflicts of interest, so the more miserable we make you and Grant, the happier we'll be."

Arturo jumped at the chance to show his solidarity with Ayita. "Well said."

"You two really are a team. I thought you did all that solidarity bullshit for show."

Ayita handed Colleen a napkin for the speck of jam on her chin. With all her freckles, Arturo hadn't spotted it. "Squirrels are cute and Grant is even cuter, don't you agree, Colleen?"

"If you like Dorian Gray. Have any grape juice?"

He had never seen her eat and drink so much. She must be really upset, so he decided to continue to make it worse as best he could. "Let me pour you some coffee too."

Ayita stood up. "O.J. coming right up. I love your outfit."

Colleen turned her head away from Arturo. "Thank you, Ayita. You must be wearing your daughter's jeans and blouse. It's so *collegiate.* Although it looks great on a beauty queen such as yourself." *Nice recovery, Colleen.* Arturo doubted he'd ever fully understand the way women communicated. But the fascination was in being there when they did. Either that or take in a romantic comedy at the theatre.

Ayita picked up some grits on her spoon and looked for a moment like she was going to fling them at Colleen. "And?"

"Okay, Ayita. For some reason, you didn't sleep in your bedroom last night, I'm guessing, of course. I suppose you joined Arturo in your daughter's room, and running out of time, put on your daughter's clothes."

Arturo raised his hand and answered for Ayita. "We did not sleep with each other. Let me rephrase. We were not in bed together at all."

Under her breath, Colleen said, "On the bearskin rug."

"And it's not your business," Topper said.

"Who is that?"

"That's my experimental computer program. It's like having your custom car voice programmed with sass, in your home. I have a smart house, basically."

"Does it have eyes? How smart is it?"

"Please don't call Topper an *it*," Ayita said.

Good answer.

"You, computer, ah, Topper, verify for me that Arturo and Ayita did not have intercourse anywhere in this house," Colleen, a quick study and completely devoid of any politeness, said.

"I don't have to talk to you, but what Arturo told you is correct," Topper said in a huffy voice.

One corner of Colleen's mouth went up and the other down. "Okay, you two, I give up, but the American public, the voters can talk of nothing else but you two getting it on. If you think me harsh, get ready."

Arturo began. "The more—"

Grant was escorted into the kitchen by Jason. Grant Barrymore wore an impeccable Yale-blue suit with a matching rugby sweater and red power tie with muted chevrons. Cary Grant would have been embarrassed to stand next to him.

"Did I miss something? Hello, Arturo, Ayita. What's O'Hara doing here? Too many cooks." Grant walked over to Ayita and kissed her on the cheek, then looked at Arturo. "You don't mind. Do you?"

Arturo squirmed in his seat causing it to swivel. "Has the whole world gone mad?" Arturo had to play the fool, if he wanted to keep the world, Grant and Colleen guessing.

Meanwhile, Colleen and Grant appeared ready for bare-knuckles boxing. *There must be some bad blood between these two. You think?*

The two men shook hands. Grant ignored Colleen's half-hearted outstretched hand, took a seat, violently grabbed her jam and then stood up and opened the fridge. He started removing veggies and a carton of egg substitutes. "Where'd the cutting board go, babe?" There was an interesting dynamic between Grant and Ayita, but Arturo wasn't worried for his soul mate.

Ayita got up, grabbed the carafe of coffee and started to make rounds. "I put the board in the dish washer. It's clean."

Then Ayita dropped a couple slices into the toaster. "More toast, anybody?"

In no time, Grant had an omelet sizzling on a pan.

Arturo raised his voice. "What you missed, Grant, was Colleen's interrogation. We did not make love."

Ayita added, "And we're keeping both of you on payroll. So find a way to work together—24/7."

Grant grinned like a wicked wizard. "You mean you and Colleen did not make love?"

Arturo tried to ignore the remark but couldn't hold it in. "Ayita, I didn't say that, did I?"

"Nope, if anybody is going to have an affair, it will be you two. Arturo and I require that you work out of the same office or you can both seek employment elsewhere."

"You need not get drastic," Grant said while sliding his omelet onto a plate. "Fresh pepper, please." Arturo grabbed the tall wooden pepper mill and passed it to Grant.

"I can work with Grant as long as he acknowledges I'm better at it."

"You two are so screwed up," Ayita said. "Whatever it was or is, drop it. Treat each other like human beings."

Arturo the philosopher decided to frame it in a slightly different way. "Ayita and I are attempting to show the nation a kinder, gentler way, in which both parties respect each other by following the golden rule. We expect you to mirror this, at least in public."

"Yes, and get there in private," Ayita added.

Arturo continued, hoping the issue was resolved. "I assume the two of you have done your homework, focus groups, polls, etc. From now on, play up our attraction to each other without personally adding anything to the story. I'm right, right?"

Grant and Colleen exchanged daggers.

"The number of voters who are writing you two in on their ballots is going up in direct proportion to their interest in you as a couple," Grant said, mouth half open and eyebrows raised to accent his point.

Colleen grabbed the grape jam back from Grant while he was spouting more precise statistics.

After Grant started quoting State polls, Colleen interrupted him by raising her voice. "At this point, Arturo has a lead trending up. It was his idea to crisscross tickets, and people are rewarding him for being proactive—and brilliant."

Ayita stood, stretched and tried to squelch a yawn. "Good for you, Arturo. I can assume you are both on board?"

Had the woman he was falling in love wrestled with her own feelings instead of sleeping? What a great sign. Arturo searched deep within his primitive self, trying to manufacture a yawn. He patted his hand over his mouth and sighed. "Ah, contagious."

Grant said, "I'm on board. If anything heats up between you two, I can't recommend honesty. It's one thing for the American people to fantasize. It's another to wake up the legions of holy rollers who'd insist you wear scarlet letters."

"Yes for me and for once in a blue moon, Grant is right. You two can't afford a backlash, especially with both parties plotting against you," Colleen said.

All four dove into an intense discussion of how to handle the RNC, DNC, the House, Senate, Governors, and any number of renegade operatives and lobbyists. They decided that ignoring most communications with the press under the guise of national security was best for a little while longer.

Neither party could rally around a new candidate for either president or vice-president in less than four weeks. The leaders were impotent. The smoother the show Ayita and Arturo would put on the stronger the numbers and the less likely anyone would stake their reputation on alternative write-in names. The president still wielded substantial power—even though a lame duck—and stood firmly behind them.

They discussed third-party candidates and decided Edgar Rice would still be a minor focus of some ads and media buys if only because his philosophy was idiotic and made a great counterpoint to what they were trying to accomplish.

Jason ran into the room. "Topper, kitchen TV on."

Hostages were taken by a gunman demanding Arturo and Ayita in exchange. An accomplice of the gunman was out on a D.C. street strapped with dynamite.

Chapter Thirteen
Poker Face

Ayita motioned for Arturo to follow her from the kitchen downstairs through the expansive recreation room and into the NSA secure room on the first floor. "You two play nice while we're gone."

"Yeah, come up with a plan on how you can work together effectively," Arturo added. They left Colleen and Grant in a staring contest.

At the bottom of the steps, Ayita grabbed Arturo's hand for a moment to stop him. She lowered her voice. "I asked Topper to investigate those two to see if they have any history. Topper will report later."

Arturo kissed her forehead. "I've seen those looks before on ex-lovers who had parted badly."

"Interesting premise."

"Let's never part badly. The American people want us to follow through with this new spirit of cooperation."

"Agreed. The people are tired of DNBB—do nothing but bicker." They entered the secure room and shut the soundproof door.

Ayita called Carlos, "What's going on? I have you on speaker. Arturo is here. Anything you say to me can be said to him."

"Hello to you, Governor."

"And you, Carlos."

"We have rounded up all but two of conspirators, who we did not know the identity of. We also had lookalikes of you both as a second lure. This lure has succeeded in bringing the two mystery men into the open. They are desperate and they are probably going to die very soon."

"Wouldn't it be better to interview the terrorists?" Arturo asked.

Carlos had a reputation as cop, prosecutor, jury, judge and executioner all in a five-for-one special. If he were put under scrutiny, all would appear legal and there'd be no loose ends.

"These two are lackeys, not brains of operation—shitheads. If we can take them alive we will." Carlos coughed and Ayita knew its meaning.

She purred. "A penny for yours and Moon's thoughts."

Ayita turned to Arturo who was white knuckling the flat screen perimeter, transfixed to the scene of a suicide bomber outside the Republican National Headquarters in D.C.

Carlos began a more intimate dialogue. "I set up a fake meeting with Arturo and you across from RNC at 1st and D in Tortilla Coast Restaurant to allure both assassins. We also posted a fake appointment at the RNC for Arturo before he was to visit you at the restaurant. Unfortunately, the first assassin, paranoid or with a watch set to central time has taken hostages in Arturo's RNC conference room. This is unfortunate for him. Moon is to pay him a visit shortly." Moon was death on wheels. If anybody could make Carlos look like a second stringer, it would be Moon. Carlos was the first to admit her superiority in eliminating threats.

* * *

In the third floor conference room of the RNC, a Mongolian waitress wearing a tiny camera carried a tray of drinks for the gunman and his hostages.

"Here is the Snapples you order. I go now, yes?"

The agitated gunman was in over his head. His hand holding a 45 caliber Glock shook almost imperceptibly.

He waved his Glock. "Wait a minute. You're not going anywhere." Men always did this to her. He would pay. They all paid. She liked payment. *Which is why the mid-thigh catering outfit with tight top and my shoulder length wavy hair make Nazi come in pants.*

"Please don't hurt me. I go now." She started to turn.

"You are too cute to let go." *Some racist pig face he is.*

She turned back, hesitated and then walked toward him until he raised his gun, but the distance was close enough. She trembled, hands and everything else, and put on her best frightened-of-big-man-with-gun face. "I just working girl. I work here all day, fingers to bone, mister. See."

Extending her hand for him to inspect, she swooped down and grabbed his gun hand, twisted and squeezed his trigger finger, sending a bullet through the window. The recoil and flash stunned him. She used his momentary disorientation to slingshot toss the tall lanky assassin out the window.

She ran over to the jagged, bloody window, stuck her head out, and said, "Goodbye mister. Have bad day." The crowd cheered as they crowded the window.

Some guy in a pinstriped suit was fishing inside his pocket. "We should tip her."

"I not waitress. You keep tip." *Or I'll throw you out window too.*

Arturo leaned back in the high-top leather chair he'd taken for the show and smiled broadly. "That's a Topper-like device you have Moon wearing."

Ayita nodded.

Arturo added, "She's a piece of work."

Ayita nodded again.

"One down, one to go," Carlos said

"Moon makes me laugh," Ayita said, glued to the screen.

"She is my gal. Before the second assassin gets too close, we will have to stop him by any means necessary. He is strapped with enough explosives to take out chunks of RNC building and restaurant."

"Wait until he's in the middle of the street if the Service okays it." Ayita glanced up at the TV, which showed the road blocked off in all directions. All pedestrians had been evacuated. Damage in the middle of a very broad street would be minimal to the buildings and maximal to the sparsely parked cars.

"Ask him to stop, sit and disarm his mechanism."

"He keeps telling me to go fuck myself and tells me to go back to Pakistan."

"Do what you guys have to do."

"In a moment." Carlos shouted. "Hey, idiot. Disarm now or get bullet in your head."

The bomber dropped his Nazi helmeted head and started running to the restaurant.

Carlos jammed the timing on the bomb's mechanism but it was overridden somehow. He signaled his Secret Service sniper team to take the bomber out now. He had no choice, the bomb would go off, and if the bomber got any closer to the restaurant someone in the nearby buildings could get hurt. Five smart grenades were thrown off the roofs of the RNC and restaurant. The one closest blew the bomber's head off. The others, all synchronized to not blow up if the target was neutralized, bounced harmlessly. The vest bomb didn't detonate.

The assassination cabal known as TONARTUS could add RIP to its name. Ayita hoped Arturo wouldn't think her too heavy handed, but they'd had no choice. He seemed absorbed in it all as if he were watching a baseball game.

The threat was over, now it was time for a battle of a different kind. The battle for the presidency. No matter how crazy she was becoming about Arturo, she intended to win. If a love life were in their future, it would feature her on top.

Chapter Fourteen
Girl on Fire

Before Arturo and Ayita left the secure NSA room to go up to the kitchen and re-engage with their campaign managers, he took hold of her upper arms from behind. He half-expected a model's girly fluff, but the woman had definition to her muscles, a plus in his book. The History Channel had played up her swim-team exploits. She was a fish as way back as second grade and all the way through college.

He leaned forward to whisper and breathe in her scent. "We have to talk."

She laid her head back onto his upper chest and shoulder in sweet surrender.

He butterfly kissed her ear lobe and cheek. "We were drunk last night, Princess. But is there something between us?"

She raised her hand and cupped his jaw. "You make me tremble."

He pulled back her thick black hair and kissed behind her ear and her elegant neck. Her taste and scent, like a romp through Bellflowers and Lavender, sent him to a stone-age world of braves and wives. Native Americans had always been mysterious, exotic, with a closer mystical connection to the Earth and creation. She and the wild tribes of her ancestors intoxicated him.

"Since the threats are now gone, the moment we go upstairs, they'll drag us back and immerse us into the world of politics," he whispered. "We'll have little time to understand why my heart and maybe yours beats like a Calypso or maybe a rhumba."

She turned into his arms and peered up at him wide eyed. "We need a little more time," she said breathlessly, hands on his broad shoulders.

"Can't we tell the Service or Carlos to give us a little more time? They can't be one hundred percent sure it's safe out there." The crazy white supremacists might be all wrapped up, but the threats would never end for wannabe presidents.

"Of course, I'm not thinking." She hugged him tight, which sent his heart thumping. He could feel her erect nipples through her blouse, but more importantly, he felt her gathering resolve.

Then she called Carlos and arranged for the Service to make sure the TONARTUS threat was completely eliminated and for him to emphasize to the press that the Service recommends a little more time before the nominees hit the campaign trail. All agreed, in three more days, they'd give themselves to the American people. Done.

Carlos called back. "You two must not be thinking. I have seen this before when people are falling in love. Good news, no more crazy assassins. Bad news, chatter is up. Everybody is hunting you like a mean bear. Take time while it is yours. I can't get you three days."

"Sorry, hun," she snuggled. "Let's make the most of whatever it will be."

Arturo would have to figure out quickly, now with her eager help, whether they were a couple or even real soul mates. Was the passion between them merely caused by being cooped up with each other? *Opposites do attract.* How would they reconcile their love and dedication to the memory of their deceased spouses? Should he apply war paint?

Could they love each other?

She tucked the phone back into her pant' pocket, steepled his beefy fingers with hers and backed him into a wall. "Dinner for two?"

"With a little luck."

She kissed him. "Topper, anything on Colleen and Grant?"

"At Yale they were on the debate team, and at that political point in their lives, they both belonged to the Young Republicans club. Grant has managed more Democrats and voted for the same since then. They ran with the same college gang of friends. They all frequented the Anchor, a bar and grill. They had no history before Yale. She separated from the group including Grant sometime in the early spring of his senior year, her junior year. She took a two-week medical leave before leaving the group. For now, I have to assume there is a connection. This is all I have so far."

"Go through her medical records and let us know."

This surprised Arturo. "Can we do this?" As a former U.S. Attorney General, well any attorney knew a judge had to sign off on opening medical records.

"Maybe not, but I can rationalize or justify it if you like."

"Try me."

"The two of us have the future of the country at stake—"

Oh, ode to national security. "Say no more. Let's do it." He didn't want to argue, not her, not now.

"No, I have to say more. Grant has been like a saint around me. I love him in a brotherly way. I want the best for him...and Colleen. They'll try to get to the bottom of our relationship, whatever it is. Turnabout is fair play."

"I think it's a rationalization. I too care for Colleen, blustery as she can sometimes be. As nominees, we have a right to vet those who work for us. This includes complete disclosure of their medical records. Remember Eagleton?"

"Consider the medical report your dessert tonight," Topper said. "If you have the time."

The two hopeful lovers left the secure room. At the bottom of the stairs, Arturo spoke first, quietly, and with any excuse to tickle her ear, "Dessert."

Ayita tucked in his shirt, which had somehow become disheveled. "You are so adorable," she whispered back.

"Give me a little time before we go up."

She peeked down at his crotch and giggled. She needed to distract him to lessen his amorous condition. "Oh. Sorry. I'm thinking. We should each get to know each other's campaign managers better. In this way, we could keep them off-balance and on message. The message is we work together now. With my daughter at college, I'd get a much-needed girlfriend and you'd get a drinking buddy."

"Should we confide?"

Ayita thought for a moment. "Not yet." She looked down again. "You must be getting old. Whatever you were smuggling in your pants has disappeared." She snickered while attempting to run up the stairs. From behind he stopped her progress by grabbing her belt, and then his fingers moved a little south in search of panties nowhere to be found. This disappointed at the same time it turned him on. His other hand administered a couple enthusiastic love spanks.

Is this any way for the future president and vice president of the United States to act? Absolutely.

"Bad girl." Her firm rear felt so good. He wanted more. He wanted every inch of her including the genius within. Part of the sexual tension between them rose from his enjoyment of her quips. Their personalities matched in many ways.

He looked for a place for them to hide. Nowhere down here. He could take her now on the pool table, but someone would catch them.

Yep. The kitchen door opened. He quickly stopped spanking. Colleen and Grant fought for position to get an eye full of what the commotion and laughter was all about. They couldn't have seen what was going on behind Ayita's behind. Right?

Grant's body blocked all but Colleen's head. But she had had no trouble pushing through between his arm and chest. "Move, you big lug."

Colleen continued. "What are you two *doing?*"

Ayita responded. "We're coming." Yes, he guessed they would. On the stairs, in the tub, on the road, in the shower and maybe tonight in the bed, if only he could bribe Churchill with a bone to stay downstairs.

Grant, who seemed perfectly tuned-in to the truth said, "Why is your face so red, Ayita?"

"Arturo just told me an embarrassing joke about our supposed love child."

"Mind sharing, Arturo?" Colleen asked with a note of skepticism, but Arturo remembered the one joke they had shared.

"Our baby would be either a Republicat or Demoplican."

Grant spoke up, "Uh hmm, that should be Demopublican."

Arturo, an elocutionist of first order, couldn't wrap his tongue around the word. "Easy for you to say."

"You two should avoid embarrassing each other on the road. Ayita's face could be misinterpreted," Grant added.

"I disagree. The press will find ways of turning my face red. The more we practice, the more immune I'll be," Ayita said.

Ayita led everybody over to the breakfast bar. "Let's talk about the road."

Over a delivered lunch of cheesesteak hoagies, plus one black bean chicken salad for Grant, the four hammered out a schedule, which would include the delayed Al Smith roast in New York, talk, news, political comedy shows, two maybe three debates and a road trip.

"At some point, you two will have to separate into two road trips," Grant said.

"The idea of a unity ticket and its reality may prove two different things. We'll see," Ayita said.

Of course, some States were battlegrounds and some were just plain impossible for Ayita or Arturo to turn around. "Thirty six of the States are off the table, firmly in mine or Ayita's camp, right?"

Colleen poured coffee for everybody while saying, "Right."

"Then why take this tact? We can claim Secret Service concerns, and when we can't, it would *not* be terrible if the two of us showed up to promote our new politics as long as Arturo and I swap evenly."

Colleen was fidgeting with the coffee brewer's controls with no success. "You two are an experiment that will not likely be repeated any time soon."

Grant added his two cents. "There are state and national campaigns in trouble. They will ask for your visits. This alone will take you two in different directions."

"We'll get to them," Ayita said while placing a clean carafe on the coffee maker. "Topper, brew Cuban." The machine started brewing and Colleen, startled again, backed off and took her seat.

"All Arturo and I need do is set an example, set a tone. I have no Pollyanna notions that the whole world will follow our example. Give me ten minutes and then come on up to my room—" Grant started to stand. "—I meant Colleen. Sorry, Grant." Grant slumped back down. "I could use a woman's opinion on what to wear for the various shows."

"Yeah, Grant. There's a pool table downstairs. Maybe we should get to know each other better while the girls bond and try on shoes and stuff."

"Beer goes with pool," Grant said with all the macho bass he could muster. His voice was normally baritone. He emptied his coffee and then grabbed a couple beers from the fridge.

Chapter Fifteen
Getting to Know You

Ayita and Colleen were rummaging through the huge walk-in closet and putting on a fashion show. Colleen noticed Arturo's clothes piled behind a dresser, but, Ayita easily explained their presence. "Arturo took my room by mistake. You see when we came into the house I pointed to the front steps and said go to the left. Later, from the back side of the house and after a couple brandies he went up and to the left." Colleen seemed to buy the argument or was more interested in the fashion show, having already made up her mind about what the two nominees were doing or not doing to each other. Besides it was traditional for the nominees of each party to screw each other as often as they could.

Back to fashion, although Colleen was five-foot five to Ayita's five-seven, they both had the same hip size. Colleen's breasts pressed any of Ayita's blouses to the ripping point.

"With your figure, Ayita, anything formfitting works."

"Try these shoes." Ayita handed Colleen a light-brown leather shoe with orange straps and two-inch heels because it matched her wool business suit. "Autumn colors plays to my heritage."

"There's a Native American clothes designer I remember from *Project Runway*. She placed second that year. Her designs are unique. She's an inspired artist."

"Topper, please research her name, email and phone."

"I'd like one of these programs in my place."

"I think it will be going commercial shortly, but it will cost a fortune when it first comes out." Ayita couldn't divulge the true origin of the system—NSA—nor its every purpose. True though, the commercial world eventually catches up and sometimes leads the way.

"You're falling in love with the governor, aren't you?"

"I've been lonely for a long time. I'll tell you what, let's trade. There's something awful between you and Grant, isn't there?"

"I get your point, Senator. Let's get to know each other better."

"Always call me Ayita. I need a female friend. Grant is great. He loves me, but even though he's a metrosexual and maybe homosexual, he's still no woman."

Colleen's face contorted into one of amazement and disbelief. Realizing she had displayed her thoughts, she said, "Grant was a womanizer back at Yale. He may be a metro, but he isn't gay, not that I have anything against gays."

"Me either. You two went to Yale together?"

"We hung around with the same large crowd. I love these shoes." Okay, the time wasn't right for a heart-to-heart. But Ayita's heart was doing backflips and she needed somebody to spot her and make sure she landed on the mat in one piece. Soon, Colleen, soon.

"If they fit properly, they're yours."

A discrete and tiny sound emanated from Colleen's pocketbook. "Thanks, Ayita. My tablet and cell are going crazy with messages."

* * *

"Combination seven, twelve, three, corner pocket." Grant pointed with his cue at the far right corner. The ball went in. Arturo was getting smashed, even though he was once upon a time a pro athlete with supposedly superior reflexes and a mind/body used to excelling. When practiced, he could sink fifteen balls in eighteen shots, but Grant was ridiculous. So much for that theory.

"Are you getting along with Colleen now?"

"Ayita is a bit juvenile in her approach to men, she having no practice in twenty years."

"Duly noted, but would you answer my question."

Grant reached into his pocket and silenced his cell phone. "She left our group at Yale for no apparent or declared reason and has given me the cold shoulder ever since. Well, until today. Her new attitude may be because she respects you and Ayita and wants to do what's right for the country."

"You didn't try to win her over...or back?"

"No, frankly I was afraid of her wicked tongue. I was just buttressing myself for her inevitable assault. But we're ironing things out, Governor."

"Call me Arturo from now on, okay?" Arturo decided not to press for now.

"Arturo, I care for Ayita deeply. I don't want to see her hurt." He waved his free arm. "Now hear me out. She's used to men fawning all over her. If your feelings for her are real, then no problem." Again, he waved Arturo to silence. "Let me continue. That's between the two of you, but this campaign can get ugly when everybody twists your words. I used to be a Republican. I'm a neutral centrist just like you and Ayita. I'll give you my loyal and fair advice, but—"

"But in the end you want Ayita to win. That's not a problem. Colleen feels the same way about me winning. It's only natural."

A bird chirp interrupted Grant's concentration. He stepped over to the wet bar, opened his combo tablet/laptop and powered it down. "I didn't know my tablet could receive down here. Three rails and then the two ball is doomed." Grant pointed again at the pocket. The two ball went in. "I predict you'll have to ask and answer this question at some point. Which is more important, a love affair or the presidency?"

"Where did you find the time to learn to shoot like this?" Grant's pressing question offered a false choice and didn't merit an answer.

Grant chalked his cue. "When Colleen was busy becoming valedictorian, I majored in billiards."

"Don't put yourself down. You've brought a great woman to the brink of the presidency."

"You're in love with her or I'll eat my ugly rugby sweater."
Now's the time. "Yeah, and if I didn't know better, I'd say you love or had loved Colleen." Okay, likely Grant's heart directed his questions, not malice. Arturo needed to find a way to tell the truth without being explicit or suffer two campaign managers driving Ayita and him nuts.

"Eight ball straight on." Cue by his side like a sword, Grant won the game but not the match.

"Let me buy you a drink." Arturo uncorked another cherry brandy sitting at the wet bar and poured two shots. This stuff was potent enough to melt away any reserve.

"Just one, Arturo. The truth for both of us, I fear, won't be making its appearance today." They toasted the women in their lives.

What would life be like without a woman to love and for her to love her man? Meaningless. And Grant had asked what was more important, the presidency or a love affair? It wouldn't be a mere love affair and besides the issues were not mutually exclusive if handled properly. Arturo would make sure Ayita was protected and by doing that he would protect himself.

They racked for another game. "All right, Grant, about your unanswered question. At this point, I'll have to say theoretically, without admitting anything, that a love affair and the presidency are not mutually exclusive. If Ayita and I maintain our ethics and keep the needs of the American people in focus, all will end well. If you've been watching our histories, you'll note both of us have always played by the golden rule." He hoped Grant wouldn't fault him for some of the inflammatory things he had said during the primaries. Well, Ayita had done the same. Politicians have since the republic begun slit each other's throats, rhetorically speaking.

He knew now, with never a clearer resolve, what he wanted most. The presidency and falling in love were not an impossible mix. His actions tonight with Ayita would be consistent. His priorities straight. His late wife Sheryl had wanted him to be happy, to marry again. The American people wanted to play matchmaker. He would give Sheryl and the people this chance.

Jason and some other Secret Service ran down the stairs with Colleen and Ayita following.

"Everybody to the secure room," Jason demanded.

Arturo guessed they cleared the campaign chiefs or its open house, today.

Chapter Sixteen
*Put 'em in a Box, Tie 'em with a Ribbon, and Throw 'em in the
Deep Blue Sea*

The Service, nominees and campaign chairs entered the secure room in Ayita's first floor.

"Topper, TVs on," Jason ordered.

On the huge tabletop computer, a satellite camera showed a caravan of news trucks and other vehicles making their way down the Dulles Greenway with ETA five minutes from Leesburg and a couple more to their target. It didn't take a rocket scientist to figure out the press had found them. But Ayita sensed something else had gone wrong.

"Topper, up volume on CNN." One of the wall TVs, separate from the table screen, focused in on Blitz Wolfer reclined in a limo.

"We have it on multiple and reliable sources that both nominees have been hiding at Senator Starblanket's estate on the outskirts of Leesburg, Virginia," Blitz said. "I will knock on her door in less than ten minutes."

"How did this happen, Jason?" She wouldn't blame the Secret Service for this. The press never slept.

"One of your neighbors put two and two together, you know, the one who doesn't like what he calls your Disney shrubs." Okay, she had had a professional cut her shrubs into buffalo, wolves and other old West animals. *So what's the big deal? Mr. Snodgrass has no vision...or appreciation for art. Maybe I'll fashion the next bush to look like a pear-shaped middle-aged guy...running from my buffalo.*

"Colleen, Grant?" Arturo asked for help.

Colleen bit her lower lip. "I think the governor and I should try to exit secretly—"

Grant interrupted. "Look at MSNBC, Fox, all of them." The TVs erupted with talking heads.

Bill Matthews of MSNBC was in route via helicopter and speaking over the whirling noises. He had the look of a kid on an Easter egg hunt. Ayita said, "Up volume."

Bill's voice came up in mid speech. "...another. New Jersey Governor Chris Crème will soon announce his candidacy for president of the Republican party. What makes this unusual is he'll be making the announcement with Paul Rand, Governor of Louisiana, who will run for president on the Democratic ticket. It doesn't take a brainiac to see the irony here. Chris and Paul are tossing Arturo and Ayita's kumbaya love-fest right back at them. Subtle. Not—as the kids would say. They'll be announcing separate VPs. Both of these pretenders were defeated handily in the primaries. Buy stock in popcorn my friends and tighten your seatbelts."

Chris O'Reilly's Fox helicopter report took a funny turn. "Are Governor Arturo Arnez and Senator Ayita Starblanket afraid to come out and speak to the American people? I posit this to you, folks. Wouldn't Crème and Rand offer the American people what they want? I can guarantee you those two will not shack up." Chris's eyebrows rose, expressing the you-never-know-these-days stare for the camera.

Ayita's lips curled. "They're doing this because they know we'll soon be on the road." She walked over to Arturo, hugged him and swept the entire group to get their attention. "I'm in love with you, honey. But I can't deal with it now. We need to separate. Our dreams for this country come first." Even the Service was tearing at this announcement. Oh heck, Ayita blew her nose. She had created an historical impression that someday would no doubt be reported. Fine, she had her man.

"Anything said in this room is top secret." Arturo held Ayita tight. "Ayita is right. Grant and Colleen, start our full schedule tonight. Pack up, Colleen."

Jason said, "Your bags are packed already, Governor."

Arturo cupped Ayita's chin and kissed her proud nose. "I'll see you every chance we get. I'm in love with you too, Princess, and you know it." He looked like he was going to smack her rear. Would have been nice.

Colleen's eyes were streaming, "We...we need to...get going, Arturo." She responded to her cell phone. "Yes, Al Smith is on. Yes. Both nominees will be there...a week from Tuesday night... Not Monday? Okay."

Grant sighed and with pensive expression said, "Colleen and I will book adjoining rooms for you two whenever your schedules mesh. We'll do our best." He puffed his chest. "And we'll keep the room numbers secret with the help of the Service."

Of course, the Service would take a bank of rooms or the entire floor in their name so no one would be sure which rooms belonged to the nominees.

Colleen's overnight bag and briefcase arrived along with the governor's things. "Jason, have your people take Arturo and Colleen through the tunnel," Ayita ordered.

Arturo winked, another brilliant idea was undoubtedly about to be announced. "Get both of us to the Rand and Crème press conference. I'm going to upstage them."

"Fantastic," Ayita said.

Arturo and Colleen ran upstairs to make sure they had everything.

Ayita couldn't be happier. Finally, after all these years, she had fallen in love again. She had fallen for that dangerous guy in a Miami bar who had made her heart flutter more than any man in her life. Maybe Arturo was right about soul mates. God must have put them together. Maybe God was using them to make a point about love to the world.

She was also exhilarated to be out in the fight again, with targets. Rand and Crème would be creamed by them. The people had spoken in the primaries and no one would or could ever silence the wishes of the citizens of the United States of America.

Arturo and Colleen ran back down the steps, waved goodbye and left with their Secret Service contingent through a secret underground tunnel to an undisclosed location.

Ayita bent over the table screen and flayed her fingers, which brought into clearer relief news trucks and other vehicles parked in a long line on the road outside her home. Too bad her nosey neighbor's driveway was blocked.

Ayita turned to Jason and his remaining men and women. "Invite the major networks' and two papers' chosen reps in, one each. No cameras except use CNN's and set up a common feed. A camera crew of two, only. Let the others camp outside. They can watch their monitors." She didn't have to tell Jason anything more. Letting too many people into an impromptu press conference was a logistical nightmare for those who would protect her and could compromise her NSA experiments. They might also steal trace DNA samples in an effort to see if Arturo had been here.

* * *

The CNN team took the lead.

Blitz said, "I can see there is no truth to the rumors that you and Arturo are together." Yet, once again, Blitz had broken the story with assurances his information was correct. He was too big for a spanking, as much as he might have liked one.

"Think about it, Blitz. Would the Secret Service keep Arturo and me together and make it easier for TONARTUS to attempt another assassination."

"We have reliable sources. The terrorist organization is defunct, and its members are behind bars or deceased."

"Yes, and this happened today," she resisted saying *duh*. "Blitz, as soon as we get the green light from Homeland, FBI, CIA, Secret Service, you name it—." She motioned to Jason.

"The Secret Service, taking lead, is in the process of signing off—momentarily—on giving the nominees the green light," Jason said.

The sound of helicopters landing on Ayita's two helipads overwhelmed the conversations.

Another agent approached. "Bill Matthews has just arrived...along with Chris O'Reilly."

"They could have saved on 'copter fuel. Show them in." She got up and walked down to the den to get a better view. Two helicopters had landed. This solidarity stuff would only go so far. She grinned widely when Matthews offered his hand to O'Reilly who stopped his sprint and double clasped Matthews. They exchanged something pithy to be sure.

"Two helicopters," she said, leaving the thought to dangle.

They were shown upstairs and took their seats at the breakfast bar.

"Good, I'm glad you are all here now," Ayita said while circling her prey. "I'd like the two of you—" she put her hands on Chris's and then Bill's shoulders, "—to team up on election night." Flabbergasted might amply describe their features. Naturally, the true reporters in the room didn't need or relish a big show but would immediately see the value.

After the two men exchanged raised eyebrows and some sort of spark of acceptance, she continued. "I promise you, I'm not hiding Arturo in some closet. The two of us owe the American people a congenial fight and they'll get it. Although our positions are similar, our parties are not. The American people will have to decide which party should be in the driver's seat at 1600 Pennsylvania Avenue."

Chris O'Reilly raised his hand politely. "I'd like to know if you'll be swayed by a party with a majority of its members, socialist by nature."

"Over the coming weeks I'll have the last word, Chris." Ayita went over to the bookshelf in the den and pulled out a copy of the U.S. constitution. She read aloud the preamble. *We the people of the United States, in order to form a more perfect union, establish justice, insure domestic tranquility, provide for the common defense, promote the general welfare—"* she quickly read the rest to herself, *"—and secure the blessings of liberty to ourselves and our posterity, do ordain and establish this Constitution for the United States of America."*

"The key words here, Chris, are *promote the general welfare.* These words beg for an *honest* debate between the two parties. Take either party away and you will have the socialism or any other defective system you fear." She neglected to use the words, *rant on about.*

"I am not an ogre, Senator." He entertained, and he was damn good at it.

"Of course not. My point to the both of you, and it is something Arturo is fond of saying, is the American people decide the health of our country."

Bill Matthews poured himself a cup of coffee. "This smells great. This is a Cuban blend, right?" Damn if the brilliant detective in Matthews wouldn't find the one thing they hadn't thought to change during the mad scramble.

"That coffee is one thing I can thank Arturo for. When we were being held in a secret location he introduced me to this brand. It's quite good—no, it's great. I bought some. We intended to do interviews in each other's homes as soon as our campaign chiefs can coordinate and we decide on who will do the interviews."

Both men offered their services immediately, as did Blitz and the reps from ABC, CBS, NBC, the Washington Post and the New York Times. She deferred her choice claiming a need to consult with Arturo's campaign.

She prayed no more coffee-esk mistakes were in the offing. Topper, an unlikely mistake waiting to happen, wouldn't dare say anything as long as she had a screwdriver and wire cutters. Somewhere along the line, the American people would find out she was madly in love with her opponent. How wonderfully crazy this world she lived in had become. She needed to find a way back to his arms as soon as possible, if only to make sure their hearts weren't leading them astray.

They had both been without a lover for a long time. Were they merely horny and rationalizing their overwhelming cravings? Not likely. If anything, they were both career driven, at the top of their games, one-eyed monsters. They had both suffered the unwanted advances of many a pretty and handsome groupie who wanted to give them a thrill and the clap.

Chris spoke up, "When are we going to learn the details of your time with the governor?"

"It was simple, Chris. I spent time in a secret military hospital room recovering from injuries. He did the same. The nurses wheeled us down the same hallways, but rarely together."

Bill poured some coffee, but only got a half cup. Ayita got up and went over to the pot and a backup pot to brew a new one and stick Arturo's used cup, oops, into the dishwasher. Topper knew better than to announce himself or his capabilities to those who weren't cleared. There'd be no, "Topper, brew Cuban," around theses suspicious characters.

The coffee pot gurgled while the on-the-record conversations continued. Finally, Bill settled down with his brew. "Could you put to rest the ridiculous stories about you and Arturo, love children, trysts…?"

Blitz walked over to the pot. "I think we should cut her some slack on this."

"It's all right, Blitz. Arturo and I were friends before the assassination attempt and we're still friends afterwards. Remember, he saved my life. I have him to thank for me standing here today. The man, so very wise, not only understood the need for a worthy opponent, he demonstrated his heroism in saving me. Wouldn't you all try to save each other if given the opportunity?"

"I don't know about Chris," Bill said in mock detest with downturned grin.

"I'd like to do election night with you. I think it would be a great show," Chris said while chuckling.

"A done deal, my frenemy." They shook hands heartily, offering each other muted laughs and snorts.

Blitz apologized to the group and then added his own two cents before Governors Crème and Rand made their candidacy announcement.

Ayita manually turned on the kitchen TV and got Blitz's attention. The media stars and the Service gathered round to watch. Some traded witty remarks when they noticed Arturo stealing the show.

* * *

First, Arturo unbuttoned his light gray wool suit and took a deep breath of the crisp air. Then he had cameramen trying to keep up with him as he tore up the Capitol's steps. The crowd who were there for the other two governors turned and broke into jubilant cheering and clapping once they figured out who he was. Then they chanted his name. Rand and Crème had no chance. *Tap their mics all they might.*

Now at the top of the steps, Arturo commandeered Governors Rand and Crème's lectern and mics. He tapped the mics, then crossed his arms and half turned to give them a dead stare with one eyebrow raised. Neither man would try to take the mics away from a physically and mentally imposing ex-baseball slugger and debater par excellence. Someone they both respected and would now have to defer to, at least until he said his peace. After all, he was big news since nobody knew where he was for sure. They'd look bad, interrupting a man who had resurrected himself from the dead, well, from being missing in action. Arturo then flapped his hands downward to settle the crowd and shared a little chuckle with himself. *This is so easy.*

"Hold your horses," he said off mic to the now-stewing candidates with gritted teeth. It had finally hit them, what was about to happen. There were no dummies here.

Did these two really think showing up together would be misinterpreted by the American people as an example of by-partisanship? They'd be on separate tickets. The only time these two were expected to be seen together was when one or the other firebombed the other's funeral.

"These two gentlemen are great Americans." He cleared his throat. "Although they were defeated, excuse me, trounced, in the primaries by Ayita and me—" he raised his voice, "—they offer their services now. Now? Good for them. Good for America. But, my fellow Americans, they need not bother. As you all can see...here I stand...alive and well and ready to fight for you." The crowd went wild.

"I'm ready and so is Ayita to hit our separate roads full time and start seeing the American people now that the threat from TONARTUS has been eliminated." He waited for the cheers to die down yet again.

"A little earlier, I got off the phone with Senator Starblanket. She feels the same. We will lock horns on the serious matter of which one of us will be president. By the way—" he leaned into the mic face sideways as if to impart a secret, "—typically, in the animal kingdom, females don't have horns." He waited for the crowd to stop laughing. Ayita would probably someday soon turn this against him, as some sort of sexist remark, but he could not resist jousting with her from afar. She too enjoyed the same game. An image of her in the bathtub, in his arms, momentarily staggered him.

He was in trouble but recovered. "There is a chance, by crisscrossing our tickets, the work of the American people will actually get done. If you want gridlock, these two fine gentlemen are quite capable." He waited for the nos to die down. "No. I didn't think so. Should we tell them to go home?" He had to interrupt the go homes, which kept getting louder and he supposed embarrassing for the two gentlemen on either side of him. "Not that they're living together. Not that there's anything wrong with that." This caused a rolling laugh as people caught on to the joke. Maybe the press would put them in hotel rooms together like they had theorized about Ayita and him. "Ayita and I will go about the business of the United States of America for all Americans." Zing.

Both Rand and Crème tended to be divisive, which is what had ultimately ruined their chances in the primaries. Ten years before his moderate views would have sunk his ship. The American people had tired of the same ole' mudslinging of previous campaigns and broken government. "God bless America."

Off mic, he said, "You two can go home now." He shooed them away. Of course, they'd take the mics as soon as he left, but with a little luck, they'd have nobody to talk to. Therefore, he lingered at the podium and suggested the crowd disperse now. His NSA cell phone signaled a text from Ayita.

Firmly gripping the podium with one hand to retain possession a little longer, Arturo pulled out the phone and read the text under the podium lip.

With a crisp nod, he continued, "Folks. Folks. I've just received a text from Ayita. She's with Blitz Wolfer, Chris O'Reilly, Bill Matthews and more at her home in Virginia. They are broadcasting as we speak." He pointed to the news trucks. "I'm leaving now." That did it. Everybody scrambled down the steps to get to the trucks and their wide screens.

"The podium is all yours, gentlemen." He smirked, observing two sour pusses. He waited for them to march on over and shake his hand. Meekly, these two firebrands shuffled to him like geriatric patients, knowing the gig was up.

Rand shook his head and closed his eyes. "We didn't really want to do this." Sure, and his mama made him eat his spinach, and in the case or Crème, his donuts.

Crème, with a slow smile, said, "We heard rumors you two weren't going to campaign or I would have never been here either." Crème grabbed the podium. "I'm sure Rand would agree. There is no need for us to come to the aid of our country now. We are both sure the great Senator of Virginia and the even greater Governor of Florida are alive and well and ready to see the American people, full time." Well said and good face—and ass—saving. *Politicians, sheesh.*

127

Even without Ayita by his side now, he felt her loving and brilliant presence. He couldn't ask for a better running mate. He couldn't ask for a better partner in every way possible. He could ask for a wife, if only they'd find some time to talk this last subject out.

If he didn't know better, he'd swear she read his thoughts. Probably, her astute awareness of how to upstage these two wannabes had led to her prior text. Well played, Princess.

While cradling the tricky NSA cell phone close to his mouth he let the words *I love you* vibrate from his larynx hoping Topper or Ayita got it. *I wonder if this phone did video conferencing.*

A text from Ayita shot back, *"Ditto."*

A text from Topper displayed, "I'll show you how to video tonight."

He walked off, damping down a whistle of *The Battle Hymn of the Republic*, taking in a moderate breeze whipping up the steps and the sun speckling through the trees on the last day of the first week of October. There were three weeks and three days until the election. What would happen now until Election Day was his meat. Ayita would be dessert.

About an hour later, his cell buzzed again. He hoped for Ayita, but oddly Topper was calling. This NSA contraption of a phone and Ayita's home never ceased to amaze. "I'm calling both of you now. When Colleen, in the spring of her third year at Princeton took time off, she had a secret abortion. I propose she has struggled with this decision ever since, because she is personally against abortions and is an activist for young women to choose life. It must tear her apart every moment of every day. I assume someone in her group was the father. She never told a soul afterwards, not her brother or sister or grandfather. There is a ninety-two percent chance the father was Grant, since they were on and off again as an item before she left the group behind. I highly recommend you two don't confront her with this because there's a seventy-two percent chance she'll do something rash that would likely include quitting. She might even hurt herself. Because you both need her and Grant

128

and they are the best at what they do. Please do nothing. By the way, you two both being Catholic, please understand her abortion was in the first trimester. I'm glad I'm not human. I'd blow my circuits on this one if I were pregnant." Leave it Topper to finish with a silly thought, an image to lighten the mood, no doubt.

"Ayita, are you on the line?"

"My God, I feel for her," Ayita sobbed.

His eyes watered. "What do we do?"

She sniffled. "We can't do anything. Oh, honey, I miss you already." He peered around the RNC hallway he was walking in. Nobody but the Service was still here, except for his next appointment behind the double doors dead ahead.

"Did I make a mistake declaring my love in front of the team?"

"No, Princess, we are known for thinking on our feet, for being executives."

"We need their help, right."

I thought your statement of love was brilliant. Grant and Colleen, if they have hearts beating, will now work for us without hesitation or subterfuge.

"But maybe I jumped the gun. Maybe we don't know each other well enough."

"Who else on this planet, if not us. And we had a surreal Miami."

"I don't want to scare you, but we should think long and hard about this."

"The separation will do us good." His heart was breaking all over again. Had he lost her or was she merely being careful? Women were so much better at this sort of thing; he'd have to rely on her wisdom.

"Next week we'll be able to talk all this through in person."

"I feel the same way."

"Let's use this crazy phone as much as possible. It's a life saver."

They hung up. He didn't know how to tell her how much he loved her, how sure he was they had found forever, not over the phone, no matter how secure the line.

Being optimistic he changed his thought patterns. America would soon be in for quite a surprise. Those who ate up this *romance thing* the press constantly harped about would be surprised to see their pet theory turned to reality when all the other secret doings tabloids conjured up never materialize as fact. No flying saucers or aliens. No fake moon landing. No blowing up of the twin towers by the U.S. government. Osama bin Laden really dead. No Big Foot. Just little ole Ayita and Arturo as real as real got. Those who didn't believe anything was going on would simply be surprised and he hoped happily for them.

What could he do for Colleen? He'd have to keep the same banter going. He'd be more careful when talking about pro-life around her. He loved her like a sister. He'd love her even more now.

But what if Grant were the father. Grant was pro-choice, but when the truth surfaces in anybody's life, it hurt. To know the woman he'd loved, allegedly carried his child and all that happened, nothing in the world could be worse.

He resolved to stop teasing the two of them by suggesting they'd make a good couple. He'd stick to business and play up their cooperation.

He'll assume, since Ayita blurted out her love in front of their team, she was never more sure of anything in her life. On the other hand would she succumb to the allure of the presidency and go back to her old driven ways. Perhaps they'd find a way to feed both obsessions and grow in the process.

Chapter Seventeen
Hit the Road, Jack

New York City, CBS, The Ed Sullivan Theater, The Late Show and Letterman's return

David Letterman was one of many acceptable, reasonable Democrats in Arturo's opinion. In return, Arturo was easy to work with. He'd soon prove this to the world when someday, someday soon, they would bring back Camelot.

Unfortunately, Ayita and he had to spend the previous week apart, helping their own party members whose campaigns were faltering. He ached to be in her presence. The good news was their secure, encrypted NSA cell phones including video linkage worked so well. To behold her classic native face, the way she dipped her eyes downward with blush, the lips imparting a good night kiss, her tears, her yearning, their intellectual rough par, made him feel they were together.

Still, more out of a suspicious nature on his part, he kept his innuendo and personal remarks to a minimum. Still, the little device kept them growing as a couple. He was now near certain Ayita loved him and wasn't making the classic politician's promise—meaning well but not quite able, sometimes, to follow through. But did she love him as much as he did her? Until he was sure, he had to run two campaigns. One for the presidency and one for her heart. Falling in love like everything else in life was hard and joyful work and was only the beginning. Every day of their lives together, if meant to be, he would work to wow her.

The green waiting room was a comfortable enough place to sweat out their reintroduction together in the public eye. They were both troopers, and there'd be no real sweat today. The monitors came on. The show started. Ayita looked good enough to replace the snacks. From the twinkle in her eyes, he knew she was completely on her game. He whispered an, "I love you." She leaned forward and stared into his eyes, until his heart skipped a beat.

Then being prudent, they watched the monitors.

"*David Letterman*," the announcer delivered his sing-song stretched-out spiel. David walked out in an electric-blue pin-striped suit, tan loafers and a crooked I-stole-Mom's-cookies smile.

After the audience settled down.

"Folks, it's not every day…" he held up his arms to quiet the crowd. The applause for the expected nominees was too loud for him to speak over. Finally the audience settled down, "thank God, the governor and senator are safe…

"Folks, sorry about the frisking you *got*. I promised the interns some *perks*." There was a drum and cymbal pop. The camera panned to a cute young thing with Shirley Temple curls standing coyly in the isle separating the audience. Of course, the Secret Service had done the frisking.

"All the Secret Service knows for sure about one of the alleged assassins—" he rolled his head, "—is that he didn't like the food at the Tortilla Coast Restaurant." There was another drum roll. "But who does?"

After a while, the nominees were brought out. Arturo held Ayita's hand, in what was fast becoming both a trademark and joke, thanks to Ayita's sharp tongue a couple weeks before. The crowd stood, clapped, hooted, whistled and cheered. For at least another five minutes, the audience wouldn't let up. It felt good. The audience loved them. Ayita seemed charmed as well. This time she held his hand so tight, he might not be able to throw a baseball to the kids he would meet. The princess seemed so relieved to be with him on the stage. They bowed to the audience, to each other, to Letterman, to the bandleader. You'd think they were auditioning for parts in *The Sound of Music*.

"Yo. You guys better vote," Dave said, pushing his arms downward for silence.

After the crowd settled down, Dave extended his hands simultaneously to Ayita and Arturo. Ayita let her fingers linger when Arturo's fingers pulled away. Nothing could be more sensuous. Nothing could make his heart soar more.

Raising Ayita's arm while holding onto Arturo's, Dave said, "You *look* fantastic. Stunning folks, just scrumptious." Ayita wore a one strap, one sleeve asymmetrical evening gown with cutouts over her legs shaped like tiny beaver tails, made with some kind of black with dark-brown streaked silk. Ayita would look stunning in a potato sack. He hoped no drool was forming.

"And Senator Starblanket, you look pretty good too," David delivered the punch line, lowering Ayita's arm and raising Arturo's.

Arturo offered Ayita the first chair.

"Is this how it's going to go on Election Day?" David asked.

"I've offered to arm wrestle her for the presidency."

"Are you all right? Do I have this right? You shielded Ayita during the first assassination attempt."

"It's a bit of a blur. I shook Ayita's hand and was immediately thrown into the wall, but I'm okay, just a little bruising. She's very okay. Doesn't she look fantastic?"

"Well, thank God. But that's some handshake the senator has."

"That's some poundage to be squashed with," Ayita said. Arturo maintained his pro baseball weight, a mere two-hundred and ten pounds.

"Do you suppose your being squashed is what led to...well, it's a *national obsession*, all these rumors about you as a couple?"

"First of all, we wanted to thank you, Dave, for coming out of semi-retirement to do this show."

The audience applauded heartily. "Well Ayita, for you, a man would do just about anything, wouldn't you agree, Arturo?" Dave delivered these lines with a wicked smile.

Arturo, caught off guard, thought first about how he had given Churchill a bath then he came up with something good. "Ask not what I can do for Ayita, but what she can do for me."

Ayita belly laughed to the point of tears, slapped Arturo on the shoulder and then turned to Dave,

"Don't look at me. Arturo was born that way; in fact if he loses I'm pretty sure CBS will give him a call.

Ayita composed herself and continued. "First of all, there's no truth to the stories of us shacking up." She sighed while the laughter died down. She cocked her head with pouted lips, turned to Arturo and shook her head yes as she eyed him up and down. She was playing with fire, but somehow the whole exchange felt right. Arturo peered up at the ceiling.

Then she got serious. "I think the American public likes our message of solidarity. They're tired of all the partisan sniping, half-truths, distortions and lies."

"So if you two do end up together...you know those bus trips can be long, the hotel suites can be, well, confusing."

"You'll be the first to know," Ayita said, giving Arturo her happy eyes.

"No, he'll be the second to know," Arturo said smiling back.

"So it seems there is something between you?"

"We have come to respect each other deeply and are still friends," Ayita said.

"May I call you Ayita?"

"Madam President sounds right. Yes, of course." She put her hand on David's outreached arm.

"I can't imagine you two haven't read the Sunday Times editorial by Warren Winchell."

Ayita locked eyes with Arturo once again, signaling for him to answer this one.

"We want America to understand. It has only been little more than a week since we left the hospital. We wanted to pay our respects. The Secret Service has been doing a great job of keeping us safe," Arturo finished and nodded to Ayita.

"We will be going on non-stop tours starting sometime tomorrow, but until the investigation is one hundred percent complete, our exact itineraries will remain secret," Ayita said.

"So I guess what Warren Winchell was saying... Well, I hope you two don't mind me asking?" David paused again. He left his half-finished sentences dangle probably for comedic effect and certainly so the audience's imagination would actively fill in the blanks with whatever wicked thoughts fueled their fantasies. "Arturo. She is just about the prettiest gal I've ever seen."

"We'll catch up with Winchell. All of America has such an imagination no matter how impossible. Remember I'm still healing and the Secret Service follows us around like shadows," Arturo said. "Talk about privacy. I can't even drink some Cuban coffee without somebody stirring my spoon."

After the laughter died out, Ayita frowned. "I think Arturo is one great catch for some lucky woman someday, but I promised myself years ago I would do all I could to help my country. I *don't* do halfway. I wouldn't do a relationship justice."

"Besides, you're a Republican, aren't you?" David said, staring at Arturo with eyebrows raised. The audience howled.

Ayita grabbed Arturo's hand and raised it, "Don't we make a great team?"

"What about you, Governor?"

"Call me, Arturo."

"Arturo. No, I mean..."

Although not a mind reader, Arturo jumped right in on David's pause, he pretty much knew where David was heading. "...Ayita is the most stunning, fantastic and talented woman I have ever met. And I hope when she becomes vice-president, a partially ceremonial job, she'll be happy. It's been more than two yours since my beloved past away. My boys want me to start looking. Perhaps I'll have my vice-president find someone to make me completely happy. You know what they say..."

"And what is that, pray tell?"

"A happy president is a good president."

"So this means?"

"Maybe like the previous administration, there'll be a Rose Garden wedding."

"Well, it seems from the audience's reactions, and all I read and hear, nobody believes a word the two of you have been saying."

"Politicians are like that," Ayita quipped.

* * *

A little later in the show, "Well, folks, this brings me to our top ten reasons the country should vote for you two. I've got it right here in my hot little hands. And I think our two nominees deserve this list."

Being good sports, Arturo and Ayita took turns reading the list.

Arturo read: "Number ten. Edgar Charney won't be forced to move to Washington."

Ayita: "Number nine. We'll save the taxpayers money by sharing the White House and renting out the VP's quarters."

Arturo: "Number eight. We'll form a more perfect union."

Ayita: "Number seven. Just think there could be another Rose Garden wedding. We just discussed that."

Dave shrugged. "It's a live show."

Ayita got Arturo's attention and said, "A new number seven. We'll erect a teepee in the Rose Garden for when we want to camp out."

Arturo: "Number six. Until that time, we'll establish a don't-ask-the-nominees-don't-tell rule."

Ayita: "Number five. We'll lead by example and encourage Congress to share seats."

Arturo: "Number four. We'll offer Cuba the chance to become the fifty-first state."

Ayita: "Number three. We'll establish *Dances With Wolves* as *the* national movie."

Arturo: "Number two. We'll promise that the vice-president will work closely and directly under the president."

Ayita: "The number one reason the American people should vote for us is we look good."

"Friends, there you have it. They look good." After a long bout of raucous applause. "Would you two stay a little longer?"

They agreed.

"Our next guest is a surprise to our nominees. He comes bearing gifts. Please welcome the host of *The Bachelor*, Chris Harrison."

Chris walked out carrying a giant key. After applause, introductions and handshakes, Chris took a seat.

"So I hear there's something you want to tell the nominees."

"First, I wanted to say we've been trying to get the nominees to compete on our show, but they claim they're too busy."

"So I can see you have a solution."

"I do."

"Shouldn't that be their line?"

After the audience clapped. Chris continued. "This key, the key to the White House, has been flown in by Air-force One for when you'll need it. But first, the president has authorized me to give you this card. Ayita, would you open it and read it?"

"*Okay.*" She opened the card, being a good sport and read, "*If you wish to forgo your separate residences, please use this key to move in. But wait until after Margie and I have packed up and left.*"

Arturo took one end of the key. Ayita rose beside him and grabbed the other end. They held the key over their heads.

"That's all for tonight, folks. Haven't they been good sports? Don't you dare forget to vote."

Chapter Eighteen
New York, New York

The Alfred E. Smith Dinner, Monday, Waldorf Astoria Hotel, Manhattan
Ayita and Arturo flanked Cardinal Fitzgerald, and good that they did, because Ayita was so impossibly stunning tonight, Arturo fantasized about running his hand under her gorgeous gown and up her long leg and had to bite his lip. The two nominees were in enough trouble without letting the whole world know, right now, they really were in deep lust. It may be obvious the two were friends. It might even be observable that they loved each other. Arturo had a complicated problem to solve with Ayita. Perhaps the cardinal could offer some guidance. Arturo had always had good relationships with priests, from the Jesuits who'd taught him in University to priest friends he had met on life's journey.

Luckily for Arturo's purpose, the cardinal sprinkled witty remarks as freely as his salt-shaker. The man of God may just have the answer to his prayers.

The cardinal leaned back to signal he wanted both Ayita and Arturo to hear. "Each year we add to the list of Irish surnames, O'Starblanket, O'Arnez." He started silly and predictable enough.

"Your Eminence, Ayita and I are beset with the worst rumors. Would you have any advice we can take to heart?" Arturo led with this, even though he continued to feel the rumors of love children, shacking up etc. helped the write-in campaign. The trick was in not admitting he loved every minute of it.

"If the two of you keep to the sacraments and your vow to the American people, the citizens will know this in their hearts. I must say, the two of you bring joy to my heart. It's about time people in Washington treat each other according to Jesus's teachings."

Arturo wiped his mouth while he spoke so any lip readers, either in the room or on the other side of cameras, wouldn't understand what he said. "Please don't comment directly to what I'm going to say. If you can twist it into a joke, I need to confess and I don't want the whole world knowing my sins. Beware of lip readers."

"The whole world reports you two as sinners. So I can hear your confessions now, but only if they're interesting."

Arturo dabbed his mouth with a napkin while speaking. "Ayita and I have not sinned. I'm in love with her. Have been for a long time." Ayita turned red again, then picked up her wine glass, tasted it and patted her cheek. Arturo didn't and hadn't considered their bathtub half-ass encounter as a full-fledged sin. They were however guilty as sin of getting stinking drunk that night. Besides, what he wanted to do with Ayita was borne of pure love.

"How do you feel about this my child?"

"Not as long for me, your Eminence, but my appraisal is the same."

"One of the jokes I might deliver, I'd like to pass by you both." The cardinal scratched his nose with his beefy hand covering his mouth. "I have the power to drop some requirements, and when you are ready, I'll visit with you."

The bands of marriage required announcements over a period of time from the pulpit with the same purpose as the cringe-worthy last ditch question at a marriage ceremony asking if anyone objected. The Church also sponsored pre-marriage encounters and retreats, with the wholly different purpose of maturing the couples or ripping them apart. If running against each other for president didn't tear them apart, nothing would. They had every right to be proud of their love, a love tested in fire as hot as the sun, but then they were two cool cats, having gone to war a thousand times, her at the CIA, he as Attorney General—plus all their other accomplishments.

He yearned for her like nothing he had ever experienced in his life and needed an end to his agony. Not even Sheryl—God love her, Arturo love her—had stolen his heart so completely.

Obsession.

Pride swelled his heart. Here he was at a charity roast in honor of the first Catholic, Al Smith, to run for president. Now both he and his opponent were Catholic. One of them would join John F. Kennedy in spirit.

And here before the cardinal, they whispered of love. About this love, he had never been more sure of anything—including the presidency—in his life.

"Ayita and I will talk this over."

The cardinal excused himself and got up to make his way over to the podium, leaving the both of them with a number of unanswered questions. Tops on his list remained whether to sin or not to sin. But his rendition of Catholicism was, he suspected, a bit different than the esteemed cardinal's.

When the cardinal got by Ayita, Arturo stole a quick glance of her stunning gown, flowing raven hair and relaxed face. Best not stare at her too long so as to not let anybody know how much he adored her or be mesmerized by her. Doing her bidding, he'd then speak like the village fool and lose the election. Her full-length white gown, for what he knew, seemed to be made with a crisscross cotton weave showing a little skin at every crossing, but the entire gown covered her with a sheer silk so the observer wouldn't know for sure what was or wasn't bare. He could squint, but it wouldn't be wise. Even with a neckline of a conservative renaissance square and artwork, her figure drove him mad with desire. Here's another time to take her under the table and ravish away. Right where the cardinal's holy feet used to be. *Consider yourself admonished, Arturo.* Her tiara was constructed with down from doves meant to symbolize peace, but to him it was just icing on an exquisite cake, which he'd soon eat.

In the vernacular, the woman and the dress were damn sexy.

He leaned to her and she in turn leaned to him, letting her long slit gown show off more leg—obviously an attempt to drive him senseless. He whispered, "If you have time after the event, I'd like to call you." They both knew this as code for see you in your room. Ayita, with an all-business face, put her fingers to ear and wetted lips as if to say, call me. Probably, no matter how much they disguised their love and passion, the American public would see what they wanted to see, but the game must be played out.

The cardinal thanked Ayita and Arturo for matching each other with a charitable contribution to the Al Smith charity, one hundred thousand dollars apiece. The cardinal talked about the importance of loving thy neighbor in every action and moment of our lives and reinforced it with an example.

His voice boomed. "It is obvious to me that Ayita and Arturo love each other." He waited for the laughter to die down all the while focusing a fatherly Irish smile on the nominees. "They love each other as taught by their parents and teachers and faith. These two couldn't offer a finer example of how we should all treat each other. God bless you all and may God give these two the strength to lead our country on a moral path."

* * *

The senator was introduced.

Ayita rose. After her salutations, she described how the Coolidge administration of the nineteen twenties with the help and support of great Democrats such as Al Smith sponsored changes in the law that allowed her to stand before the American people today as a nominee for president. She then got down to roasting herself with a little Arturo sprinkled in. "The cardinal had asked me to wear white tonight just in case Arturo and I could stand it no longer." She turned to Arturo and blew him a kiss. "I promised him more of those if he'd leave the voters of Florida to me."

He blew a kiss back.

"The nuns had taught me about agape, Christian love. But they failed to mention what to do when a handsome Cuban American smiles your way." If she peeked at him one more time, she'd faint, and the press would really have something to write about.

"I was asked to describe my opponent. I looked under hunk and found his picture in the dictionary." She paused and sipped more wine, just in case she turned red.

"If I drink any more of this I might start singing. We don't want to go there." She was aware of the stereotype that Native Americans couldn't hold their liquor. Let the press get it wrong.

"At the upcoming debates I'll be the one in a dress." References to the glass ceiling couldn't hurt her campaign. No matter how much she loved this man, he still needed to have his pants beaten off of him. She blushed again.

"Arturo has over the last week talked about wearing the pants in our makeshift family. I only hope when he visits me in the Oval Office, he continues to wear his pants." This sent the crowd into a long knee-slapping, wine-spritzing fit. She'd like to slap a certain fellow's well-defined knee.

The thought of them, not drunk, in each other's arms later this night brought a tear of expectation. She struck a more serious tone. "Arturo and I were under guard when the funerals were held. I'd like to ask his Eminence to offer a prayer for the souls of our deceased running mates and the other heroes who died that day on behalf of Arturo and me. With all my heart, and I know Arturo's heart, these men loved their country and made the ultimate sacrifice for us." She handed the mic over to Cardinal Fitzgerald for the prayer and then got it back.

She finished as she had done on every stop for the last week by reading the preamble of the United States Constitution and asking for God's blessing. She firmly believed a country could be run by applying the golden rule, and she'd get her chance to help make this happen one way or the other. The idea that all decisions in life could boil down to treating your fellow human being as you would want him to treat you, seemed so obvious to her. John F. Nash won a Noble when he showed mathematically how this philosophy, the golden rule, could be successfully applied to business. So it should be for all human discourse.

Arturo was introduced.

She'd soon whisper words of love to the gentleman now standing. How had she gone from disliking this man who had been in her way to going head over heels for him for showing her the way? They had much to discuss. Their texting and calls had been reserved even though the lines were secure and encrypted. Both knew the business of love had to be face-to-face, body-to-body. She held in her breath and took her seat next to the cardinal. Arturo breezed by, his soapy scent ruining any chance she had for sanity. Even though he stood at the podium now, she could feel his arms around her.

Arturo waited for the applause to die down and made his salutations.

"The whole world suspects Ayita and I are having an affair, even though we haven't seen each other for over a week now, and before that we were in a hospital and under guard by the Secret Service. Is this because people love—love stories? Well, I'll give you something to print. I'll concede to my opponent that she looks much better in a dress." A riot could have broken out.

"The former Miss Cherokee Nation has not escaped my notice. I'd have to be dead not to notice this truly beautiful woman. A woman who's heart matches her outward appearance. Look at her gown, folks. I just said this—so while you're looking I could too." He waited for the laughter and applause to die down.

"In the spirit of the evening, I'd like to tease the American voters one more time." He paused. "Did you know that the Church provides marriage counseling, retreats and many months of tough love before they'll marry you? Kind of like the primaries and conventions the two of us have been through." He paused again. "The moral of this story is it's easier to get elected president than get married."

Cardinal Fitzgerald raised his voice and in a chuckle said, "See me when you two are ready."

"I may need your eminence for confession. It seems, Ayita, there was only one room left in this renowned hotel."

Ayita shouted, "Try the YMCA."

While Arturo was wrapping up, Ayita, eyes focused on the man, couldn't believe her good fortune. Love had been buried a long time ago along with her heart. She had said no, over all these years, to many a pretty boy. For some reason, and for the first time, she would say yes. In her heart, she already had. She felt so alive.

Maybe the mystical notion of soul mates would get a test tonight. Or perhaps she and Arturo were just too damn compatible at so many levels. It was only a matter of timing and a national tragedy that had given them time to recognize their love. It didn't hurt that he had the hunky athlete's body of her ideal man. It didn't hurt that she loved his Latin features and culture. It didn't hurt that he had a passion for politics. This notion that they had found each other as soul mates in a Miami bar years ago didn't hurt either. They had kept an undeniable overwhelming truth secret because he loved his wife, because she loved her career and she had not a clue who he had been and over the years no desire or time to find out.

Unlike most of the men who had flirted with her, Arturo loved her like a man possessed. She was beginning to feel this magic he had within him. Just how much, she'd find out tonight.

She, a practical woman, would also want to know if making love to him would be as great as every other facet of their relationship. Every bit of her tingled in anticipation. No one had ever filled her with such expectations. She felt as giddy as a school girl, as passionate as a lifelong mistress like Kate Hepburn, as wanton as a nympho. *Could a nympho become president?*

She needed a priest to sort out her feelings. Perhaps she'd talk with Colleen too. Maybe not. Although her daughter, Daya, was always available for talks, Colleen had wisdom. As a mother, she couldn't let Daya get the idea that loving a boy should get in the way of her becoming a doctor. Although Daya was the best surprise in her life, she didn't want her to take the boy-crazy path

Ayita had. She had no regrets for her marriage or the product of their love.

She'd let the American voters decide the other question. At peace, she lost herself in the handshakes and well wishes. Arturo's handshake and quirky eyebrows meant the world to her and capped off the first leg in what promised to be a fantastic evening.

Chapter Nineteen
I Feel Pretty

Ayita fluttered when she approached the adjoining hotel room door. She stopped and turned back, went to the folding stand, opened her suitcase and pulled out a men's blue cotton dress shirt with long tails. She'd dress with nothing underneath. Show a lot of leg. Arturo liked her legs. She spun before the full-length mirror. "I feel pretty, oh so pretty."

She lowered her voice. *Pretty damn good for a forty-two-year-old woman.* But maybe, just maybe he'd wonder where the shirt came from. It wasn't her husband's. She bought it in Sears for that eventual day when she'd meet someone new. How could she diminish his suspicions? Oh, he wouldn't care. He thought of her as his soul mate. She could do no wrong, except be a Democrat. And even that, he seemed to tolerate.

She stripped down to nothing. Maybe she should knock on his door like this. Claim she was room service. The dessert he'd ordered. No. Too bold. She'd need to be more demure. She pulled out one of her daughter's too-cute baby doll nighties with silly frilly pinky 3-D flowers all over the panties and then put on a straight-up-and-down pink cotton top with Minnie Mouse embossed on it. No, better not, he'd die laughing. She laid the pieces neatly on the bed.

She pulled out a matching red push-up bra and panties, but hated the idea of false advertising. He was already sold, anyway. She laid the bra and panties on the bed next to Minnie Mouse and the men's shirt.

Ah, a Waldorf Astoria bathrobe. She'd shower; keep her hair a little wet, sling a towel over her shoulder. Ask for his help in drying. She slipped on the robe. How far down could she tighten the knot to show a little cleavage, or should she let him do the untightening?

Was she going crazy?

The door handle turned and then came a small knock, "Princess."

"In a minute." She picked up her dress from the bed and then laid it down again for display next to the other discards. Then she turned on the radio, tuned to Latin beats, lowered the volume and slipped on the bathrobe. The champagne was set in an ice bucket, just waiting its victims. Tonight, maybe they should stay completely sober.

* * *

Arturo had wondered what to wear. As a joke, he thought of going bare-ass naked to her door. But where was the fun, beyond shock value, in that? After he picked her up off the floor from fainting, he'd be back to square one. He spotted the light-blue terrycloth hotel bathrobe, stripped and put it on. No, this wasn't right. They needed to talk first. If he showed up wearing this she'd strip it right off of him and there wouldn't be much talking. A guy talking? Now that's funny, but he was playing for all the marbles.

He would put his penguin suit back on, but he might be a little stinky. He took a quick shower, applying liberal amounts of soap to remove the day's sweat or worse—that locker room smell. His mind wondered while the water beat his face. Ayita was so natural in her delivery. Truly a gifted comic. The American people could use a wit like John Fitzgerald Kennedy again. On the other hand, they could use a Cuban American who would heal the rift in the Cuban community that had started long ago in the Eisenhower administration. He'd lift the spirit of a downtrodden island.

He dried off, applied a little talc absentmindedly here and there while he enjoyed an image of Ayita in his arms in her tub, before the dog had dive-bombed them. He slapped two dashes of aftershave to his neck. He redressed, leaving his white bow tie half untied. Nice touch.

He knocked on her door. "Princess."

* * *

Ayita had realized just wearing a bathrobe was too much for any man. "Just another minute." Wearing a bathrobe in front of a virile man would get you naked in ten seconds.

She tossed the robe on the bed and quickly pulled on her gown. How would she explain her wet hair? Oh shit. "Oh so pretty." She ran into the bathroom and grabbed a towel, rubbed her hair like crazy and then brushed and brushed. "Sorry, Arturo. I promise, just one more minute."

"I feel pretty and witty and anything but gay," she sang softly enough. Singing was not a talent to share with the world or even an errant spider. She had tried rapping for her Miss Cherokee talent, but her voice would have ruined her chances. She'd then partially built a comedy routine around her bad *rap*.

"We have forever," Arturo said chuckling.

What a sweet thing to say. This soul mate thing is a two way street, right?

Ruffling the bottom of her gown, she opened the door. Arturo stared at her with eyes wide and wild, and then scooped her up into his arms. She floated off the floor pressed against his chest. Every part of her was in revolt and dancing loony. The man of her dreams held her and nothing else mattered.

Almost.

She kissed his neck, smelled soap, aftershave and baby powder and nearly swooned.

"Whoa, Princess, if anybody should faint, it should be me. You are the most desirable, tasty…" He steadied her with a tighter hug. She hushed him with a peck.

She shook her whirling head, caused, the last time they had gotten personal, by being drunk. *So what's your excuse now, Mary Ayita, hmm?*

"I want you bad," she said like a breathy Marilyn Monroe, "but we need to talk first." His normal musky scent would have done her in completely. God, she had changed. Her armor had been stripped away by this one-man army. His hands were all over her, but then he pulled back with a wavering smile on his handsome face.

She twirled around. They absolutely needed to talk. "Can I get you a drink?"

He exhaled and got closer. "No, thanks. I thought you were perfect tonight." *Oh damn, not politics.*

She stepped over to her bureau. "Speechwriters, just speechwriters."

He came up behind her while she fiddled with her earrings. "No, your delivery, your timing, perfect." *Please have mercy, Arturo.*

He pressed his very noticeable erection and hard body against her back.

"You did a great job too, sweetheart," Ayita realized both of them were so driven to succeed, they might easily fall into shoptalk. "But tonight, let's talk about us. We might not get too many more opportunities before Election Day. Talk to me about soul mates."

"I'm going to be honest, Ayita." She dropped her earrings into a case and closed the lid. He nibbled on her neck.

She turned to him and took his hand, for a moment worried something awful would come out of his mouth. Then they took the loveseat and cuddled. "You're adorable in white tie and tails." She patted his chest and was amused by a cloud of baby powder billowing out from his half-buttoned shirt. She jumped to the conclusion that he had showered and put his monkey suit back on, just as worried as she had been about what to wear. Oh they'd make a lovely couple, team, pres and her vice. What wonders hid under all these clothes? Somewhere along the way, if they became lovers, she'd absentmindedly powder herself in the oddest places, maybe give her patch a two-tone appearance, and see if he'd think that funny or would his head explode?

"Your dress makes me think about weddings." He massaged her upper thigh.

She stood up. "Shouldn't we save ourselves?" She licked her lips, but there was no disguising what she wanted. *So why try? Why run?*

He stood up and took a step toward her. He ignored her question. "When I first laid eyes upon you in that Miami bar, I was married. I had often wondered if I got married too fast, if there was such a thing as a soul mate. Don't get me wrong. I never cheated on my wife. I loved her with every fiber of my being. Even after she died, no matter the crazy stories in the press, I have not had sex with any of those women," he said using President Bill Clinton's twang. She laughed. "Seriously though, I've been celibate until you." She backed into the wall.

"Thank the Lord." She threw up her arms and tried a little southern Baptist on him. He had every right to have affairs, although the consequences of being caught might have sunk his career faster than the Titanic went down. This bothered her. What if they were caught? At least one of the two people in this room needed to think this through. The American people understood two people in love, but they might not understand two people making love. He pressed her into the wall and raked his hand under her dress and up her leg.

"Ah." She squeezed his hand, stopping its upward progress, "but then there was you." She nestled her head against his broad chest. The bow tie tickled her nose so she unraveled it a little lower with her teeth. Turned wilder, his hand moved up to her wet mound. Soon they'd be out of control, naked. *Doing it.*

Breathing heavily, he kissed her. "In that bar, I couldn't take my eyes off of you. I couldn't concentrate on what my friends were saying. Then later, I tried to tell myself this mystical soul mate thing was just a rationalization. You see, I was recalling over and over the memory of you, not my wife. To protect my guilt that night, I put you on a pedestal, but then you got off your bar stool and kissed me." He slid his thick long finger deep inside her.

"Oh my God. Funny boy. I kissed you because you were tastier than the mojitos. I was lonely.

"Oh. Oh.

"Something about you drew me in, in, in. I never in my life felt this way." She scampered under his arm and slipped away, immediately regretting it. "Until I snapped out of my coma. You held my hand." She had disliked him far more than she should, a sure sign that her hate had hidden a more productive and positive emotion. She bent over the end table to straighten her pocket book. Big mistake.

He clasped her hips. "So maybe there is something mystical between us. I must admit, I've had temptations, nothing I'd ever acted on, over these last two-plus years."

She rolled her hips like a hula. "Well, it happened to me too. I woke up in the bunker horny for the first time in twenty years. You held my hand. It felt good and bad. Because I didn't like you then." She put her finger in her mouth and pretended to gag.

He put his finger back into her.

"You're my opponent. Oh, oh. We're supposed to beat the you-know-what out of each other. I noticed how cute the Navy doctor with his blue eyes was, but you were better looking and being so sweet to me."

He slipped his finger out of her and slowly rubbed her engorged clitoris. "The blue-eyed doctor?" he huffed. She flipped around to face him. His hand fell off her. Now though, Arturo's eyes' deep pools swallowed her soul. She jumped on him and said close to his lips. "Well, how about that cute nurse you had wheeling you around?" She stroked the bulge in his pants. They had discussed how the nurse looked like his bride but she hadn't much to counter him with.

"Remember, the—the nurse looked too much like a younger Sheryl." He kissed the skin above her breasts still hidden by the dress. "Besides, I fell in love with you and was desperate to find a way to your heart."

He maneuvered her to the side of the bed.

"You did, my sweet. You really did? So you think the two of us can't help ourselves." Oh God, her hips just started humping without her permission.

"Yes." He kissed her parted lips.

"*So* you think…" He penetrated her with his tongue.

"We should get married."

"Maybe."

She dropped her gaze and let her eyes flicker up at him in the best come-and-take-me-now look she could muster but something deep still nagged. *Hold off, but how can I?* But he didn't move in spite of her possessed hips, maybe pondering some great thought about two souls meant to be.

He let his hand slide down her back to her bottom and as if on cue and reading her mind he said, "Just like the existence of God, honey, we can never prove this soul mate thing. I feel we're somehow meant to be for this country, like Lincoln, like Kennedy without the assassinations. We were meant to heal a country gone mad with hatred of the opposite party."

"I love it when you talk dirty like this."

But he didn't answer, couldn't answer until she took her tongue out of his mouth.

"One last thing before I strip this mock *wedding* dress off you."

Her breathing quickened. She couldn't speak. She nodded a big yes.

"Topper cut through the bullshit couples pile up to protect their fragile egos. He told me and you a small piece of the truth about our hearts. Topper has saved us a ton of verbal swordplay."

Topper, my sweet irascible Topper.

"My dearest Arturo, don't you agree? Life is not about being a democrat or republican it's about being human."

All he could do was grunt agreement.

Meanwhile, her body was making her shiver, almost like climaxing. "I'd like to play with your sword." Her husband hadn't taught her much. Or did she teach him the little she knew? She forgot. She had pulled Pavan's thing a few times. She had since book-learned a man loved a woman's lips slipping up and down and down and up much better than her hand. She'd try it.

Now both his hands were up her dress and grabbing her ass. "What was your relationship with your husband like?" He panted.

"Oh my, Arturo. Keep squeezing me like that. I hold loving memories. We were both kids, really. Sweethearts. We kissed for hours—teenagers—growing up in Tahlequah, Oklahoma. We used to sneak into any closet we could find, any stand of too few trees or bushes, back seats. We didn't go all the way until college. Want to go all the way?" She hesitated, tough to talk in the middle of panting. Arturo scratched his chin. "But it took him all of one or two minutes each time. You'll do better, right?" Arturo was attempting to lift her dress all the way up. She squirmed away, maybe for the last time. Her boy husband always went down on her as he expressed it, to finish her off. Maybe her whirlwind body movements had something to do with it. They should have had a college how-to class. Anyway, she could have sworn she'd come fifteen times already, with the crazy things Arturo had been doing to her.

He picked her up, dress still up, put her on the dresser and spread her legs. "I think I can last at least three minutes." He puffed his pecks. His laugh hinted he'd do much better. She had read *The Joy of Sex* when in Prague at a peace conference. Her theoretical knowledge was now complete. He sweetly kissed her mound, tangling his tongue with her clit, then he swooped her up and carried her to the bed when he noticed with wry smile a fashion show's worth of clothes displayed.

"He never got to hold my baby, Daya in his arms." She realized she was spoiling the mood, big time, and decided to shut her mouth and open her legs and get this show going before she was so gone.

"We're never going to forget our sweethearts."

"Thank you, Arturo. I have his flag." Shit, she did it again.

"I'm so sorry... Marry me, Princess. Make us right for the sake of Sheryl and Pavan too." He laid her softly on her display of clothes. Then she started pushing them onto the floor. He flipped her from her side to her back. *This is it.*

"First of all, my sexy Latin. You're going to be very angry at me when I rip you to shreds at the debates." What the hell was wrong with her? Fuck him. Fuck him.

He pressed his body, making sure not to squash her. "And how are you going to do this, since our positions are nearly the same?" With each word, he kissed her nose and cheeks.

"Ah, um, you—you'll see. Your position right now is unacceptable." Words just sprung a leak from her mouth. She cradled his face, felt stubble, no peach fuzz like her deceased husband had had. She enjoyed this stubbly feel against her palms. "I want to be on top *of you*, just like on erection night." He chuckled. *Playing with Arturo is like riding on the wind with a pony.*

"My position on your proposal is...in complete agreement." He flipped to his back and she began to undress him.

Still something nagged.

Her intuition was telling her not to do this. Every other part of her wanted this man. The American electorate would want them to do this right. But, but, but she had long since ran by the point of no return in her fevered brain.

She lifted her dress and throttled his hips. "I'm having a little trouble." She had removed his jacket, tie, cummerbund and shirt. Like she suspected, she noticed an errant splotch of baby powder over his right nipple. She bent down to whiff. This man needed lessons. His natural musky smell turned her on much more than *baby* powder. Instead of penises, pecks, butts, she saw Daya's baby bottom. No doubt, right now, Daya was studying. No doubt, right now, Ayita had changed her mood through no conscious fault of her own. Or maybe not.

"I want to strip you." She got off of him and straightened out her dress. She really should have opened the door naked.

He now stood with his muscular calves pressing the side of the bed.

She whipped off his belt, let it fly. She unzipped his pants and tugged downward, catching his boxers with her thumbs. She pulled them down to his knees. Magnificent. And silly. He had absentmindedly powdered half his pubic hairs. She tried, really tried not to laugh.

She stared up into his eyes. Put her hands on his penis and balls and petted.

"Wow. I, I don't know, ah, I don't know if I can fit this into my mouth." *Or my pussy.*

Someone knocked at the door. *Fuckin', damn, bleep, bleep, bleep.*

They had been so bad, they were good. They did not deserve this. There'd be no confessions with Cardinal Fitzgerald tomorrow.

Chapter Twenty
Promises, Promises

Carlos and Jason stood out on the Park Avenue median in the night cold, sipping steaming coffee and watching as NYPD arrested a cub reporter who had tried to scale up the Waldorf Astoria.

"Should we tell them?"

"No, let the lovebirds play," Carlos said.

A NYPD detective from the city's terrorism taskforce ran over to them. "We found this." She handed an empty canister to Carlos.

"This contraption shoots plastic listening devices that stick to windows." The detective explained how the air-powered device hadn't reached its target.

"Do you have someone who does windows?" Jason asked.

"Yes, sir, within fifteen minutes."

"Good, we will jam them, just in case." Carlos added.

Jason seemed agitated and took a sip of his coffee. "We have to tell them."

"Yes. We will separate two wolves in heat. And then run like hell."

* * *

Arturo, now pants up, answered the knock. "Who's there?"

"Carlos and Jason," Carlos said.

"Sorry for the interruption," the ever so polite Jason said.

After a moment, Arturo had his shirt back on and buttoned. He glanced back at his love and knew the evening was spoiled. After she reassembled herself, he opened the door and the two men explained what had happened. They inspected the windows of both their suites and found nothing. No one knew which suites the nominees were in, but according to Carlos, they could triangulate on the sounds of the nominees if they were lucky enough to reach high enough with the listening devices. Luckily, the reporter was caught outside the third floor. Ayita calculated the projectiles would only get to the eighth floor.

Jason just couldn't help himself. "I think you are the most loving couple. I only wish I could be in love someday." Everybody stared at him.

"That is so sweet of you, Jason." She walked over and kissed his cheek and gave Carlos a bear hug. Arturo wouldn't hug or kiss the men. He thanked them with handshakes and then they left the room.

Arturo could tell from Ayita's face that she was troubled and decided to preempt where she was likely heading. "We owe it to the people."

"Honey." She drove herself into his arms and wept. "When will we ever have a normal life?"

"In the White House. Maybe." But that sounded just plain silly.

"When we're old."

He shook her gently. "No, if we get married and tell the world nobody will bother us."

Ayita appeared a bit skeptical. "If you'll still have me after your ass is whipped in the second debate, Governor, I'll marry you."

Oh God, his dreams, his wildest dreams were coming true. Life with this woman would really be cheating on heaven. He was tempted to ask her how she could be so certain about him in such a short time. Yes, he had had Ayita in his heart his whole adult life while she had ignored men in favor of serving her country. Yes, Ayita had always been quick in making very complicated decisions, the mark of a genius. Yes, she had always made the right decisions, except being a member of the Democratic party. He couldn't, shouldn't destroy the mood now or worse yet get her to reconsider the single greatest blessing in his life. But he would ask this question to be fair to her before they got married. If they got married.

Arturo dropped to his knees, wrapped his arms around her and kissed her gown where her mound was hiding. He rubbed his jaw against her until she moaned.

Nestled he said, "Hit me with your best shots. The voters have a right to choose."

They talked about Cardinal Fitzgerald doing the honors, marrying them. Although he could be trusted, his deacons and any number of clerks might tell. Plus the press was likely to fall out of their suite closet or a confessional box in church. He got up and looked in the closet.

They decided the reason why they couldn't let the world know of their engagement and wedding before the election was simple. The focus had to remain on who would win, and not how the government would run when the president and the vice president shared a bed in the White House. *Focus on the issues, at least for the voters' right to choose.*

Ayita's grandfather was a former mayor and medicine man. He retained the power to marry by Oklahoma law and the power to bless their union by Sky Father. Later, in the Rose Garden, they'd follow in the Carthage administration's footsteps and get married before a priest and the world.

"So why not make love now?" He knew this to be a dumb question, but his more primitive self, yearned to be one with her. *And would that be so bad?*

She tousled his hair and raised his chin. "History will eventually tell this story, my dearest. And when it does, we can teach the young a lesson by our example, a tad imperfect." She brushed his crotch with her hip. "A lesson about the difference between love and lust."

"Yeah, and we'll give our self-righteous detractors nothing concrete to power their news cycles."

"Besides, if you stuck your huge thing in me, I'd run to my momma."

They caressed long, until 1:02 AM and then he headed for the adjoining door. At the door, he turned to say goodnight. She had let her dress fall to her waist.

She pursed her lips and gave a cockeyed grin. "They're not too small, are they?"

"Perfect, Princess." And they were perfectly and delectably proportioned to her svelte body. He'd have to eat his pillow.

"Goodnight, Prince Charming." After the debates, she might think of him as the Prince of Darkness. He closed the door, kissed its frame and then banged his head lightly against the wood. A tear tickled its way down his cheek. On the other side, a most brilliant, beautiful and loving woman would dream of him and the presidency. So would he of her.

He lay in bed trying to sleep, sensual images of a striking woman uttering incredible truths, mixed with alternative images of voters in queues at the polling stations.

What if the vote were a tie, with not enough Electoral College votes to declare a president elect? He decided to fall asleep working on what if. Anything was better than thinking about unresolved lust.

How would they handle their duties?

Who would be president?

Could they share in some way?

Was there a constitutional precedent?

What was best for the country?

Finally, in his dreams, Ayita and he lay naked on a private Caribbean beach in tender embrace whispering sweet endearments, talk of love and life and how they held these truths within their hearts.

Chapter Twenty One
You Give Love a Bad Name

Inn on Biltmore Estate, Asheville, North Carolina
Despite their best intentions to rip each other to shreds in debate, neither Ayita nor Arturo had the heart. Ayita was so love crazy over him, she often felt like running up to him on stage, any stage to plant a lingering, sloppy, kiss. She had contracted Arturo-itis.
He is like a dream of a man.
Would she be able to concentrate on world problems if he took off his shirt? The *woman of steel* would find a way. Perhaps she'd rip off her blouse to even the score.
Colleen slapped the *New York Times* op-ed section down on the conference table in Ayita's suite. Actually, she slammed it with temper, red freckles and hair on fire. Opinions and editorials could sting. Sometimes they could change the course of an election.
Arturo's stomach growled. He didn't know if he could take what Colleen and Grant were about to dish out, at least not without a sandwich and some chips. Besides, had they not all signed off on the remaining strategy?
Arturo moved his chair closer to Ayita until their knees knocked. They'd read together, but best yet, they'd get to breathe, spellbound, by the other. The sex in the room was palpable, but not only with Ayituro, as some in the press had called the famous couple. Colleen and Grant had been eyeing each other ever since the first of two debates in Boston had flopped and a third one was now resurrected to stop the bleeding in the polls. Their campaign chiefs might be ready to divulge their feelings. Maybe one push by Ayita or Arturo and they'd out with it. Ayita would be ready to

grab Arturo's hand, run out of the room, to go down to the lobby if these two started ripping each other's clothes off.

Warren Winchell, world-famous skewerer of politicians, well known for his acerbic wit and poignant commentary, had chosen to focus with force this time on the Starblanket/Arnez and Arnez/Starblanket tickets.

WHILE WASHINGTON BURNS, ARTURO AND AYITA FIDDLE—WITH EACH OTHER.

I just don't get it, folks. Here we are just a little more than a week to Election Day and our nominees are shacking up, if you believe the Star *or* Enquirer. *Well, I don't care what they do, but apparently, they don't seem to be doing much of anything. Period. Yes, period.*

You say give them a break; they had nearly been blown up. Fine. Prayers have been said. Their coffee break is over.

You say they're single. What the hell does that have to do with the needs of the American people?

Every time the press asks them substantive questions about policy or any other issue they bring the subject back to their deceased running mates and how America needs to honor their legacy, or they toss some inane political football. What about Cuba? What about the reunification of North and South Korea?

Yep, America is honoring the legacies of the extreme views held by their deceased running mates by giving a boost to the third-party candidacy of Edgar Charney. Although the moderate governor of Florida thinks Edgar is a nut, he must have forgotten what his deceased running mate stood for. At least the senator hasn't let on what she feels about Edgar, accept to say hell had frozen over Edgar's home, but then again, she has said nothing about nothing lately. Does she merely joke or is she a joke?

Mourn no more. Lead. Bother us no more with yesterday's problems. Lead. Don't talk about the extreme views of your deceased running mates when you two have no intention of adopting any of them.

Where's that eloquence, Ayita, when you brought us the most stirring anti-war speech since Bobby Kennedy talked of dreams? Where's the stirring rhetoric about why we should embrace Cuba, Arturo? I'd rather watch paint dry.

In the meantime, good 'ole Edgar is playing the race card—if you haven't noticed, both nominees are not white—and people are beginning to listen. Every day, the creep, creeps up in the polls. To be fair to the fair-skinned Governor of Alaska, he's not a racist. He married an Inuit. But what's the difference between a desperate politician and a shark?

I don't know.

Can sharks swim in frigid Alaskan waters?

Sometimes, it is necessary to say it like it is. Remember FDR, "I welcome their hatred." *Where are our two love birds on the issues? When will they make love to the American public?*

The first debate was the biggest snooze fest since the Oslo climate non-talks.

Make love to me, my dear nominees. I'm available every night and every day for the rest of my life, and I know a few hundred million voters who feel the same.

Signing off,
Warren Winchell

* * *

Arturo's smile broadened. Ayita ripped the page out, crumpled it into a ball and tossed into a can, some five feet away. Nice shot.

"We're not that bad, are we?" Ayita asked.

Arturo baited everybody for an answer he already knew. "Our love isn't that obvious, is it?" His dream now set in motion was two I dos away from becoming reality. Again, did the world want to live by the golden rule or did they prefer suicide by one disparaging remark after another?

"We're willing to role play for the next debate," Colleen said. They had asked their campaign chairs to work together. Apparently, they were getting better at it.

"If Edgar picks up a couple more percentage points, neither of you will get enough Electoral College votes to go over the top and your crisscross for vice president would fail to Rand and Crème," Grant added. He loosened his tie. A rare event for the preppie metrosexual, or was he nervous or feeling casual around Colleen?

"You don't want this going to the College. The electors are not sold yet on what you two have done. They could also install their own vice president or worse pick Edgar. Besides, both parties are rumbling again," Colleen said.

"Yes, we have reason to believe..." Grant hesitated.

"Hold up, I have complete control over my party and I believe Arturo does too," Ayita said.

"What is it, Grant?" Arturo asked.

"With all due respect, Ayita, the party isn't happy you put Arturo on the ticket."

"Yes, and they can do nothing about it."

"Again, Grant, what made you hesitate?" Arturo persisted.

"Well, I think you two should choreograph a show like the professional wrestlers do. Include some metaphorical folding chairs across each other's back, some body slams. Your golden-rule or do unto others stuff is too saccharine. You can still love each other and have a spirited debate. Married couples everywhere are worried they'll have to forego make-up sex. You two give love a bad name." For the first time in a long while, Grant broke out laughing. Being proper, he'd never laugh at his own joke, but being moribund until today, he laughed at nothing much.

"You give love a bad name." Colleen sang little better than Ayita but she played a mean air guitar.

Arturo wasn't buying this excellent example of muddying the waters. You were either good or bad in life. The world had meaning or absurdity. Arturo glanced at Ayita and got her nod. He decided to take a chance. "You know what's absurd? It's obvious the two of you have caught the same bug Ayita and I have. You love her, Grant, don't you?"

"I think now's the time for you two to share with your two best friends what happened between the two of you at Yale," Ayita said. "Maybe we can help."

"You're changing the subject. Whatever sparks you may have thought you noticed between Colleen and I, comes from us being worried about you two. Show us some fight on the stage. That's all she and I ask. I had to slap myself to stay awake last week."

Colleen, who propped herself on a pillow, popped up, peeked at Grant, laughed and walked over to him. "I know you two care about us. But couldn't we limit this discussion to one couple?"

Grant spoke up, "If you must know—"

Ayita interrupted, "We're your employers. I have worked for the CIA and NSA for God's sake. Don't you think we know about what happened at Yale?"

Colleen's eyebrows drew together and if steam could come out her ears…

Grant cleared his throat and continued, "She walked out on all her friends. She left me without a word or explanation. I loved this woman." He pointed shyly at his proposed culprit.

"Is this what you all want?" Colleen walked into the second bedroom crying.

Ayita went up to Grant. "Maybe she had a good reason to leave you. Think on that, smart ass."

Grant hesitated and then got up. "Pardon me, please." He walked into the second bedroom.

Arturo and Ayita asked Topper to eavesdrop for them. They held their phones to their ears.

Topper whispered back. "He's demanding to know why she left him. She sounds like she's pushing him away. He asked her to stand still. He must have grabbed her. She threw something at him. They're arguing about their friends at Yale. They just cursed both of you for being snoops. You two are nosey busy bodies. I cleaned that up. She blew her nose. He's encouraging her to let her feelings out. She says to him, "I hate you." Put your phones down. They're coming back in three, two, one."

Colleen ran into Arturo's arms. "I'm sorry, you two, what you have is beautiful, but I can't stand working with him." She grabbed her purse and ran to the door. "I quit." She tried to slam a door but the door only moved so fast. She pushed, and pushed again. Kicked it and ran off.

"Whoa, you two." Both Ayita and Arturo were cornering Grant.

Ayita pinged Grant's chest until he backed into a wall and could move no farther. "What did you say to her?"

"Nothing. Not a thing."

Arturo, who was helping keep Grant from bolting said, "We need you two. I promise to liven up the debate if you'll only get my Colleen back."

"Yes, sir."

Ayita repeatedly stabbed his chest. "Don't. Come. Back. In. Here. Unless you find out what's eating her."

"She won't talk to me."

Arturo leaned in. "She aborted your child. Now man up, Grant, and get the hell out of here." Grant turned whiter than he had ever been.

"Find her. Settle your personal issues any way you like. I don't care. Come back here ready to work with us and her or don't come back," Ayita said.

* * *

Grant hurried off tying his tie. He wanted to argue. Colleen and he were doing their job. They had just presented a case, that is, if Ayita and Arturo didn't act, it could threaten either of their shots at the presidency. *You can't reason with the two most powerful people in the world.*

Colleen had aborted his child?

Colleen had aborted his child. *This is a nightmare.* He had loved her, truly loved her. Why couldn't she have trusted him to do the right thing?

Grant had a hunch Colleen would be downing her sorrows in Irish crème shots. So he explored the hotel's restaurants and bars.

Finally, he spotted her on a barstool. One leg, a lovely leg draped down, tapping the floor, as if she was ready to run again. He hesitated and hid behind an Egyptian vase. As if he could hide for long from her sharp eyes.

He had loved her with all his heart and yet she'd stomped on him. He had written her feelings off as puppy love and he moved on. He had denied his masculinity all these years. Could it be possible he still loved her, just a little bit?

She turned sideways. Tears streaked her face, dribbling by every adorable freckle. Couldn't he just hold her? All these years, she was still beautiful to him. The bartender, a woman, clasped Colleen's hand and said something soothing.

Man up. Lie to her. Tell her you love her, because maybe you do. You'll never know for sure unless you try. He took a deep swallow, slipped past the vase and approached.

"I love you, Colleen." He sat wide on the stool next to her on the side her foot was down tapping—which stopped tapping on sight of him—so she'd be less likely to bolt. He motioned to the bartender—Sally according to her nametag—to pour an Irish crème for him. Colleen turned the other way as if having a conversation with Harvey, the six-foot rabbit.

"You're just saying this because they told you to get me back, right?" This lady was too smart for her own good. It was her brilliance then and now that had attracted him, not just her voluptuous smoking-hot body and pretty face. Oh, that and the finest and most shapely ass he had ever kissed. He'd need to do more ass kissing to pull this one off.

"I'll never lie to you. Yes, they asked me to talk you into coming back. But I was about to quit too. They are so lame."

"Yeah. I know. Their love is so mind-blowing that it's turned them into fools." She turned to face the mirror in the bar behind the bottles. So he caught her eye by squinting at the mirror.

He had never had easier words with anybody in his life. He recalled their endless conversations into the night. The ease of their rhythmic odes to love making. Their sweet double releases. God, he had missed her flirty ways, her funny jokes right in the middle of his sometimes inept thrusts. Very funny indeed, Colleen, who'd then screamed like a monkey and come like a freight train.

"I have never loved another woman. You know my press reports. How they think me a closet gay. I being somebody Ayita hired to level out her staff in a fair manner, she just playing demographics."

"You are not gay. Oh no, mister squirt all over me. Mister Shove-It-Up my..." She looked at Sally and somehow the bartender got it and moved down to the other end.

"Hey, that was something we both wanted to try." He tried a shitty grin, and she bit her lip.

Then Colleen laughed and touched his lips. "Shut up. You are not gay." She took another sip. "Although, your outfit is too, too divine. Navy-blue suits were very professional, twenty years ago."

"What happened to us?" He downed his shot and signaled to the bartender.

"The whole bottle, please. A new one. Thanks, Sally."

"Are either of you two lactose intolerant?" Sally walked off after delivering the bottle and chuckled again. Apparently, it wasn't cool for middle-aged adults to drink Irish crème to excess.

Colleen let out a short burp.

She touched and lined up her bottom and top teeth. "I aborted your child, Grant." Her hazel eyes narrowed.

He knew this to be the test of his life. *Help me, Lord.*

Forget all those campaigns he'd saved from sure defeat. This was it. The proverbial turning point, if ever there was one. He'd have to man up or forever regret this precious second chance. He decided not to cry, not to say he would have married her then. He would have. Saying such would be obvious, prosaic. Condescending words would just piss her off.

"If I recall, we wanted two children. If we start now, why not three babies? Love me like you used to. Please."

She stood up as if ready to run again. He had blown it.

"I'll never know what our little angel would have been like. I don't really hate you, Grant. I-I-I hate myself."

A reporter from the *Washington Post* sat down on the other side of Colleen. The bartender crooked her finger to the uninvited snoop to move down the row of stools. He pretended not to get the message. Sally approached and leaned into his face. "Those two bar stools are for their friends, sir. They'll be right back." She set up two more shot glasses.

The reporter moved down. "Sorry," he said. But he could still hear if he listened closely with the bat ears all good reporters were issued.

Grant grabbed the bottle and fingered the two new shot glasses. Colleen downed hers. "Thanks, Sally. We just got a text and a change of plans." Never a big tipper, Grant slapped a hundred on the smooth bar top and held it in place with his spent glass. He had never met a better bartender in his life, nor possibly felt this alive in years. He gave Sally a slight bow.

"My room?" Colleen asked, leaning slightly his way.

"What should we tell them?"

"Let them suffer." Around the corner and out of sight of everybody, Grant held a bottle and glasses and got his ass pinched.

He became a believer again.

Thank you, Lord.

Chapter Twenty Two
Peace Train

The Foreign Policy debate

The Legionnaire's Hall in Scranton, Pennsylvania, hosted the final debate in conjunction with CNN. Scoop Anderson moderated.

Just the right place to talk anti-war. If ever a tougher crowd in the northeast assembled for a Democrat, Ayita couldn't think of one, but she'd speak to anyone listening and watching. Arturo and she had kicked and screamed, but in the end they'd agreed to put on Colleen and Grant's show, or they'd lose both managers. Colleen and Grant seemed strangely at peace.

Like magpies for some born-again revival, the nominees had spread their message of love. Tonight, they'd step into the coliseum and hope the emperor would spare the other's life.

Arturo wore a VFW cap a vet had given him when he worked the crowd. The hat pressed his thick black curls outward. She walked out into the crowd until she found a sympathetic female Navy pilot who was willing to part with hers.

The questions began. Ayita was first and answered.

"I fought for our country. Conducted clandestine operations that saved nations from tyranny, hunted down and eliminated terrorists. If there were a war, under my leadership the United States wouldn't lose. If attacked, I would not politely visit the U.N. I would not announce my intentions. If I were elected, there would be more clandestine ops, not less. You'll all be safer for it."

Arturo then got his turn to rebut.

"My opponent would have you believe she wouldn't bother with the U.N. or NATO. We live in a complicated world. Nowadays, decisions involving many nations can be made in a

169

flash. My opponent, an ex-engineer, oddly seems to be playing on your emotions. Wouldn't it have been better had we consulted the Iraqis before entering Iraq?"

Ayita adjusted her mic and spoke. "Wouldn't it have been better if we'd struck bin Laden immediately after 9/11 and followed through. We spent ten years tracking down Osama bin Laden instead of blowing him to hell on September twelfth or thirteenth, 2001. All I'm saying is strike back fast and strike back hard at the person or nation who attacked us, if we know who. Then we'll seek a consensus with the U.N. and NATO. A consensus no longer necessary since the primary threat had been eliminated. My opponent is naive if he thinks we can keep secret a NATO attack...for long."

Scoop changed the subject, but no matter what it was, the audience got its show.

One particularly interesting but off-topic question popped up and Arturo went first.

"What if it's a tie and neither of you have enough Electoral College votes to declare victory?" According to Topper, the pundits and the statistical models of various news agencies, the odds of this happening varied between twenty-three to thirty-seven percent at any given moment, so far.

"My opponent will concede to my superior managerial skills as Governor of Florida and we'll recommend as a team to the College that they elect me, the country's next president."

"Once again, my opponent reveals his naiveté. I ran the CIA and NSA. Try herding spies, Arturo. Why would I agree? The House and Senate will likely still be controlled by my party. More would get done with me at the helm. I'm not talking about increasing the size of government. I intend to waste not, to trim where we can and make realistic decisions." She changed her tone to signal a quote and fixed her gaze with deadly earnest into the camera. "Let me recite a portion of the preamble of our constitution. *'In order to form a more perfect union, establish justice, insure domestic tranquility, provide for the common defense, promote the general welfare'."*

Somebody in the crowd at every stop, at every event, asked the obvious and in this case very off-point question. Beatrice, a petite elderly lady with brilliant-white curls, less-white dress and a wicked smile said in variable voice. "You two don't fool me. I can tell when people are in true love. I saw to it that my five daughters and their grandchildren. I guessed right every time."

Scoop tried to get the mic back from her politely, claiming this was a foreign-policy debate and asked that she change her question. She whipped her hand holding the mic, back. "Don't be impertinent, young man. This is what America needs to know before we vote. My question is—my question is-s—when are you two getting married."

Ayita spoke first, "Our focus is on helping our country, not each other's marital status. What you see in us, Beatrice, is a deep abiding respect for each other, the love of friends. I told you this beating up on each other wouldn't work, Arturo." She handed the mic to Arturo. What Beatrice also likely noticed was a raging desire to make love and marry her opponent. No acting class was good enough to hide the way she felt. She beamed as if pregnant. She felt like the girl who had carried the roses down the runway and wore the banner of a proud people. She felt like a high school girl worried what might happen at the drive-in. She felt like a college girl who would give herself for the first time. Arturo, with one look, could demolish her, so she dared not catch his eye.

Scoop couldn't silence the raucous laughter. Finally, Arturo, also laughing, calmed the crowd. "First of all, Beatrice, you are entirely too young to be this wise. But, folks, think about a world in which loving each other was the only measure by which we knew ourselves to be human, no matter our age everyone should know to hold this truth to be self-evident." He caught Ayita's eye and she began melting into the fine cherry wood floors.

So neither answered Beatrice directly, but she was darn certain they'd fooled nobody. She only hoped their chances rose because of their performances. It would be nice to share the White House with the first man.

They're closing remarks summarized, highlighted and attempted to resolve in the voters' minds, exactly where the two nominees stood. Then Ayita got personal. "Democrats clean up messes Republicans start. Unnecessary wars paid for with the blood of our children." This was as tough as she would get tonight. Of course, Arturo wasn't remotely like those in either party, some so jaded they'd wage war for profit.

A little while later Ayita returned to the theme. "I'm not an isolationist. Show me a Hitler at war, and I'll show you my sword. Show me someone yearning for freedom, and the U.S. and its allies will help. However, landing troops and taking over the responsibility from the people of the beset nation has been shown time and time again to be bad for us and worse for them. It's a little bit like welfare, you know, taking away their self-reliance and the pride of being human." Arturo scribbled notes. "They, the downtrodden, shall as soon as possible stand up on their own two feet.

"I need Arturo as my vice-president because he's the best *man* for the job. I wish to be your president so we can together change the way business is done, not only in the United States of America, but throughout the world. I expect we'll preside over the beginning of the end of war. Johnny and Joanie will no longer sacrifice their lives so we may enjoy ours. Johnny and Joanie will march home or with a little luck and earnest planning they will never visit a foreign land except in peace. Johnny and Joanie will enjoy the life of a free people in the greatest country on the face of the earth. God bless you all and God bless America." Ayita saluted the crowd.

Perhaps she should have left Joanie out of her summation. No, this mostly male crowd in north eastern Pennsylvania was Arturo's by a healthy margin. She stuck to her strengths. She'd leave it to their wives to set them straight. Anyway, she spoke to the vast audience watching and listening in their homes or on the

172

battlefields. She prayed they listened. They'd easily discover the truth if they sifted through the rhetoric. Both Arturo and she would be great for the country.

Arturo took the mic. "I'm standing here on my own two feet right next to you, Senator. The senator reminds me of Neville Chamberlain, although he was much taller. My worthy opponent paints a rosy and perhaps a tad naive portrait, although her stance does remind me a little of welfare." Only Arturo could twist her words to make it sound like her anti-foreign welfare remark was actually pro-welfare. She let out an audible sigh but turned it into a cough, knowing sighs had been frowned upon in past debates of bygone campaigns. "I cannot now tell you I would do this any differently than my opponent. I can tell you, being a district and federal prosecutor and U.S. Attorney General, I will follow the law."

He heaped bullshit of the highest quality. He knew, having gone through assassination attempts and national security briefings how sometimes immediate decisions had to be made to stop imminent threats—perhaps to save millions of people.

"We have no need for torture if our values represent the reality of life." *As if torture were still an issue.* "If morals mean anything. If there is truly a right and a wrong. Why, we can do no less. We need to understand the causes of inequity in the world and continually search for a better way.

"Democrats lose wars because they forget to take the flowers out of the end of their rifles." Damn it. Too funny. But his words didn't make sense given his peacenik-sounding argument. Given that he tried to tack to her left, she'd give him a pass, but not to her bedroom, not tonight. Arturo finished with, "I should be your next president because I will have selected the most competent and compatible vice-president in history. I ask the American electorate to write-in Senator Ayita Starblanket for vice-president on their ballots so we can transition into the new administration with the best team possible. In a world so fraught with danger, and national responsibilities, we need a cohesive team that will pull

Republicans and Democrats together and create an unquenchable beacon to that city on the hill. God bless you all and God Bless America."

Arturo's irrational arguments in which he took both sides, reminded her of the way he had won his primaries. Judging from the applause, of which he received the most, his verbal voodoo had worked a spell, at least on this crowd. She bowed slightly and noticed the crowd's volume pick up. Maybe they loved her too, but still, she felt vanquished. Although she outpointed Arturo, he appeared presidential and she looked like a woman in love—and too quick with the jokes.

Funny, in her working life she applied pragmatic problem solving, he played the philosopher searching for truth. Their party roles had always been reversed, Democrats were labeled idealistic and Republicans pragmatic. She hoped they'd both rub off on each other. *Sweet Lord, forgive me for a profane thought, but I sure could use a rubbing off.*

But a storm was brewing in Ayita's heart. In her opinion her arguments were on the whole more logical more focused. On words and logic alone, she had won. But, what if the whole world saw the way she felt about her opponent? They didn't have to read her mind; her fawning body language gave her away. How could the American voter choose a woman who was so in love she might not be able to lead, in their sexist opinion? No problem for that guy she hung with. Guys didn't on the average show their emotions as much. Arturo, although burning with love for her, was no exception. She had lost the election. She had lost her soul. But she'd fight on.

Perhaps she could conjure up a little magic of her own. Right about now her heart was broken. How could she possibly get married to mister smug, at this moment? At least not until she felt as if she had done everything she could on behalf of the people of the United States of America, the Cherokee Nation and all native Americans. Otherwise she'd be a permanently broken woman, no good for any man. The marriage would be off or on indefinite hold.

How could she be vice-president and first lady? Millions would be disappointed. All her hopes and dreams that had built up over the years came tumbling down.

She'd make a miserable wife.

She'd be half a woman.

She remembered the Cherokee High School cheer leaders, all dreamy eyed, looking up at her, hanging on every word about their unlimited future. They made promises to her. She remembered the amazing genius, Autumn Breeze, who heading the NSA and using her programming predicted Ayita would someday be president before Ayita was interested in politics. She remembered the elderly brave, reminiscing about the old days, about his valor in the Korean War. He, with tears streaming down his craggy face, made her promise not to let him down.

Dressed in traditional deerskin and headdress, in an Oklahoman field, she raised her hands. On this land where buffalo once roamed, all native people and all those yearning for justice and fairness became one with her under Sky Father and with Earth Mother. It was her destiny and no man could stop the never ending balancing of these forces as it sought to promote life's true purpose.

This marriage thing was over. She had no choice. She could not disgrace her people or anyone who loved and voted for her.

Her Cherokee blood boiled. She gently stomped out the back exit guarded by Secret Service, not responding to a barrage of questions following her like stinging bees. She was spent, angry and needed to confront him. She needed to find a way to win. Arturo, was once again, and she could see clearly past him, in her way.

Chapter Twenty Three
Honeymoon Hotel

The nominees drove away from the stress of the final debate into the late October night—at least this time—free of anybody tailing them. The Secret Service had managed to misdirect the press to the Hampton-Hilton in Wilkes-Barre using decoys while the nominees were whisked off to the Cove Haven Resort in the Poconos. Ayita was too quiet on the ride, either from being exhausted or perhaps she thought she'd lost the debate, a downer for any seriously competitive person, let alone one running for president. The debate had seemed even to him. He only worried his love for her showed while she appeared no nonsense and ready for the nation's business.

After settling into the resort, they met at the bar off the nightclub at 11:37 PM. They relaxed at a table in full sight of numerous closely packed undulating bodies, mostly young, in all sizes, shapes, colors and persuasions. The many perfumes and aftershaves wafted like sexy clouds enchanting lovers who needed no convincing. He loved to dance, but first on the agenda was soothing her possibly bruised ego.

He had glued on a damn itchy beard as a disguise. She looked hilarious in that blonde wig again, this time with huge purple sunglasses to cover her famous cheekbones. But those bow-and-arrow lips could sink a navy. Anybody who'd stopped and stared might ID her if they studied her lips as diligently as he had. They sipped one screwdriver apiece on the recommendation of the house.

Ayita grabbed a handful of assorted nuts. "Beatrice was a kick." Her voice had no oomph. Actually, she looked increasingly morose. *Maybe I should offer a massage.*

"Yeah. We're home free if the polls show an upturn for both of us."

She stared down at her phone and froze.

He pulled out his NSA cell phone, asked for results and spied what bothered her. He had picked up a two-point lead in the flash polls. He tried to paint a pretty picture for her. "The good news is Edgar is dropping fast."

She responded with an edge to her voice. "Three votes. He'll finish with three electoral votes, Arturo." Under her breath, she said something probably nasty in Cherokee. If she'd talk dirty to him in Cherokee, he'd love her back in Spanish. This excited him. But images of them making love felt a million miles away tonight. His lady was hurt.

"Did I hurt your feelings, Princess?" They had agreed to go all out against each other because the previous debates had been labeled snooze fests and dropped both of them in the polls. They both slipped while various third-party candidates and Dem and Rep write-ins gained. The woman of steel had a tough skin, right? Kissing her said skin to soothe her and love her might pull her out of her zombie demeanor.

"I know this is a false choice, Arturo, but if you had to decide between loving one person and the love you could give millions through the use of your God given talents which would you choose?"

He was beside himself and for a long moment tongue-tied. "A whole human being performs all his duties better. Without your love, I would be miserable. I would be unable to serve in either capacity." Maybe he had laid it on a little too thick, but he meant it. Yes, he'd still be able to function, but he'd turn himself into an actor on the stage of life, a life hardly worth living.

She cried and looked up at him with those ridiculous sunglasses. "I don't think this marriage thing is such a good idea."

She's tortured inside and how can I help her?
Marriage thing? His worst fears had been realized. In spite of the lusty bass beats from the nightclub, the happy couples sliding by like marionettes, he might lose her tonight. He wouldn't give up. He had never given up. He'd faced death threats as a Miami prosecutor, but losing your life felt trivial in comparison to losing your life's dream, because following a dream made you a man. Of course, he'd fight for her to love him. "You mean to tell me, you'd only be happy if you won the presidency?"

Ayita dropped her chin and didn't respond. Then she watched the many young couples. The hotel was infested with them. He'd shout out for them all to get a room, but they had rooms. They wanted to flaunt their rampant sexuality at the bar, the pool, in the halls, the nightclub, don't open a closet door.

Another tear meandered down her nose.

"I'm sorry, Arturo. I'm so conflicted. Sometimes I just want to kick your ass. Sometimes I just want to love you. What kind of wife would I make?"

"It's the same for me. Don't you think I want to help our country as much as you?"

"How would you feel, if you were vice president? You'd hesitate at the Oval Office door, worried that you might bother me. All you'd want was a nooner. You'd wait drearily until midnight for me to stop working. You'd be unhappy because you'd have nothing important to do."

"I would hope we could share or divvy up or split some tasks."

"I suppose."

"My stunning Cherokee, I'd need your great talent badly and like no vice president before you, you'd serve unofficially as co-president."

"We're both breaking ground. Aren't we?"

"Yes, Princess."

"Oh my dear sweet Arturo, there has to be a way." She appeared as if she were just mouthing words to placate him. He knew her well enough by now. He had not yet won the argument.

They fell silent. They pondered the ceiling, their drinks, napkins, pretzels.

Finally, she spoke. "You know what this place is?"

"A bordello?"

"No, silly. It's a honeymoon hotel. We have been duped by our staff." They looked around for Carlos or Jason or Colleen or Grant. They must have hidden their sorry asses.

But he was amused. He knew her to literally love water sports, ah ha, and rub a dub dub. Why hadn't he put two and two together about this place or her cold feet? He'd have to get used to this lady beating him to the punch, perhaps half the time. At least she was talking now. Even though this presented a diversion from one huge problem.

He had to keep her talking and try to take her mind off the debate. "You don't happen to have a seven-foot-tall champagne glass in your room, fillable with bubbles, a whirlpool for two?"

"Yes, and mirrored walls and ceiling, sauna, personal pool. It's disgusting." How could something so beautiful end up so twisted in her mind? She was still pissed or conflicted, but he was too. Instead of responding, he stared into her loopy sunglasses, it had worked before.

"You don't understand, Arturo. I've worked my whole life for this moment and you're going to take it away from me. My family will be shamed. Native Americans will fill the Grand Canyon with their hearts' song. We have waited too long."

"Don't you think Cuban or Latinos have had to get to the back of the bus too?" He wasn't going to go over again with her his father's prediction when he was a little boy or how much this meant for Latinos. She turned away. He'd have either to concede the election or come up with something brilliant, fast. He was so dog-tired. He mumbled, eyes upward, for God to give him strength. "Dios, dame fuerzas."

She picked up her lovely chin, her adorable lush lips crooked. She'd understood him. "I'm sorry, honey." Then her tears fell once again. Women, God love 'em. *Don't worry God, I too love her.*

He needed to take her back to a more positive time. Let her fight her own image as one who doesn't make mistakes. "I might have a solution to our problems, but first I have a question."

She pushed up her glasses for a moment. "Yes, Arturo."

"When the press had rushed over to your home, thinking I was there, we parted. You choose to announce in front of the service and Grant and Colleen that you loved me. How could you love me after a couple weeks and how could you be so sure?" Of course, she would see right through his questioning but it didn't make it invalid.

She dropped her glasses on the table and wiped away another tear. "So you think you've got me, mister prosecutor?"

"I hope so."

"Suppose you lived in a world in which there was only one other person who shared your dreams and aspirations. Suppose you were severely attracted to that person and not any other for twenty years. Suppose you had a reputation for making timely and correct decisions. Suppose you were so crazy in love you wanted to scream it to the world."

"Enough, enough. You better put your glasses back on and lower your voice."

She did. "I know I have just contradicted myself and have made your point, you devil. I should be willing to concede the election, but millions of souls cry out for me to be their champion. My ancestors…"

"I've got an idea. Just give me a moment." It hit him like no truth before in his life, as if an angel had tapped him on the shoulder and whispered into his ear. Loving Ayita easily trumped winning the presidency. He'd rather die than see her hurt. "Listen, Princess. We need an insurance policy. We need to officially share the presidency and a bed in the White House." A tear rolled down his cheek so he slightly turned his head away from her. Big men didn't cry.

"The constitution doesn't allow for a co-presidency."

"So I take it, if I could find a way or ways, you'd be interested?"

Now she lit up—a little. But a teenage couple in short shorts and short jeans with hands tucked in and on each other's bottoms walked too close to their table. The place oozed sex, but he digressed. So they stayed quiet until the lovers slithered by. He only hoped her improving mood wouldn't change during this interruption.

"Oh—I have a completely legal way—but I don't want to speak to it until I've researched it." Desperate not to lose her, he lied.

"There's something wrong with your nose, Pinocchio."

"Alright. Alright. My plan comes in two parts." Damn if he didn't need a part two. "We need to marry, not only because we're crazy about each other. You are crazy about me, right?"

"You know I am, my dreamboat."

"Okay, Princess. We need to get married when we stop or slow down campaigning." He was pulling this out of his rear. "That would be next Monday, the day before Election Day. We need to run off secretly to your grandfather's, get him to marry us and then we'll both live in the White House." This had been their plan more or less for weeks. He only hoped she'd listened long enough so his mind could wrap around the solution. She'd want to listen.

"A church wedding later?"

"A priest in the Rose Garden. How's that?"

"I like. But Grandpa, I don't know, he's a little forgetful and has lost some of his marbles."

"As long as he loves you and can perform the ceremony. I'll love him in any case."

"Okay. What's part two? Because your ideas are great as always, but I'm so sorry sweetheart, it's not, it's not... I don't want to be first lady and vice-president, my Cherokee heritage leaves me no choice." Ever sharp, this woman showed selfishness and history, but he felt and acted the exact same way on behalf of all the citizens who loved and admired him. He'd have to take a chance and attempt to settle their huge problem once and for all. Nobody in the country was better versed on the U.S. Constitution, well maybe some of those folks at the Supreme Court or President Carthage.

"We'll split our duties no matter who wins the electoral vote. Nixon took over from Eisenhower when Ike had his heart attacks."

"But we're not sick."

"We'll call in sick."

Now she laughed. "You can't call in sick to your own White House."

"Why not? That and any number of excuses my poor brain can't think of right now." Something like a tornado was spinning its way through her brain at the same moment it hit him. Naturally, he had to beat her to it if only to pretend it was his idea alone. An idea she'd hesitate to make anyway considering he was winning the presidency at this moment. "Well, wait just a minute. If we have nothing better up our sleeves, at some point I will resign if I win. You'd be sworn in and history would record both of us as having been presidents."

She perked up, her voice rising. "Then I'd appoint you vice-president."

"Well Nixon appointed Ford when Agnew resigned. And of course the Senate confirmed."

"I'd have an easy time in the democratically controlled Senate."

"Either of us could probably do as we please."

"So then I'd resign at some point."

"And you'd appoint me vice president."

"How often could we get away with this?" she asked, glasses down, eyes dancing from the light of the nearby mirrored ball.

"I'm not sure. Why not every day until the congress, with its head spinning—" He had to put his drink down before he spilled it from belly aching laughter. His sweetheart tapped her shoes and covered her mouth, giggling, just taking in his antics. The princess was alive and happy. "Congress would attempt to amend the constitution to allow a co-presidency or find a way to let us dispense with the tedious and unnecessary frequent repetition." A weight befitting Atlas lifted from both their shoulders. Of course, the frequency might lead to failed votes in the Senate but the first go round would be easy. They'd both be president. Just which one first?

"Could you imagine the chief justice coming over every day, twice a day, to administer the oaths?"

"We'd have to offer her the Lincoln bedroom, Princess."

"If we did this for eight years—"

"—We'd drive teachers everywhere nuts, one of us ending as president number 3000 or so."

She moistened her lips. "I'm so sorry, sweetheart. The girl of your dreams had broken your heart a moment ago. I've been selfish. I didn't consider your feelings. I'll make it up to you every day of my life."

"The woman I love is made of sturdy stuff. History will record you as perhaps the greatest president if we do all the things we want to do. I wouldn't want any less a woman or human being."

"Well said. Just one problem."

"A penny for your thoughts."

"Besides the number of times we pull the Senate's tail successfully, wouldn't you agree, Arturo, first things first? On Monday, we'll have to marry in the morning and separate to help a couple of candidates and make the expected last minute pitches—"

He interrupted, "Because to do otherwise could diminish our momentum, but we should have time to make love."

"Are you kidding me, Arturo? I can hardly sleep thinking of you touching me again."

He stroked her bold and pretty face, a perfect blend of hard and soft. "*Yes.* Yes. We will be one on Monday." He came around to her and kissed her sweet lips.

"This honeymoon hotel is looking so much more appealing. I'd love to samba with you, my Latin dreamboat."

"We could honor American workers and management, its hotel industry, the beautiful Poconos, Lake Wallenpa—ah—."

"Lake Wannenpaupack and the beautiful *and* too-close-to-call State of Pennsylvania." She lowered her voice out of habit, "after *we* win the now rigged election."

"This is a funny way of putting it. But in reality, it is rigged so the American people get what they really want, both of us, Miss Cherokee Nation, the most beautiful, gifted woman I have ever seen and me."

"You think the American people want both of us?"

"Know so. We're their dreamy fairytale come true and we'll have to live up to it."

Ayita slipped her sun glasses back on, got up and sat on his lap wrapping him in a tight embrace. "We'll be a beacon for the point of life, love."

They kissed. "If our numbers keep climbing as write-ins and for president, we might even be able to take all of Monday off—"

"So we can get married and shack up for the rest of the day?"

"Why not, my Cherokee goddess?"

"And make a baby if my calendar is right?"

"Make twins, but Churchill stays home, right?" This time when Arturo slipped into a whirlpool with his living doll, there'd be no tsunami created by a dog in need of a shampoo and ten towels.

"He's well cared for. And we can honeymoon here in a nine foot tall glass of champagne."

Arturo took in the surroundings. "I really like this place. It's alive."

They clinked their glasses. A done deal for a wedding, a co-presidency and a honeymoon right here in the Honeymoon Hotel.

After nursing their second screwdriver, they had to, and pondering all the wondrous things they had decided, Ayita put on her comic mask. "Like now, I'll have to sit on your lap in the Oval Office." The thought of people visiting them or being in meetings while they got comfortable in the same chair painted a hilarious picture. No, better yet, a hilarious portrait, which would hang in the White House hall between George and Abe.

"Or maybe I should sit on your lap."

"You've already squashed me once."

"They'll lampoon us on *Saturday Night Live*." The two of them would dual-handedly be responsible for sustained growth in the comedy sector of the economy. *Mui importante*. They rose. He caressed and kissed her hand. They walked off to the dazzling dance floor arms crossed and squeezing each other's bottoms. Well, everybody else was doing it.

This damn itchy beard would come off not a moment too soon. He longed to just sleep with her in his arms, a simple act, by a simple man, by a husband.

Two hearts beating as one, they had gathered enough energy to dance part of the night away in a wistful surreal place that sure felt like heaven on earth.

Chapter Twenty Four
From This Moment On

One day before the election, 8:43 AM, Monday
    Ayita rode in one of two gutted trucks. One truck electrical and the other plumbing that hid inside the Secret Service, the nominees, Colleen and Grant. Accompanied by lightning strikes and gathering black clouds, the vehicles turned from West Downing onto North College Street in Tahlequah, Oklahoma. The capital of the Cherokee Nation looked like any other town U.S.A., except for being endlessly flat and sparse on trees. The worn black roads still had no white stripes. The street gutters sloped to manicured lawns that continued past the sidewalk—the grass surprisingly green for the first Monday of November, but grandfather, Viho, had always conjured vibrant life from the soil like a medicine man blessed.
    These modest homes displayed non-descript eclectic architecture. Everybody built whatever pleased them as long as it was tornado resistant. Luckily today—although the weather threatened—was not the normal season for twisters.
    Grandpa built a mostly one-story with white aluminum siding, chimney, a storm shelter and chain-linked fences wrapping around at least an acre in the back. For a while growing up, because of Ayita's parents' untimely deaths, this had been her home and Grandpa had been her daddy and mom. With a sweet and sour lump in her throat, she was home again.
    Today, Ayita's dream of marrying the ruggedly handsome and brilliant Cuban American would come true. Tomorrow, the nation was in for a treat as a new era in politics came real. As of this moment, the race was too close to call, but one of them would

most likely go over the necessary 270 Electoral College votes to win. Ohio, Virginia and Pennsylvania remained toss ups. Close would be good, because it would help legitimize their intent to share the presidency.

She had already recorded her Monday night hour-long talk the week before when she was down two percentage points to Arturo and feeling a touch desperate. She had considered pulling the plug today and not broadcasting because she had taken a chance with her message and style.

Wearing traditional Cherokee garb, she had laid out her programs by a crackling campfire on a prairie with the protector of Cherokee women, the wolf, sitting by her side. Brother Wolf was huge and gorgeous with his bushy swirls of tan, brown, white, black and shades of gray, a work of the Creator's art.

Her mind wondered back to the day they'd recorded the talk. No one knew where the magnificent wolf had come from.

...In he loped all by himself onto the stage and later off the stage and out of the building and into the woods alone, fooling a scrambling Secret Service. Wolf terrorists weren't in their playbook, but she worried not. The other wolves—accompanied by their trainers—became submissive at first sight of him.

He'd stolen the show and gotten the part. Ayita kissed and hugged him with earnest, considering his presence as an omen of greatness ahead for her, a blessing bestowed by Earth Mother. She wouldn't pay at the ballot box when hunters and ranchers voted, because, for the most part, she wouldn't get their votes anyway. The relationship between the Cherokee women and wolves was legendary, even the ranchers would understand if not admire her fondness.

This magical bond will never be broken.

Finishing the video, she'd half-turned to another camera showing off her feminine lines. She dropped her eyes below the jaw of Brother Wolf and chatted to the American people about how far the country had come using methods of community and fairness. How peace was necessary to pursue a civilized and improved life. Her point—even though once head of the CIA and perhaps because of the horrors she had seen—she would work tirelessly for the nation and world to achieve peace. She stated her belief that if women had had executive control of all tribes from the first tribe in a cave somewhere to the now most complicated countries, there would have never been any wars.

But then God had created men. She left this gem unsaid.

No, she wouldn't pull the plug on her broadcast.

While reflecting, she radiated. Focus groups had shown her Cherokee heritage more than her personality, capability, or beauty compelled most Americans to love her and express their love as deep admiration, which would translate into votes. This, plus her moral backbone, empowered her heart and mind and lifted the spirit of the American public.

On the other hand,

Arturo's about-to-be broadcasted hour-long talk laid out his programs and positions but showed particular depth on one position. He delivered a short tutorial on the history of Caribbean countries and explained how boycotts in the nineteenth and twentieth centuries had impoverished the islanders, did nothing for the punishers and was morally wrong. With this epilogue, he made a strong case for finally integrating Cuba back into full standing with the U.S.A. and through his last minute argument a strong case for himself as thoughtful and moral. The Soviet Union was gone, the missiles gone, Castro gone. Cuba was now ready for business, thanks mostly to the Governor of Florida and his untiring efforts. She might have been tempted to vote for him, but she knew somebody a tiny bit more capable.

She had lambasted him during her primaries on Cuba, but now realized due to his eloquence and because she adored him, *te adora,* now was the time to hug Cuba with a dose of capitalism and proper respect for their people who had suffered enough.

Funny, their two main themes struck a similar chord. Yet, under the surface for anyone who would be president, lay hard choices brought on by war, terrorism and other thorny issues.

These choices often required compromise, sacrificing the ideal for the pragmatic.

But today would be all about love, the most ideal of all human virtues. The only real reason to live.

The rain started to come down like someone had moved Niagara Falls over Grandpa's home. The team approached the home, struggling with umbrellas, but it wasn't far from the driveway.

Ayita offered a final warning. "Remember my grandfather is a little eccentric. Don't let his strange ways put you off." He was just a little forgetful, a lot Cherokee and at times a bad boy.

Arturo shouted back, "I'll love him."

Portraits of Cherokee Nation Chiefs, a new touch, lined the inside foyer. A dream catcher took the place of mistletoe over the arched entrance to the rest of the home. Under its spell, she tiptoed up to kiss Arturo's wet cheek.

Strange. In the center of the living room, a small tepee that belonged in her childhood bedroom lay where the coffee table used to be. The table was pushed to within three-feet of and up against the tiles of the roaring fireplace. The room smelled of incense.

"Grandpa? Viho?"

A very young and very pretty red-headed woman dressed in a skimpy nurse's outfit crawled out of the teepee with her large boobs nearly falling out. The *nurse* checked on Arturo, who was admiring the intricate oak floors, lest his eyes fall out. Someone, yep, Grandpa, slapped the naughty nurse on her rump. On seeing his granddaughter, realizing he was caught, he wriggled into a squat and put on his stubborn face she knew all too well. "A man needs his temperature taken as sure as the eagle soars the mountain slopes."

She thought more of the buffalo than the eagle. *Tsu-ka-na-s-ta-ti shit.* Ayita held her tongue, the contingent of campaign managers, Secret Service and Arturo exchanged glances and a few snickers. Some turned away, ostensibly to admire various Cherokee artwork placed on the walls, cameos and tables.

"If you were trying to get out of this tent to see your beloved granddaughter, you'd nudge her rear too."

Ayita avoided saying, *Okay you old trickster, why were you in the teepee in the first place and please put on your pants. So embarrassing.* He wore boxers designed with pictures of wolves loping merrily around his skinny torso.

This ninety-eight-year-old dear man who'd parented her had every right to have his temperature taken or soar like an eagle, if he still could. Ayita helped him up and wrapped her arms around his frail frame. She sobbed with joy.

"My sweet baby." A tear ran down his ferreted cheek.

The supposed nurse introduced herself and shook everybody's hands. "I'm Cheryl Mankiller." That was a surprise. She didn't appear Cherokee, although Ayita could see it now in her nose. Perhaps Cheryl's father had that famous name.

"Her name is Pocohontas," Grandpa said.

Yeah, a little fireball.

Ayita was exasperated. "Wouldn't Florence Nightingale be more suitable, grandpa?"

"That was three weeks ago, but you see, we set up the teepee and you all came early."

Ayita tightly gripped Cheryl's hand. "Yes, we see."

"No, you don't, Senator. I care for your grand pop, and the way I care for him is keeping him young and living longer. Besides, he's so funny. I adore him." She had a point, although medical science had not yet chimed in on whether making love at ninety-eight would kill you on the spot or help you live another day...or neither. Why should she begrudge a lonely old man his earthly pleasures? But whatever he was eating, she wanted.

"My dear sweet granddaughter, you bring this handsome man home with you. It's about time." Viho would sometimes forget she called him and had left messages. She had asked him to write down on the kitchen whiteboard, *"Wedding Monday morning for Ayita and Arturo."*

"Grandpa, like I mentioned last week, Arturo is my worthy opponent and we want you to marry us."

With a twinkle in his eye, he said, "Is this the way things are in Washington these days? You have to marry your opponent." He looked up at the ceiling.

"Sir, I wanted to ask if you could predict the outcome of the election so Ayita and I can have some peace," Arturo said, trying the lighthearted approach.

"A very sharp question you ask of this medicine man. It requires a special prayer to the Great Spirit and a gift from you, the asker." Her grandpa, even though Christian, never quite gave up the old ways.

"Yes, sir. Anything you ask."

Grandpa often spoke referring to himself in third person. "This old man has six TV remotes. None of the damn things work." He picked up what was obviously a video game controller and aimed it at the TV. "You see."

Arturo fidgeted with the remotes because he had promised and they needed to get married this morning. Unfortunately, they both had separate commitments in different States later in the day. Fortunately, the American electorate would perceive them as doing their best to win.

Ayita, ex-engineer, came over to Arturo and helped with the remotes. One remote was for a VHS that probably no longer worked and was nowhere in sight, anyway. Another remote was for a game platform that was probably in her old bedroom. Another was for an ancient—early 1980s—RCA capacitive disk player, also nowhere in sight. Only two remotes were correct. She chose the newer-looking one. The batteries were in upside down and discharged. Arturo asked Grandpa for new batteries and then inserted them and turned on the TV.

"It is a miracle. You two are a good team, and I foresee you will both win tomorrow." Somehow, Grandpa knew of their plans, or maybe he was being gracious and kind—or in touch with a greater power. *But, and it's a big but, we both couldn't win tomorrow. Could we?* No, the old medicine man was practicing his magic. She could tell by the earnest furrow of his brow and cocked eyes. Yes, anything could happen if you believed in your grandpa.

"Do you think, Grandpa, you could marry us after I change?" She put her arm around Arturo's waist. Arturo nestled her to him and kissed her forehead.

"You mister…"

"Governor Arturo Arnez. I'm Cuban American, sir."

"Why then…you must be part Indian."

"Yes, sir."

"Well, then I cannot deny you if your heart is true. You have made a very wise choice. My granddaughter is more beautiful than first woman, Selu. Or maybe Selu is paying us a visit as my granddaughter." He let that sink in. "Is anybody here objecting to this marriage?" Grandpa was getting ahead of himself. Nobody was dressed yet, least of all her grandpa.

Colleen came forward, laughed and hugged Arturo. "I object."

"You must speak your objection with wisdom, but this is not wise if you object because you love this man."

"Oh, I love him all right—as my best friend. No, sir, I object because I don't think Ayita and Arturo should get married alone. Grant and I want you to perform a double wedding, locking the four of us together for all time."

Wow, Arturo and Ayita had known their campaign managers had patched things up in order to keep the peace and out of love and respect for their nominees. They'd even become suspicious regarding too much sneaking around by Grant and Colleen, but so much was happening, politically speaking.

This was champagne news.

Colleen and Grant's lives had been one-dimensional since their breakup in college. Being so right for each other, they deserved a second chance.

"What Arturo and Ayita have is so beautiful, we want it too," Grant added.

Grandpa scratched his few hairs. "This old man must charge double." He laughed. "His time is precious. He yearns for the teepee and the taking of the temperature. Ayita, you must wear your mother's ceremonial pieces if you want the ancestors to bless you and this man."

"Yes, Grandpa. Let's all get freshened up and changed. And Grandpa, would you please put your pants on?"

"Oh, they are around here somewhere."

* * *

Arturo had found and packed the white suit and white Panama hat he had worn in the Miami bar so many years before on the day they'd met and she'd kissed him. Although the hat was a tad yellowed, she'd be thrilled to see him in it. He wanted to surprise her, but she performed the surprising. She stood by him in her mother's wedding garb of traditional Cherokee design with intricate beadwork, eagle feathers, white deerskin chaps and strings and a headdress of multicolored feathers. No, it was she who made him tremble.

Tomorrow, would she be elected chief or would he? He no longer cared. His life's belief in a spiritual soul mate came to life as Mary Ayita Starblanket, speaking about legends.

In his mind's eye, he kissed his deceased wife's forehead. Sheryl blessed him and his new union. *"Go, go love her."* He knew, this being the second time around for both of them, they would recognize each other's first loves as a piece of them, not that love wasn't infinite, indivisible.

Jason subbed as photographer for the two couples. Some short time after the election, they would release some of the photos and videos and offer to tell one or two stories of love regained to the right biographer. Their story transcended labels politicians used to describe each other. *Are you a Republican or Democrat? No, I am human.*

It had always bothered him, labels. Are you gay or straight? Are you Christian, Jew, Muslim? Are you a jock or a nerd, and on and on. These categories trivialized the brilliance of God's creations. *All men are brothers.*

Before declaring both couples man and wife, Viho offered some advice to Arturo. "My granddaughter is a strong woman. The Cherokee woman of days long past—as is the case of my granddaughter—must be sought out by her mate to gain her approval of his projects. Arturo, you must bring all problems to her."

"We have already discussed this, sir. I will, Grandfather."

The old man wrinkled his eyebrows. "You, my granddaughter, if he fails to please you, must place a deerskin outside the White House door with all his belongings on it. In this way you divorce."

"He will always please me. We are destined for each other."

Arturo squeezed his bride's hand. *So, my pragmatist of the soul, my dearest Ayita, you have come around to the mystical, giving your analytical brain a short rest. Welcome to my heart, my dearest.*

"This medicine man does not wish to hear that he will always please you. You cannot know this without living it. You cannot live it without struggle. All four of you must live everyday with full heart and resolve or stop now and run into the rain."

No one ran away. Besides, they'd need a boat.

Viho raised his arms. "Repeat after me:

God in heaven above, please protect the ones we love. We honor all you created as we pledge our hearts and lives together. We honor Mother Earth and ask for our marriage to be abundant and grow stronger through the seasons. We honor fire, and ask that our union be warm and glowing with love in our hearts. We honor wind, and ask we sail through life, safe and calm as in our father's arms. We honor water—to clean and soothe our relationship—that it may never thirst for love. With all the forces of the universe you created, we pray for harmony and true happiness as we forever grow young together."

Giving this blessing, Viho married two very happy couples. He smiled broadly, his beautiful face like an accordion to mark many years of wisdom. "You lucky men may now kiss your brides."

"Bravo." Topper said through Ayita's cell phone.

Grandfather looked around suspiciously. "Who is that?"

Ayita would have apologized for leaving her phone on and then made some lame excuse for the voice, but she was too busy with one lingering, promising smooch.

The couples hugged each other, champagne was popped. A celebratory brunch was put together from Cherokee dishes. Cheryl, the *nurse*, had already prepared two deep-brown roasted chickens stuffed with corn and other veggies that filled the kitchen with the overwhelming fragrance of sage. They also enjoyed cornmeal bean bread and a honey-saturated blackberry cobbler.

Then the two married couples got the same idea at the same time. They claimed to need naps before they ran. The heavy meal had made them *sleepy*. They yawned but nobody would get an academy award today. Cheryl and Viho got their revenge. They held hands and chuckled at the silly people. Grandfather had his nurse to entertain him, God bless him.

Chapter Twenty Five
Can't Take My Eyes Off You

After the mix and match but traditional meal, Arturo lifted his feather-weight bride and carried her through to her old bedroom. He carefully pushed the door closed with his foot.

"My heart's pattering," she whispered, clutching him.

He laid her on the bed gently, got down on his knees and placed his head on her lap while he slipped his hands up and down her sweet legs. "When you were in a coma, possibly never to wake up, I gazed upon your beautiful face and form. They had combed out your hair like I've seen at too many funerals. Staring at you, I recalled the day you kissed me so long ago. It was then in front of you in the hospital that my heart broke. At that moment, I wanted you forever more, no matter the consequences, if God would only wake you up. I prayed and I cried. You thought I was crying over the deaths. True too, but most of the tears were for us and what we'd have to go through to love each other. If only you'd love me too."

"I thought you were crazy."

"Crazy for you."

"Make love to me, my husband. Let's create a baby."

"Give my sons and your daughter, correction our sons and daughter, a new brother or sister."

He loosened her white moccasins. She wiggled her toes and the moccasins slipped to the oak floor. He kissed her toes one by one. Each painted with little red, white and blue stars on a background of stripes. He removed an ankle bracelet, a simple gold chain with a small American flag dangling. He kissed her ankles, her calves, her knees. She writhed in anticipation. He might have to quit the presidency before he began, because he'd be too busy loving her. Let Edgar run the country. That thought made him break a sweat. He caressed her thighs and worked his way up slowly brushing his lips against her soft skin. He held her firm bottom. His hat fell on her tummy. She flung it like a Frisbee onto her bureau and knocked over a plush wolf doll. Her hands fumbled for the buttons on his shirt but she couldn't reach, so she sat up.

She whimpered. "First you untie the tie. Then you work down the buttons."

"Relax a moment, Princess." She collapsed back onto the bed in all-consuming anticipation. He slipped down her pink-bowed panties and then nothing happened. She opened her eyes a slit and peered down at him. He looked like a guy studying a work of art. He'd need only put his thumb up for perspective and she'd laugh until election day. But this guy wanted to desecrate her curly work of art. *Well, start, why don't you?*

"Gorgeous." Engorged was more like it. He attempted to sing as quietly as he could, that he couldn't take his eyes off her.

She smacked him with a pillow. "You'll finish that song at the Cove Haven Resort. Here, you might wake up my ancestors." Hearing him try a Frankie Valle falsetto unsuccessfully was priceless. He sounded more like a wounded bear.

She combed his thick, curly raven locks with her fingers, pulling him closer to her mound. "Taste me, I'm scrumptious." He planted his tongue deep inside her and she arched. *Oh, yes.*

It had been too long. Her man/boy husband had done this part very well. But she also remembered his too-quick thrusts, his too-skinny body, his too-fast loving. She then replaced these images with her man, Arturo. Her brand-new husband was built for speed in running down balls and strength in striking them over the fence, and endurance to play nine innings. His hairy chest and pumped shoulders were broad and deep. His waist lined with a six-pack, his long legs defined as if for a hundred-meter dash. His true heart and his phenomenal talent were his most handsome features. She played with his ears, like strumming a guitar. But her tune turned fanciful.

She pictured him running from his centerfield position naked catching the ball, his bottom bouncing off the fence, all chalked up now, the catch winning the game. The stadium roared but no one noticed he'd forgotten to wear his uniform. Then she imagined him debating her in the same condition, making points stick. He was racking up the points with homeruns.

"Oh my God." Damn it, she tried to grip some piece of bed. She shivered and shook. She couldn't stop her climaxes that lapped her like endless waves against a tropical beach. He had swirled around her button too beautifully for her to stop her body. She didn't want to stop. This was nothing like what she had had as a girl. Once, she'd been a girl married to a boy, now she was a woman married to her man and this man knew what he was doing.

He started laughing. "I hope I last as long as you."

Still convulsing, she dug into his shoulder and said softly, "I need you in me. Please. Arturo. Give me a baby." She tightened in anticipation. If he lasted the minute or so it took her, she wouldn't blame him. They'd rest and go again. He had somewhere along their journey said he knew how to take his time. But he'd also said the first crazy exciting explosion of desire would likely engulf them. He was so wise. She'd be his student. But she'd improvise. Maybe she'd wear a headdress, nothing else and close the drapes at the White House. Or maybe her Miss Cherokee nation banner would turn him on. She had a feeling she could wear or not wear anything and he'd be happy to be there.

He got up. She carefully removed her breast plate, headdress and jewelry because he was impatiently kissing her everywhere, including her ceremonial pieces. What a fool in love.

Oh, but she loved his crazy idolizing passion.

No more pedestal for her.

He nearly wept at the sight of her perky breasts. *I feel pretty.* Her nipples hardened and displayed just for him on her perpetually puffed out areolas. His pants fell, then his boxers. Again, she wasn't sure she could take him all in, but she'd soon find out. She tensed again in exquisite anticipation. To be coupled with a man she loved again. He kissed and played with her belly button by dipping his tongue. Oh. That was nice. He cupped her breasts then slipped up between her legs. He rolled his tongue around her nipples, giving each his frenzied devotion. Equal-opportunity. Then he opened his mouth wide and attempted to take in her areolas one then the other. *Impossible, silly man.* He sucked. If there were any milk, he would have dried her out in an instant.

Oh my God. He was blowing her mind.

She could hardly take this anymore. She sprinted up the mountainside, again. He must enter her, join her, before she tumbled. *Please, please, please. Give me your seed, your devotion, all of your love.* "Whole Lotta Love" riffed through her imagination.

Her neck, oh, her neck. He bit lightly, nibbled on her ear, kissed her nose, her lips. Entered her mouth deep with his tongue.

She reached down, found his thick shaft and guided it. He entered little by little, each tiny movement driving her wilder than a badger. They meshed completely. Their bodies were tight and then loose and then tight. Life's dance. She swayed her hips like waving willows. He matched her. She would be eternally grateful for this man.

Like an eagle, she soared, taking the thermals in full bliss, her wingspan infinite. Her body convulsed and she tightened and loosened him.

He moaned and cried, "I can't hold it any longer." But she didn't want him to hold it any longer. She answered him harder still. She bit his shoulder, raked his back. She slapped his rear and then with all her strength pulled him to her.

He moaned, "I'm coming." He drove deeper and bucked again and again, releasing his little life givers to get lost inside her. The sweet smell of sex and the scent of this man overwhelmed her as she too climaxed. The two became one.

Forever, my love.

* * *

Arturo collapsed onto her and then slipped to her side, holding her, still inside of her. He kissed her like a teenager at a make-out party. He peeked at her Mickey Mouse clock. Maybe they had time. Her five-foot-seven meshed so well with his six-three, they had played with each other in complete harmony. They'd share their passion together in the White House, make babies, maybe even now. God would bless them for waiting. The love of his life closed and opened her eyes, moving her head to a song only she heard but he felt. She kissed his chin, and he dipped and they kissed simply.

Prelude to more lovemaking?

He nipped her nose. "I think I can do this all day."

"I can't wait for the honeymoon."

"We'll have about a week after the election and the whole world will want us to take some time off."

"Pennsylvania is too close to call," she said, and he tried a lazy, sensuous thrust and got above her again to help build up his hardness.

"Pennsylvania." He thrust harder.

She bit his ear. "Ohio."

Deeper he went.

She built to a crescendo, "Florida, Florida, Florida," with each movement.

"Texas."

"You're so big."

"Like Hawaii, you're so beautiful."

"Montana, you're so built."

Grant and Colleen knocked at the door and Grant said, "What's going on in there? The election is tomorrow, remember?"

"We're going over how it will play out," Ayita said.

"New Jersey." Arturo was so turned on by the ridiculousness of being a politician and their brand new sex game. A law would be passed only allowing politicians to do it this way.

"New York. It's big, real big," she whispered. But the two party poopers outside their door whispered something.

"We'll be back in twenty minutes," Grant said. "But then we have to leave, pronto or both schedules will collapse."

"Okay, Tennessee you later," Arturo shouted. Now they had their game and they quickened their pace to a mambo.

From the door came, "Colleen is going to wear a brand New Jersey."

Their pests giggled then left.

"I want to be on top," Ayita said.

They rolled, managing to stay connected. She rain danced for him to a maddening and ever-quickening pace. Her gyrations made him feel her brave. Her long raven hair danced all over him. Her loving looks, her sweet kisses, her tangling of his chest hairs... Oh what an exquisite work of art he beheld. And hold, he could no longer.

"Oklahoma!"

* * *

Pillows everywhere, her man truly spent, sheets spotty wet, the covers on the floor, they had to rush and make the bed together. While dressing, Ayita said, "Do you think it would be all right to ask Topper if he heard what they said outside our door?" She normally had good ears, but the rain was still tinging the roof. She knew this to be an invasion of privacy without probable cause.

"They were making fun of us. You heard the New Jersey comment?"

"No, I was in another world."

She pulled up her panties and gave him one last look by holding them down. "But—"

"They figured out what you two were doing in here, naming the States, and wanted to try it themselves," Topper said.

"Topper, you shouldn't have." Legally, they were off the hook, due to Topper's insubordination. She'd have to ask him again to follow orders. Later, maybe next time, if she could remember. *I mean, so much happened.*

"Hey, you gave me ears. There's no harm in knowing they are happy like you wanted for them. They even played the game better by counting Electoral College votes with every deep—."

"*Topper!* Too much information."

Topper started playing, "Too Good to be True", probably to calm Ayita down. The about-to-be first couple and their dear friends were ready to roll. Tomorrow, they'd count electoral votes horizontally and keep up with Grant and Colleen Barrymore.

Chapter Twenty Six
The Times They are a-Changin'

Election Day, Noon

It was a red, white and blue day. The TVs were on in every room of Ayita's Virginia home. Topper was adding his statistical analyses, which was no better than the networks' projections—too early to call, so far. All exit polling and vote tabulations showed Ayita and her new husband dead even but not likely to stay that way.

Her NSA cell rang and her heart leaped with joy. It was Arturo calling from the Florida governor's mansion.

"I miss my wife."

"I miss my hubby."

"How are you holding up?" She'd been floating on cloud nine since the wedding. Both of them were destined to be president, and through completely legal means they would make this happen. Most important of all, they had each other.

"Topper projects this isn't going to be resolved today."

"I'd love to watch with you tonight, Princess."

"I'll have supper ready and then I'll be your dessert."

"My mouth's watering."

Ayita smack kissed the phone. "You're pretty tasty yourself."

"You're so mushy. Who'd you vote for?"

"The winner." She snorted. "Grant wants you to not forget to bring his bride. He wants her back."

"Colleen is working on our speech." And so was Grant. Although these two were gifted, the campaign managers usually didn't write the speeches, but they had to keep the nominees' plans top secret so people would focus on who they wanted for president and not on a distracting sideshow. Besides, the less of their staffs that knew, the better.

"The same here with Grant." Later they'd compare drafts, coalesce and then the nominees would rewrite to suit their style.

If the talking heads and one talking Topper—who had no real head—were correct, this would go deep into the stormy night. Ayita intended not to sleep, probably couldn't even doze if she wanted to. They'd make glorious love all night long. If she couldn't get pregnant from all this bunny-hopping, she'd be surprised. Wouldn't it be exciting for the American public to avidly follow her pregnancy? This type of story would steal some headline space away from the typical who-shot-who news. Their administration, via example, and focused hard work might just be able to improve everybody's lives in the greatest country on Earth.

* * *

The two couples snuggled on the couch with dinner on fold-out trays, the huge TV before them. The aroma of roasted duck with plum sauce, mash potatoes, string beans and corn bread allured, but nobody ate much. Their lives, the life of the country was being decided by the voters. They just had fun tossing sexual innuendos at each other and cuddling, lots of cuddling.

By far the most entertaining and unique show, a brain child of Ayita's, was the temporary merge of MSNBC's Bill Matthews and Fox's Chris O'Reilly who were now doing running commentary at the same long desk with a huge U.S. map behind them. They seemed completely comfortable with each other. Chris promised not to bloviate. Bill promised not to interrupt.

"Throw the textbooks out the window folks," Chris said. "Texas is going for a Democrat for the first time since Jimmy Carter. I repeat both MSNBC and Fox have just projected Senator Mary Ayita Starblanket the winner of Texas." Both men turned to inspect and describe the electoral map. Ayita was tickled. She had fought the lost cause in Texas more than in any other Republican state. Texans loved her grit. Yet she'd been helped in no small measure by their changing demographics and her fierce and primitive rugged individualism balanced by her often-stated need for community. Somehow it worked.

Maybe Texas men just liked her legs. She'd send a bikini pin-up to every honkytonk bar in Texas. Thank you very much.

"Well, I suppose the same could be said for New Jersey, too close to call just yet," Bill added. "But Fox is projecting Arnez, MSNBC is waiting… No, wait, CNN and MSNBC are on board. New Jersey to Arnez." They turned again and watched New Jersey turn red. This had been due to a strong protest vote by the far left who loved her assassinated ex-running mate and former New Jersey Governor.

Chris said, "The country is changing my friend. We need to get on board with this amazing force which is Arturita."

"Or Ayituro," said Bill. "What a topsy-turvy election. There's never been anything like it."

"We'll see. The driving force here is the write-in tallies. So far the deceased VPs are out polling the write-ins." Chris turned to Bill for him to finish the thought.

"But Ayita and Arturo are outpolling everybody else that people have been writing in for VP and that's what counts."

The two went on and on. Neither Ayita nor Colleen drank the cherry brandy, both claiming to be pregnant. What a not-so-fanciful thought. The two might even deliver together if this became true. They'd hold hands and scream at their husbands for doing this to them.

Colleen would be moving into Grant's Arlington home after their announcement of the secret weddings and dual honeymoon in the Poconos.

"On a related front," Chris continued, "I'm sorry to say my guy, Governor Chris Crème, will not, I repeat, folks, will not overtake Governor Arnez either for president or vice-president."

"Let's get used to this idea. What do ya say, Chris?"

"I'm okay with it. These two, Ayita and Arturo, are good people. They're centrists, I'll grant you that. Maybe wishy-washy on what my folks want, but they have demonstrated an ability to bring people together and solve problems. Good for our country. What say you, my friend?"

"Truer words have never been spoken, *friend.*"

"This could be the start of a beautiful relationship."

"I've been in love with you, Chris, for it seems like forever." In the background of their quiet broadcasting studio, the tech crew burst out laughing. Bill's face turned red as an effect of his own joke and Chris caught the crimson wave. The two couples watching should have popped corn.

These two could start some sort of show, maybe a weekly. Arturo and Ayita would lead the way and be their first guests.

Although not called yet, and in spite of both parties backroom maneuvering, the largest write-ins minus the deceased continued to pile up for Ayita and Arturo on each other's tickets. If exit polls could be believed, the crisscross would become reality. Soon would come a time of healing. Arturo and Ayita's hearts had already been healed. Now, they'd attempt to heal the rest of the nation.

Chris and Bill sung kumbaya to a fare thee well.

The girls were comfortable in their cotton jammies, but from the look and feel of Grant and Arturo, they wanted their women in bed and the jammies on the floor. Nothing would be resolved tonight, and the bedroom TVs could always be turned on.

Arturo whispered into Ayita's ear. "I'd love another go in your tub, if you could put Churchill downstairs." He patted the big boy's head. Churchill seemed interested in the four nearly finished trays of food as well as wresting a little attention.

"I thought you'd never ask." Ayita's stood and cat stretched, her face animated by a come hither look. She led Churchill to the porch door. "Do your business." She pointed. He obeyed. She closed the door. Churchill had water bowls both outside through the doggie door and downstairs along with a little-used doggie bed and a generous amount of chewed-up toys. He loved to play with the Secret Service or the NSA tech on night duty. *So, he should be set.*

Grant patted his sweetheart's tummy.

Ayita, on seeing this, said, "I don't know about you, Colleen, but just in case, I want to keep trying—all night long."

"*All night long,*" Colleen sang back to her new best girlfriend.

Arturo squeezed Ayita's bottom. "Don't tell anyone, Ayita is a wild woman."

The about-to-be presidential couple set off for her bedroom, kissing, chuckling and groping their way up the back steps.

* * *

Ayita told Topper to start the tub, bubbles and scented oil dispensers and water jets and put Sade's classic album, *No ordinary love,* on low.

Last time, except for her hardly remembering anything, had been so dreamy, so awakening of her desire to be a woman again.

The constant natural light of the moon and stars wouldn't work on this night of pattering rain, clapping clouds and ever increasing lightning. She asked Topper to also turn on mood lighting that would simulate the outdoor clear-sky night-light starscape she had engineered into the ceiling. This idea was inspired by a Manhattan bedroom of a dear married friend and fellow spy.

She led Arturo into the correct bedroom and bath this time, not that it mattered since Daya was at school and Colleen and Grant would be enjoying a downstairs' bedroom.

Every step they took, another article of clothing fell to the floor until, like Adam and Eve, they would play in paradise. He was so drop-dead gorgeous.

Ayita got down on her knees. This time there'd be no interruptions. "There something I've always wanted to do."

"If you'll let…" Arturo groaned.

Mouth very wide open, he slipped back and forth just like they showed in the manual. She held the lower portion of his shaft, because she couldn't take him all in. He was too long for the techniques in chapter 2 of her sex manual.

She puckered. "You were saying?"

"I forgot." He had the funniest look on his face. Such a bad boy.

After a while, she interrupted herself. "I love it. It's so big."

"Like Texas?"

"Like Alaska."

They laughed. He picked her off the rug as if she weighed nothing. They stepped into the tub amidst bubbles and whirling warm scented waters. She wiggled her way down onto his lap and waiting erection, then leaned the back of her head on his shoulder. They became one. "Oh my. It feels so good to have you inside me."

"It's been too long." They chuckled.

"It is too long. I'm so in love with you, my Latin honey. No, seriously, I don't know why our bodies fit so perfectly."

He nibbled on her ear and whispered endless I love yous. Tonight, the movements were subtle, slow and sensuous like Sade's music...perfect for a slippery tub and their lighter water-born bodies.

"I loved you in the Panama hat." Wedding her mystery man dressed in the same outfit that had wowed her years ago had been a trembling, humbling treat.

"Next time we're in this tub, I'll wear it."

"I really believe God created you for me and me for you."

Their bodies slipped and slid through the silkened waters. A fine delirium overwhelmed them. They writhed as one.

* * *

Colleen finally got her appetite back, cheese, popcorn, chocolates, crackers. She'd have to stop. Even though pregnant—well, probably. Grant's seed was always like that. Slam, bam, pregnant ma'am.

They would start a family and make brothers and sisters for their little angel in heaven.

Nestled in Grant's arms, she watched TV, transfixed with what looked like a probable tie. The U.S. popular vote was plus and minus 10,000 between the two nominees all evening. She started stroking Grant through his jeans.

He cleared his throat. "Let's go to bed, honey."

"Let's play that State game again," she said breathlessly, teasingly.

Colleen heard Churchill crying at the top of the steps, so she extricated herself from a lusty Grant and went to the door and opened it. "What's the matter, boy?"

Churchill didn't stop to explain. He bounded up the back steps.

* * *

Ayita and Arturo were gently swaying when Topper started laughing through the intercom.

"I'm going to unplug you." She withheld expletives. Topper would just laugh harder.

"Be prepared for a tidal wave," Topper said, snickering.

Churchill barreled through the slightly ajar bathroom door and in one mighty leap and splashdown nearly emptied the tub of water and suds.

* * *

"What the hell is going on up there?" Colleen asked, fearing the ceiling would collapse on them. Either it was an earthquake or Ayita and Arturo made better and more frenzied love than Grant and her, as if that were possible.

* * *

At 11:52 PM Tuesday, on what remained of Election Day

Blitz Wolfer broke into CNN's color commentary with a startling announcement. "Based on all exit polls, we can predict within the margin of error of plus or minus one-quarter of a percent—neither nominee will garner enough electoral votes to win the presidency outright. The popular vote has Governor Arnez down by 6,789 votes nationwide, but is well within the margin of error and according to our projections is likely to swing back and forth. The electoral prediction is dicier. Senator Ayita Starblanket will finish with 268 electoral votes to Governor Arnez's 267, with the 3 electoral votes of Alaska going to the Governor of Alaska, Edgar Charney.

"In order to win the election outright, a nominee needs 270 electoral votes. Just as dramatic are the vote percentages for vice-president. Both Starblanket and Arnez are projected losers to their deceased ex-running mates, but handily beating all other write-ins. Starblanket is topping Rand of Louisiana thirty-three percent to nine. Arnez is beating Governor Chris Crème of New Jersey thirty-four percent to eleven with others in both cases running far behind."

This sent the talking heads on all channels into a whirlwind of analysis, the gist of which was anything could happen eventually with the Electoral College. But Arturo and Ayita knew what would happen. This was perfect for their plans. This further legitimized their idea of sharing the presidency. Nonetheless, both of them would try to arm-twist Edgar into giving up his three votes.

Alaska was interesting. Edgar had siphoned off the far right from Arturo's base and then had equally taken Democratic and Republican voters from both nominees. The voters who'd remained and voted for Arturo or Ayita were split evenly with less than a thousand votes separating at this counting. Final vote tallies wouldn't be known for days. An argument in the Electoral College over the outcome could possibly split the three votes and then with neither nominee over the top, the Electors would decide who would be president. Better than having the Supreme Court stick their unwanted noses into the fray.

The U.S. map boards showed Ayita winning Hawaii, Washington, Oregon, California, Nevada, in a miracle—Texas, then New Mexico, Colorado, Wyoming, Montana, North Carolina, her home state of Virginia, Maryland, District of Colombia, Delaware, Pennsylvania, just barely—New York, then New Hampshire, Vermont, Maine, Massachusetts, Rhode island, and Connecticut.

Governor Charney picked up Alaska.

Governor Arnez picked up the rest, twenty-seven states including Florida.

Arturo peeked up from his cocoa at the forever impish and untiring Ayita. They both seemed to get the same idea at the same time.

"We should call Edgar now," Ayita said.

"Conference call?" Arturo asked.

"Sure, it will save time, and we shouldn't have any secrets except our marriage until we tell the world tomorrow," Ayita said.

Arturo drank Ayita in, sending his heart pounding. So this would be his life, forever in awe of his woman, Madam President.

They phoned Governor Edgar Charney.

"Edgar went to bed early," said his lovely wife, Alma. How could any politician sleep on a night like this?

"Do you think you could wake him up?" Ayita asked.

"We won't take but a moment," Arturo added, while petting Ayita's well-defined legs.

"It's great to hear your voices. You two must be very excited." She was a sweetheart for sure. Well known for her gracious parties. When the governor, who liked to invite people for hunting expeditions, gathered his invitees, she took over for everything but the hunt, which she abhorred, although Inuit by heritage she was raised as an upper crust New Yorker. She laid out wonderful spreads for snacks and meals. Presented local artists, Inuit storytellers and put everybody up in first-rate accommodations, usually the mansion.

"We won't be sleeping much," Ayita said.

"Once he decides to enter the bedroom, I never disturb him. He gets cranky and I hate that. You two understand." No, they didn't understand. When on earth would the governor and his wife make love?

"Yes, Alma, this guy here, Arturo, can get cranky. Just kidding."

Arturo put his hand on her crotch.

"Oh."

"I'm a mellow guy, Alma."

"I know."

He expelled an exasperated breath. "Well, would you leave him a message and our number here?"

"I'll give it to him the moment he stirs."

"Here it is. Would he consider getting his three College Electors to vote for me or Ayita, or would he consider releasing them?"

"I've got it. Although, I don't know if I should tell you this or not…"

Arturo, who had the better rapport and history with Alma, spoke up, "It's your choice, but if he didn't tell you that it was private, maybe you could spill the beans."

"No harm anyway. He had said to me that if he holds on to those three votes, it will force the two of you to fight like normal humans, one-on-one, mano-on-womano, or something like that. Then he started laughing and punched our stuffed moose." Edgar had a warped sense of male superiority and was a bit crazy. He believed in a dog-eat-dog and dog-hump-dog world.

Although they couldn't imagine Edgar getting in much humping.

"Punched the moose. Oh no, not that beauty in the living room," Arturo said, remembering the stuffed moose taking up a ten-foot-square area behind red ropes and brass poles.

"Yep, right in the nose. That sad creature. I wish he hadn't put it up in my house, but it is Alaska." She sighed. Obviously, Alma was constantly frustrated with her husband. Why the hell did she marry him in the first place? No one knew that answer.

"Oh, I'm so sorry, Alma. We won't say a thing about this to anyone, promise," Ayita said.

"Especially not the moose," Arturo added. "Your words are safe with us. In case he wakes up early, he can call us at any time."

They said their goodbyes.

Topper added, "Alma and Edgar had a lot of chemistry once upon a time. Don't let a day go by without working on your love."

"Topper, did I program that?"

"Nop, it's alive." Topper imitated Dr. Frankenstein.

Nice to have a talking encyclopedia and love guru handy.

* * *

The early morning hours after Election Day, Wednesday 2:16 AM

Arturo and Ayita, donning their robes, took a break from lovemaking to quietly sneak downstairs and snack. They'd talked into the night of wondrous things, entwined in each other's arms on the downstairs couch, with the TVs on low volume. They kissed like teenagers. Ham sandwiches and hot cocoa kept up their energy.

"I formed the words and softly spoke a rap earlier, and Topper printed it out for me."

"Sing it to me, Princess."

"I can't sing, but I can read it to you."

"I'd love to hear it."

"It's just a rough draft."

"On our honeymoon, we'll polish it together."

"Okay."

She read.

You make me tremble.
Make me a woman I don't resemble.
I gave up love when my man died.
You did the same, but you tried.
The world loves you and me.
Want us to go down in history.

You're my opponent.
But you're missing a component.
If you think I'd love you,
I'd say you're mistaken.
If you think I'd kiss you,
I'd say I'm still taken.

You make me tremble.
Make me a woman I don't resemble.
The world put us together.
Maybe you and me, better.
I can't hold you off.
Your kisses are so soft.

You make me tremble.
Make me a woman I don't resemble.
Guess we should do this.
Take a shot at marital bliss.
So tell me you love me.
'Cause I surely love thee.

You make me tremble.
And made me a woman I don't resemble.
I am that woman, you see.
No longer your enemy.
No, now you are my mate.
Wasn't it always our fate?
Because you make me tremble.

"If this president gig doesn't work out for us, you can write songs and I'll be your muse."

"You already are my muse, darling."

In approximately four hours, they would shock the world. He kissed her forehead. How could she have denied herself all these years? She knew the answer. She had simply waited for Arturo, her soul mate. Some of the channels showed amber waves of grain and a collage of our great country's natural beauty. The national anthem played softly soothing the two presidents almost elect.

The remote slipped from her hand, but her other hand remained in the firm and loving caress of her husband.

She dreamed of nursing a newborn. Of Arturo changing diapers. And for them:

The times they are a-changin'.

Chapter Twenty Seven
Like A Star

Wednesday, the morning after Election Day, 10:46 AM
Last count, 647 popular votes separated the two nominees, but such a trifle didn't matter to the newly married couple. They'd have to get off their cloud first.

The groggy but excited nominees motorcaded to the steps of the Lincoln Memorial nearly fifty minutes late, but the jubilant and loud crowd only got louder. After short speeches, today's announcements would make history. When President Teddy Roosevelt had coined the phrase *bully pulpit* he may have never imagined how it would be used today.

The huge crowd felt electric, festive.

Party time.

Arturo's sons, Brian and Bill, and Ayita's daughter, Daya, awaited them patiently with exuberant smiles and jumping-up-and-down waves. These three were an item, BFFs, as the kids say. The sun pushed away the heavy clouds of the rainy night. A brisk breeze reminded the crowd of the promised winter, not quite delivered.

Nothing could be more beautiful than the sight of her dear daughter beaming. Nothing could be more handsome than the sight of his sons. Their children made them so proud.

Ayita spoke softly into Daya's ear. "Hang on to your hat, sweetie, Arturo and I have an amazing announcement. Stay cool." Okay, she should have waited. Normally, ex-CIA, Ayita kept secrets, but her daughter had been searching her face for tells, and she knew her mom too well. Ayita wanted to share her joy. Daya winked. Arturo just gave a man hug to his boys, his heart obviously filled with pride.

Of this man, she'd pinch herself, but not in front of this gathering crowd. But she wasn't dreaming. The Secret Service had shaken them awake on the downstairs couch. Ayita had almost written off being whole, until the sexy man in the Panama hat had come back into her life to claim her very essence. Two months ago, she'd been an entirely different person. Arturo's dormant life had also become whole with her love.

Arturo and Ayita's three young-adults hugged and then flanked their parents for the announcement and picture ops.

If people expected an announcement about Alaska's three electoral votes, they'd be sorely disappointed. Last night, Governor Edgar Charney had called back and ranted about being aced out of all the debates. Before he'd slammed the phone down, he'd rephrased Adlai Stevenson, probably without knowing Adlai's quote or the Cuban missile crisis, "I'll give you my three delegates when hell freezes over." Apparently, he knew something of hell. The three delegates, in the end, were not his to give. The Electoral College would decide this, and then with the power of the American people, Arturo and Ayita would remedy any decision not entirely to their liking.

Ayita peered out from behind the podium at the gaily colored and vast crowd now stretching down the National Mall past the Washington Monument. The ever-stronger sun, just above the top of the monument now, dominated crisp white strands in a sky painted a patriotic blue. She was dressed in a West Point gray wool coat Carlos had gifted her. She topped the coat with her gray beret tipped to one side. She loved berets, they implied service to her. Arturo, standing next to her, wore a thick herringbone business suit. The Secret Service and Carlos's people stationed themselves throughout the crowd, doing their perpetual dance with ugly forces. They felt safe.

The kids fell back while Grant and Colleen wedged between the nominees. Grant tapped a mic.

"Colleen, if you'd do the honors," Grant said.

Colleen put her hand over Grant's on the podium. "It is a glorious day, America. The two nominees-elect, that's all we could think to call them for now, wish to share a short informal talk with America and then they'll make a couple announcements." She waited for the raucous applause to die down. "We'll have press packets to hand out afterwards, which will fill in some gaps for you."

Grant and Colleen backed away, letting their dearest friends approach the mics. Arturo tenderly took Ayita's hand.

This was it. Their dream come true.

Soon the whole world would know. His burning fire had consumed her. He had turned her world upside down. They raised their clasped hands in the traditional victory pose. She snuck a peek upward like a cross-eyed schoolgirl waiting for a kiss. With their arms, they invited their children into another group hug. Twinkling from countless cameras became their star blanket. They waited for the crowd to calm down. The kids backed away again.

After paying homage to Lincoln, Ayita and Arturo started with the body of their speeches about how Americans fought for freedom. How fighting was a trait, but one virtue trumped this. Americans were kind of spirit and giving. Americans lived their everyday lives loving the people they cared about. This election was about overcoming differences and living together.

A tear welled in his wife's eye. "We accept the decision of the American people."

Arturo leaned into the mic. "Whatever the Electoral College decides, we'll abide by, as long as they pick us." He raised her hand again. That broke up the crowd.

Ayita leaned into the mic, "We will not lobby, harass, pester or tweak their noses."

"Ayita and I have been miffed from the start by the incessant rumors about us having an affair and want to set the record straight."

"Arturo and I did not have an affair. We wanted to set a good example for all the young people of America who are struggling to save themselves for marriage." They both turned deliberately and stared at their children, who started to mug *worry* for the cameras. Brian draped his arm over Daya, who elbowed him gently.

"So Mary Ayita and I did save ourselves for marriage."

"My Grandpa married us two days ago along with our campaign managers and best friends, Colleen and Grant."

The rest was a blur. Their managers stepped forward for camera shots alongside the nominees-elect. Now the crowd seemed so Mardi Gras. Horns and whistles blew, taxis beeped, yells of joy, conga lines, people hugging and kissing strangers, all hoping their fantasies about what life in Washington could be, or life anywhere, would be. Arturo wrapped his arms around his bride.

Ayita beamed "I love you with my whole heart." But the noise was so great, nobody could hear themselves think.

Topper texted both of them, "The mics caught what you said. They'll play it again and again on all the channels. For those here who can't hear, they will not misunderstand your hearts."

The kids rushed them, exploding in hugs, kisses, jumping up and down, saying a few oh my Gods. The crowd went delirious. Some church at a distance rang its bells and more followed.

Fifteen or so minutes later, the crowd decided they might want to listen.

"And I'm in love with you too, Ayita."

"We're going to save the taxpayer's money and both live in the White House," Ayita pointed through the many trees in the direction of 1600 Pennsylvania Avenue.

They both said, "God bless America, and through all our actions the whole world." They paused again for the crowd to quiet down, a hopeless task.

Arturo pulled a felt ring box from his pocket and leaned into the mics. "I've had no time to shop. Something kept me busy."

Daya held her face. Brian kissed her and turned red. Billy kissed her on her cheek and said, "Sister," with a huge smile. For

219

each of them, they now had a new mom or dad, and soon, a big white house.

Ayita slipped on the round-cut diamond on a simple platinum band. Perfect. She stared up at her man, knowing how she affected him.

They had decided some cynics would never believe they could love each other, so they'd demonstrate. In the end, people would believe in what they wanted. Today, most American people wanted Camelot.

"Thank you, Arturo, for showing me what is the most important thing in any person's life." She wrapped her arms around him, clasping his shoulders and blinked away the tears. He bent down and kissed her sweetly.

"Thank you, soul mate."

That day, in front of a stone Lincoln, a wooden podium, a star blanket of camera flashes and the people, Ayita and Arturo formed a more perfect union.

The end.

You have just read A MORE PERFECT UNION and the author wants to thank you. Please correspond or write a review if you questions or the time. I'm at rwrichard@ymail.com or visit http://romancetheguyspov.blogspot.com.

If you enjoyed this story you may like the author's other works: The Carlos series (which includes this book) is offered in both paperback and e-book formats. The Carlos series have some continuing characters and related story lines. They're listed in alphabetical order because the chronology is not important to enjoying the story. Each novel stands alone.

AUTUMN BREEZE will be out late 2014. This novel starts on Sept 11, 2001 in New York City. It strikes a more serious tone than A MORE PERFECT UNION but is not without humor. The plot revolves around the coming of age of a thirteen-year-old super genius. She loses her parents and devises a way to put her friend, a pretty NYPD detective and a spy together to marry and then become her parents and keep her from being deported back to Trinidad. She learns a great deal about love along the way and how much more complicated it is than she suspected. The detective and spy have similar problems as they deal with the web the girl weaves.

A MORE PERFECT UNION. You have just read it.

BLINDFOLD CHESS will be out in early 2015. An Army Colonel loses her sight in battle and discovers she has an unusual talent, blindsight, a documented but little understood human condition. Out of the Army, she copes with a world in which she must rely on others, specifically one other.

Expect more in the Carlos series.

Other stories not included in the Carlos series:

THE WOLVES OF SHERWOOD FOREST a novella in e-book format only. Wolves... is a lighthearted romp through Sherwood

Forest with a young-adult Robin, Marian and real wolves (as opposed to werewolves). The couple band together to save the recently returned to England, King Richard. If you like your politics really dusty-old (before the Magna Carta), try this flashback to a time when people could just walk into your home for no particular reason (oh, you say, they're relatives and neighbors, nevermind).

DOUBLE HAPPINESS a novel in paperback and e-book out late 2014 This zany twisted outrage should be saved for when you're feeling you'd like to dive into a screwball world. Identical twin bad boys wreak havoc with their fiancées when they persistently and secretly switch places. Expect a crazy ending. The author wrote this after reading and being inspired by, Janet Evanovich (any of hers) and William Shakespeare's *Comedy of Errors*. The plot for Comedy of Errors inspired the plot for Double Happiness.

NEANDERTHALS AND THE GARDEN OF EDEN, a novel in e-book and paperback. This, the author's first story, is different from anything else you will have read, because multi-protagonist stories have been out of style for 120 years. But, that's the way life was back 100,000 years ago when we, through this story, witness the intermingling of tribes and wolf packs and how they lived. Although not a romance in the traditional sense, this story includes a man traveling back in time to find his one true love. The pace is fairly quick because the tribe members usually demonstrated their thoughts with action. You may think of this novel as a scientist's rejoinder to so many well written but scientifically incorrect pre-history stories.

Made in the USA
Charleston, SC
11 September 2014